ALSO BY EMILY MCINTIRE

Be Still My Heart: A Romantic Suspense

THE SUGARLAKE SERIES
Beneath the Stars
Beneath the Stands
Beneath the Hood
Beneath the Surface

THE NEVER AFTER SERIES
Scarred: A Dark Royal Romance
Wretched: A Dark Contemporary Romance

HOOKED

A Never After Novel

EMILY MCINTIRE

Bloom *books*

Published by Bloom Books, an imprint of Sourcebooks
P.O. Box 4410, Naperville, Illinois 60567–4410
(630) 961-3900
sourcebooks.com

Originally self-published in 2021 by Emily McIntire.

Cataloging-in-Publication Data is on file with the Library of Congress.

Printed and bound in the United States of America.
VP 31 30 29 28 27

Playlist

"Lost Boy"—Ruth B.

"Control"—Halsey

"Heathens"—Twenty One Pilots

"Bad Romance"—Lady Gaga

"bury a friend"—Billie Eilish

"Blood // Water"—Grandson

"In the Shadows"—Amy Stroup

"Look What You Made Me Do"—Taylor Swift

"ocean eyes"—Billie Eilish

"Lifetime"—Justin Bieber

For anyone who has been
the villain in someone else's story.

"You can have anything in life if you will sacrifice everything else for it."
—J. M. Barrie, *Peter Pan*

Author's Note

Hooked is a dark, contemporary romance. It is an adult fractured fairy tale.

It is not fantasy or a retelling.

The main character is a villain. If you're looking for a safe read with redemption and a bad guy turned into a hero, you will not find it in these pages.

Hooked contains sexually explicit scenes as well as mature and graphic content that is not suitable for all audiences. **Reader discretion is advised.**

I much prefer for you to go in blind, but if you would like a list of detailed triggers, you can find them on EmilyMcIntire.com.

PROLOGUE

Once upon a time

IT FEELS DIFFERENT THAN I THOUGHT IT WOULD.

Killing him.

My knuckles tighten as I twist my wrist, and when his eyes widen, blood spraying from his neck and dousing the skin on my forearm, I'm hit with a burst of satisfaction that I chose to hook my blade in his carotid artery. Fatal enough to ensure his death but slow enough where I get to enjoy watching every last second of his miserable life drain away, taking his pathetic soul along with it.

I knew it would take mere seconds for him to lose consciousness, but that's all I need.

A few seconds.

Just long enough for him to stare into my eyes and know that I'm the monster he helped create. The living incarnation of his sins coming back to sow justice.

But I *had* rather hoped he'd beg. Just a little.

I stay crouching on top of him long after the high of his

bloodshed fades, my calloused palm wrapped around his neck, the other gripping the sheath of my blade, waiting for *something*. But the only thing that comes is the chill as his blood cools on my skin and the knowledge it's not *his* death that will bring me peace.

It isn't until my phone vibrates in my pocket that I release him, the weight of his control lifting away as his corpse drops from my arms.

"Hello, Roofus."

"How many times do I have to tell you not to call me that?" he snaps.

I grin. "At least one more."

"Is it done?"

Walking through the office and into the en suite, I turn the water until it's tepid, putting my phone on speaker and beginning the task of rinsing the blood spatter from my arms. "Of course it is."

Ru grunts. "How's it feel?"

My hands grip the edge of the sink, and I lean forward to stare at myself in the mirror.

How does it feel?

There's no quickening of my heart. No fire surging through my veins. No power leaching from my bones.

"Rather anticlimactic, I'm afraid." Grabbing a towel off the wall hook, I dry myself and walk back into the office, reaching for my suit.

"Well, *that's* not surprising. James Barrie, the hardest kid to please in the entire fucking universe."

I smirk as I button my suit jacket, adjusting the cuffs while I head back to stand over my uncle. I gaze down at him, his black eyes staring vacantly at the ceiling, his mouth open and lax—much like he always forced mine to be.

Funny, that.

But my innocence was stolen long before him.

I kick his leg out of the way, his hideous crocodile boots splashing in the blood that's pooled underneath his body.

Sighing, I pinch the bridge of my nose. "Things got a little… messy."

"I'll take care of it." Ru laughs. "Lighten up, kid. You did good. Meet me at the Jolly Roger? It's time to celebrate."

I hang up the phone without responding and let it sink in that this is the last moment I'll ever spend with a relative. Closing my eyes, I breathe deep, searching for a sliver of regret.

There is none.

Tick.

Tick.

Tick.

The sound jumps through the silence, scratching against my insides. My teeth grind as my eyes shoot open, my ears straining for that *incessant* noise. Crouching down, I take the handkerchief from my breast pocket and reach into my uncle's jeans, pulling out his gold pocket watch.

Tick.

Tick.

Tick.

Rage twists around my gut and squeezes, my hand slamming the watch onto the ground. My heart races as I stand, bringing my foot smashing down on the hideous object over and over again until sweat breaks across my brow, dripping along my cheek and onto the floor. It isn't until I'm sure of its silence that I'm able to relax.

Straightening, I huff out a breath, slicking back my hair and cracking my neck.

There. That's better.

"Goodbye, Uncle."

Tucking the handkerchief back into my suit, I walk away from the man who I wish I'd never known.

Now I'm one step closer to the one responsible for everything. And this time, he won't be able to fly away.

CHAPTER 1

Wendy

I'VE NEVER BEEN TO MASSACHUSETTS, BUT I'VE heard about the lack of heat. So while the temperature change from Florida is a shock, it isn't wholly unexpected. Still, as I shiver in my tank top, the light breeze blowing across my arms, I can't help but wish I had stayed behind instead of choosing to follow my family to their new home in Bloomsburg.

But I can't stand the thought of not being a phone call away if they need me. My father is a workaholic—even more so after my mother's death—and without me around, my sixteen-year-old brother, Jonathan, would be all alone.

I've always been a daddy's girl, even though he makes it difficult. I'd hoped, after the move, that he'd slow down. Make more time for his family instead of constantly searching for the next big thing to sink his teeth into. But Peter Michaels is never one to settle. His thirst for new ventures overpowers his ache for a family connection. Being named the *Forbes* top businessman for the fifth year in a row means he has a lot of opportunity in that regard. And being the owner of the biggest airline in the Western Hemisphere means he has lots of funding for said opportunities.

NevAirLand. *If you can dream it, we can fly you there.*

"We should go out tonight," my friend Angie says as she wipes down the counters at the Vanilla Bean, the coffee shop where we both work.

"And do what?" I ask. Honestly, I was hoping to just head home and relax. I've only been here for a little over a month, and I've been working so much that I haven't had a night to spend with Jonathan. Although he's in the teen stage of "I don't need anyone or anything," so he may not want me around anyway.

She shrugs. "I don't know. A couple of the girls were talking about heading to the Jolly Roger."

I scrunch my nose. Both at her use of "the girls" and at the name of wherever she's talking about.

"Oh, come on, Wendy. You've been here for almost two months, and you haven't gone out with me once." She sticks out her bottom lip, her hands coming together in prayer.

Shaking my head, I sigh. "I don't think your friends like me."

"That's not true," she insists. "They just don't know you yet. You have to actually come *out* with us for that."

"I don't know, Angie." My teeth sink into my bottom lip. "My dad's out of town, and he doesn't like it when I go out and draw attention."

She rolls her eyes. "You're twenty, girl. Cut the cord."

I give her a half-hearted smile. She, like most people, can't understand what it's like being Peter Michaels's daughter. Even if I wanted to, there *is* no cutting the cord. His power and influence reach every corner of the universe, and there isn't anything or anyone that escapes his control. Or if there is, I've never met them.

The bell above the front door chimes, Angie's friend Maria walking in, her long black hair glinting off the overhead lighting as she saunters to us.

My brows rise as I glance at her, then back to Angie. "What kind of place is gonna let a twenty-year-old in anyway?"

"Don't you have a fake ID?" Maria asks as she reaches the front counter.

"I *definitely* don't have that." I've never snuck into a bar or a club in my life. "My birthday is in a few weeks. I'll just go out with you guys next time." I wave them off.

Maria eyes me up and down. "Angie, don't you have your sister's ID? They look…similar." She reaches out and touches my brown hair. "Just show a little bit of that body and they won't even look at the face on the card."

I laugh as I brush off her words, but my insides tighten, heat surging through my veins and lighting up my cheeks. I'm not a rule breaker. Never have been. But the thought of going tonight, of doing something bad, sends a thrill rushing down my spine.

Maria is one of "the girls," and she hasn't been anywhere close to welcoming. But as I watch her grin and run her fingers through her hair, I wonder if maybe Angie is right. Maybe it's all in my head, and I just haven't given her a chance. I've never really had a close group of girlfriends, so I'm not sure how it's all supposed to work.

"I don't care if you don't want to go." Angie pouts, throwing her damp rag at me. "I'm making the executive decision."

I laugh, shaking my head as I finish restocking the cups for the morning.

"Hmm." Maria pops her gum loudly, her dark eyes searing into the side of my face. "You don't wanna go?"

I shrug. "It's not that. I just—"

"Probably for the best," she interrupts. "I don't think the JR is your kind of place."

My spine bristles and I stand up straighter. "What's that supposed to mean?"

She smirks. "I mean, it's not for *children*."

"Maria, come on. Don't be a bitch," Angie pipes in.

Maria laughs. "I'm not. I'm just saying. What if *he's* there? Can you imagine? She'd be scarred for life from even being in the same building and run home to tell her daddy."

I lift my chin. "My dad isn't even in town."

She cocks her head, her lips thinning. "Your nanny then."

Irritation spikes through my gut, and a need to prove her wrong clicks my decision into place, pushing the words off my tongue. I look at Angie. "I'm in."

"Yes!" Angie claps her hands.

Maria's eyes glint. "Hope you can handle it."

"Give me a break, Maria. She'll be fine. It's a bar, not a sex club," Angie scoffs before turning toward me. "Don't listen to her. Besides, we only go there so she can try and get the attention of her mystery man."

"I *will* get his attention."

Angie tilts her head. "He doesn't even know you exist, girl."

"My luck is bound to change at some point." Maria shrugs.

Confusion makes my brows pull in. "Who are you guys even talking about?"

A slow grin creeps across Maria's face, and a wistful look coasts across Angie's eyes.

"Hook."

CHAPTER 2

James

"THERE'S A NEW PROPOSITION ON THE TABLE."

I pour two fingers of Basil Hayden into the crystal tumbler, adding one ice cube and savoring the flavor before I turn to face Ru. "I wasn't aware we were taking any new propositions."

He shrugs, lighting up the end of his cigar and puffing. "We aren't. But I'm a businessman, and this one has massive potential."

His voice is muffled as he speaks around the roll of tobacco, but years of soaking up his words as gospel make him easy to understand.

Roofus—known to the world as Ru—is the only person in my life worthy of my trust. He saved me from hell, and I'll never be able to repay that debt. But the courtesy only extends to him, which makes it *difficult* when he decides to bring new people into our operation.

He's grown reckless with age.

"One day, your inability to turn down *potential* will get you killed," I tell him.

His eyes narrow. "I have no intention of dying and leaving my legacy to a Brit."

I smirk. All this is mine anyway; he just doesn't like to say it out loud. Doesn't want to admit the student has surpassed the master, that he only holds the reins because I allow him to. It's been the truth since the moment my uncle's blood spilled under my hand eight years ago—the day I turned eighteen. I gutted him like the worthless fish he was, then used the same blade to cut into my steak at dinner, daring anyone to question why my fingers were stained with red.

Ru may have the title of boss, but it's *me* they all fear.

Setting my glass on the edge of the desk, I sit down in one of the wingback chairs. "Your mortality is not something I particularly like to joke about."

Sometimes I truly believe Ru thinks he's untouchable. It makes him sloppy. Makes him trust too easily. Allows people to get too close. Luckily, he has me, and I'll slice my knife deep into the belly of anyone who tries, reveling at how the life drains from their eyes while their blood drips into my hands.

I guess when you've experienced the things I have, you learn quickly that immortality is only granted through people's memories.

Ru leans forward, resting his cigar in the ornate ashtray on the corner of his desk. "Then pay attention. We have someone who's interested in being a new *partner*." Ru grins. "Wants to expand our distribution. Run our pixie to new corners of the universe."

"Fascinating." I dust a piece of lint off my suit jacket. "Who is it?" I ask, purely to appease him. I have zero interest in bringing on someone new. We've been using our current drug runner for the past three years, and I vetted him personally. Watched him sweat through his clothes while he watched our pixie dust get loaded on the plane, hidden inside crates of lobster. Sat next to him in the cockpit through the entire flight, twirling my hook blade through my fingers as he pissed himself from the nerves.

If you want to ensure someone's loyalty, you have to make sure they understand *why* you deserve it. And I've made sure that people understand the end of a blade hurts worse when the person wielding it enjoys causing pain.

Ru wipes his hand over his mouth. "You've heard of NevAirLand planes?"

I freeze in place, the blood in my veins icing over. I'm quite sure I've never mentioned that name to anyone, especially Ru.

"Can't say that I have." My jaw quivers.

"Well, you must be the only one." Ru laughs. "The owner, Peter Michaels, just moved here."

My heart slams against my ribs. *How could I have missed this?* "Oh?"

Ru nods. "He's looking for a new *adventure*." He smiles, his slightly crooked teeth gleaming. "It's only fair for us to welcome him in properly, let him know how things around here work."

My hands twitch with the rage that spikes inside me whenever I hear Peter Michaels's name. I reach out and pick up my tumbler, my grasp tight around the crystal as anticipation blooms in my chest.

How fortuitous that the man I long to kill is serving himself to me on a silver platter.

"Well, I think this sounds like a wonderful opportunity." I smile.

Ru picks up his cigar. "I wasn't asking your permission, kid, but I'm glad you're on board."

"So when do we meet with him?" I sip from my drink, trying to tame the quick beats of my heart.

"*I* meet with him tonight. *Alone.*" He narrows his eyes.

My gut clenches. "Let me go with you, Roofus. You shouldn't meet him alone."

Ru sighs, running a hand through his ridiculous bright red hair. "You're too intimidating, kid. I need this meeting to be friendly."

Can't argue with him there.

"At least take one of the boys." The thought of Ru alone with Peter Michaels sends a chill up my spine.

Ru blows a ring of smoke in the air.

I lean forward, knuckling the top of his desk. "Roofus. *Promise* me you won't go alone. Don't be foolish."

"And don't forget your place," he snaps. "*I* run this, not you. You answer to *me*. How about you show your gratitude and, for once, just do as you're fucking told?"

My teeth grind at his tone, and if he were anyone else, I would thank him for the reminder right before I cut out his tongue. But Ru gets away with a lot of things that no one else does.

I first saw Ru when I was thirteen—two years after I was shipped to America to live with my uncle. Reading in the library, I heard a commotion down the hall and went to investigate the noise. Peeking through a crack in the office door, I watched, mesmerized, as a large man with olive skin and dyed red hair loomed over my uncle's desk, threatening him within an inch of his life, a gun at his temple and menace bleeding through his thick Boston accent. It was awe-inspiring, truly. I had never seen my uncle cower before anyone. It was usually his favorite pastime to see others fall to their knees for *him*.

As a politician, it happened publicly often.

As a person filled with rage and perversion, it happened in private even more.

So I found this mystery man enthralling and took to following him when he left, desperate to emulate his power. I suppose you could call it obsession, but I had never known anyone like him. Had never seen someone command obedience from a man who ran the world.

I wanted to know how to do that too.

But at thirteen, I hadn't mastered the art of being undetected, and Ru knew I was stalking him all along. Took me in and taught me everything he knew. Introduced me to the streets of Bloomsburg and kept me sane through the nightmares that plagued my sleep.

So I'll defer to what he wants, because there isn't a single soul on this planet who has taken care of me the way he has.

There was once, but that was long ago. Another lifetime, really.

"You're right," I say. "I trust your judgment. It's everyone else's I don't."

Ru laughs and opens his mouth to respond, but a knock on the door interrupts.

"Come in," Ru grunts.

Starkey, one of our younger recruits, pops his head in. "Sorry to interrupt, boss." His eyes slide to mine, widening as he quickly looks away. "There're a few girls trying to come in with fake IDs. Making a hell of a time for us downstairs."

"You come up here to bother us with this shit?" Ru snaps. "What the hell do we pay you for?"

I grin at Ru's temper and walk to the security cameras, looking at the one aimed over the front entrance. Just as Starkey says, there are three girls, one of whom is currently screaming in our bouncer's face. *Pathetic.* I continue my perusal, my eyes locking on the beauty standing off to the side.

My stomach tightens as my gaze trails along her body in a tight blue dress. Her arms are wrapped around her middle, her eyes darting back and forth between the bouncer and the cabs that line the street.

Annoyance snaps in my chest with the fact that I can't see her as clearly as I'd like. But I see her enough to know she looks uncomfortable. Innocent. Definitely doesn't belong in a place like this. And for some reason, that shoots a thrill straight to my cock, making it thicken and pulse as I imagine all the ways this place could defile her. There are not many people who inspire a reaction from me. A life of *not* reacting has bled into my skin, hardening into an impenetrable shield, nothing allowed in or out. Just an empty shell with a single purpose.

The fact that this girl has tweaked my interest even a modicum has my curiosity piqued.

"Let them in," I interrupt, my eyes still on the brunette beauty.

Starkey stops rambling, his eyes shooting to me before landing back on Ru. "Are you sure? I—"

"Did I stutter?" I ask, turning to face him. "Or maybe it's the accent that gets in the way of you understanding?"

"N-no, it's just—"

"It's *just*," I interrupt. "Clearly, you're in need of some guidance on how to handle the situation. Or have I misunderstood your reasoning for bringing this trivial issue to our attention?"

Ru smirks, leaning back in his chair.

"No, Hook. You didn't misunderstand."

"Hmm. Then it's a problem, to be sure." I nod. "Tell me, would you agree that we need to fire whoever is working the door?"

"Um, I don't—" Starkey starts.

"After all, if he lacks the ability to control a group of females, how can we be sure he'll handle anyone else?" I cock my head.

Starkey swallows, his Adam's apple bobbing. "I... They're—"

"You see," I continue, slipping my hook blade from my pocket and flipping it open. "Subduing a woman is all about control." I walk toward him, twirling the stainless steel between my fingers, the intricate brown design of the handle sliding against my skin. "A delicate weaving of power. A give-and-take, if you will. Supplying them with the absolute *pleasure* of your dominance." Stopping in front of him, I pause the knife as I grasp it in my palm. "Clearly, our bouncer this evening possesses more of a submissive gene." My free hand reaches out, straightening his tie. "I understand how difficult it must be to recognize the same trait within yourself." I lean in close, allowing the tip of my blade to rest against his throat. "Be a good boy, Starkey, and let. Them. In."

"Yes, sir," he mumbles.

I pat him on the shoulder, and he spins and rushes out the door.

Ru points at me with his cigar, amusement lining his eyes. "And *that* is why you aren't coming to this meeting."

I smile, straightening the cuffs of my jacket. "That's fair. I'm off to the main floor anyway. I have a bouncer to make disappear and a sudden appetite for something *pretty*."

Ru chuckles. "Just make sure they're legal."

Grabbing the door handle, I pause. "Ru?"

He grunts.

"Make sure Peter knows I'm *so* looking forward to meeting him face-to-face."

CHAPTER 3

Wendy

AN HOUR AGO, I WOULD HAVE SWORN WE WERE on the verge of being arrested, and now I'm sitting in the VIP room of a swanky bar, sipping overpriced champagne, courtesy of "an admirer."

Apparently, the legal drinking age is more of a *suggestion* here than an actual requirement. Embarrassment slams into me as I think of all the people outside, watching Maria yell because the bouncer didn't fall for my fake ID. I'm not surprised. I don't look a thing like Angie's sister. I was two seconds away from dipping into the closest cab and bolting, but then a blond man in a fitted suit walked out and whispered in the doorman's ear. Next thing you know, we were led to a VIP area.

I feel extremely out of place, but this is arguably the most fun I've had in years, which makes me feel pathetic considering we aren't doing anything other than drinking and people watching.

Or more specifically, watching for one person.

Hook.

I roll my eyes at the name but can't help the tendril of curiosity that's bloomed inside me. Apparently, he's the main reason they always come to *this* place over any other. Just for the hope to see him again.

Maria swears he's her soul mate, so every weekend she shows back up, her eyes peeled and her legs already half open, hoping he'll come down from his ivory tower and she can steal him away.

"So tell me about your man," I say to Maria as I sip from my champagne flute and glance around the room.

Angie groans. "Ugh, don't get her started."

Maria's face splits into a grin. "It happened about a month ago when I was at the bar getting a round, and I swear to you, the crowds parted and there he was. Sitting like a fucking god in the back booth, cigar smoke swirling around him."

"Did you go talk to him?" I ask.

Angie laughs. "Yeah, right. She'd have to get through all his lackeys for that."

I cock my head. "His lackeys?"

She lifts a shoulder. "He's always surrounded by men."

My brows shoot to my hairline. "Maybe he's gay."

Angie cackles, but Maria's gaze narrows. "We had a moment."

"A moment so strong, he never searched her out after," Angie says with a snort.

"He's clearly a busy man," Maria snaps, wiping a strand of hair from her face. "But that's why we're here now. One of these nights, he'll find me."

"And he'll take you up to his bed and split you apart with his monster cock." Angie's eyes grow big as she spreads her hands shoulder-width apart.

Giggling, I rub my face. "Well, *that* sounds realistic."

Maria's lip curls. "Girl, why'd you even come if you're gonna talk shit the whole time? You could have just stayed home and saved us all this trouble."

I shrink into myself, my stomach burning with guilt. "I'm sorry. I believe you. I do." My fingers tangle in my lap, twisting around each other. "You just make him sound so...mythical."

Her eyes roll. "It's not like he's a figment of our imagination, *Wendy*. He's a businessman. He owns the fucking bar!" Her hands smack the seat cushion.

My brow rises. "He does?"

"I think so anyway. He's not always down here, but whenever he is, he comes from the back and always sits in that same spot." Maria points to the far corner of the room, where a booth sits— an empty space in the otherwise crowded room. She takes a sip of her drink. "Anyway, luck is on my side. I can feel it." She taps her long, red nail to her temple.

I lean over, clinking my champagne flute against hers, trying to mend the bridges I've obviously torched before they could finish being built. "I think you're right. It does feel lucky tonight."

Maria grins—the first genuine smile she's ever given me—and satisfaction blossoms in my chest. Maybe I'll be okay at this friend thing after all.

Suddenly, heat pricks the back of my neck, and I twist in my seat, an unsettling feeling of being watched washing over me. But when I turn, there's nothing there.

Odd.

I drain the rest of my glass and stand, leaning in toward the girls. "Hey, I'll be back. Need the ladies' room."

"Hey," Angie shouts when I'm halfway out of the room. "The one down here is always packed. Find the hallway to the right of the bar. There's one in the back that isn't used as much."

Nodding, I commit her directions to memory and leave, weaving my way through the main area. My vision blurs the slightest bit from the champagne, and I stumble, slamming into a body.

"Shit, I'm sorry." My hands reach up instinctively, landing against a solid wall of muscle. Rough palms grasp my shoulders, goose bumps sprouting along my skin from the heat of the stranger's touch.

"Filthy words for such a pretty mouth."

The deep, accented voice slides across my skin like silk and wraps itself around me, a shiver skating down my spine. His grip tightens, palms moving until they brush my upper arms. My hands are still pressed against his chest, the black fabric of his suit soft under the pads of my fingers. My breath stutters as he sucks me into his gaze, his eyes like cerulean glass, an almost haunting chill to their beauty.

I break our stare, finally letting his words filter into my brain. "Excuse me?"

He smirks, and I take in his high cheekbones, a natural highlight falling on the sharp angles, contrasting harshly against his jet-black eyebrows and tousled hair.

My stomach clenches as I realize just how attractive this man is.

His mouth descends until it's next to my ear, his breath trickling down my neck, making heat spike through my core. "I said—"

"No, I heard what you said," I cut in. "My question was rhetorical."

He leans back, a slow smile spreading across his lips, his thumbs rubbing up and down in a rhythmic motion against my bare skin. "Oh?"

I nod. "Yeah."

My chest tightens as I glance around, taking in our surroundings. Dozens of people, and yet it feels like he's the only one in the room. His energy crackles through the air, desperate to cling to his skin. This man screams power, and for a split second, I wonder what it would be like to dive into his brand of trouble. To live without limits, just for a while.

Ridiculous.

Shaking my head, I step back, my teeth sinking into my bottom lip. "Okay, well, this has been—"

"A pleasure," he purrs. He moves into me again, grabbing my palm and bringing it to his lips, skimming them back and forth in a whisper of a kiss.

My heart skips. "I was going to say strange, but sure…a *pleasure.*"

Taking my hand away, my stomach twists. I almost feel disappointed to be leaving him, and the feeling is unsettling. I move to walk around him, but he grasps my arm, pulling me back until I feel every hard line of his body against the soft curves of mine. Gasping, I freeze in place. This man—this *stranger*—touches me like it's his right. Like I'm his to touch.

"Don't I get to know your name?" His voice rumbles against my neck. My legs squeeze together from the deep timbre of his voice.

I've never had somebody handle me the way he is. Never had someone like this give me their attention. It's both infuriating and intoxicating, the strange mix of emotion making nerves sizzle underneath my skin.

Blowing out a breath, I try to stem the tremble in my voice. Maybe it's the champagne, or maybe it's the man himself, but the urge to be a different kind of Wendy has my tongue loosening before I can stop it. "No. I don't think you've earned it." I wrench my arm from his grasp. "And for the record, these pretty lips will say whatever the *fuck* they want."

His eyes flare, and the corner of his mouth twitches, but he doesn't speak again. Just puts his hands in the pockets of his three-piece suit and rocks on his heels, his gaze searing through my back as I spin to walk away.

CHAPTER 4

James

MY HEART SLAMS AGAINST MY RIBS.

Wendy Michaels.

I know her, of course. The daughter of the man whom I've been keeping tabs on since I was eleven years old. Her father stashes her in the dark now that she's older, most likely to keep her safe from the unsavory side of his business, but when you've lived your life following a man's legacy, you learn everything about him, including the shape of his shadows.

Which is why I'm not sure how I missed that he was moving here.

Still, I've never begrudged the offspring for the sins of their father. We're all by-products of evil, some of us born into it and others created from circumstance. However, if the universe is placing her in my palms, the least I can do is handle her properly.

My cock lengthens at the thought of driving inside her until she breaks, leaving wounds that scar with the reminder I was there. Tarnishing her innocence and then tossing her at her father's feet, a defiled version of the girl he bred.

Delicious.

I've watched her from the moment she walked into my bar, recognition stealing my breath, clarity that the grainy resolution of our security footage didn't allow me.

A smile creeps on my lips as I walk back to the office, where I'll continue to follow her through the cameras. The thrill of the chase thrums through my veins, anticipation of catching her sinking into my bones.

The truth is, things have been rather boring as of late. I'm salivating for something new to sink my teeth into, and Wendy Michaels is the perfect pet project. I'm giddy at the thought of taming her until she purrs, then sending her back with a new master controlling her leash—a beautiful harmony as I conduct the symphony of Peter's destruction.

Unbuttoning my suit jacket, I slide into the leather seat behind my desk, typing in Wendy's name, watching as articles flash across my screen. My stomach tightens with excitement as I read of Peter's love for his daughter.

His little shadow.

Fitting nickname, I think. After all, one can't leave their shadow behind without missing it in the end.

A gruesome image of me thrusting inside her on top of his remains, my cum dripping from between her thighs and mixing with the pool of blood beneath us makes my cock jerk violently, a groan ripping from my throat as I palm my aching erection.

This won't do.

Pulling out my phone, I send a text to one of the cocktail waitresses on staff tonight, Moira, telling her to stop what she's doing and come find me. Now.

Clicking out of the articles, I pull up the security feed,

satisfaction burrowing in my chest as I see Wendy sipping champagne and trying to act as though she belongs.

She doesn't.

Not here, and certainly not with the pathetic group of girls she's with. Her innocence shines like a beacon—a sparkling jewel in the midst of trash, bait for my darkness to come and smother it whole.

The door clicks open and shut, the tall, scantily clad body of Moira sauntering toward me, a smirk on her ruby-red lips.

"Hook," she breathes, walking around the oak desk. "I've missed you."

I allow a soft smile to play across my lips, ignoring the way her voice grates against my ears. My hand brushes a strand of black hair behind her shoulder, cupping the back of her neck and pulling until she's centimeters away, her moist breath skating across my skin.

Her head jerks. "Sorry, new tattoo. Still kind of sore."

"On your knees."

She drops dutifully, her manicured palm rubbing over my length, her mouth pressing kisses against the fabric. My teeth grind, annoyance lancing through me from her poor attempt at foreplay. I palm the back of her head, fingers wrapping around her hair as I jerk her face upward. My free hand presses against her jaw until I feel the indent of her teeth through her skin, my thumb smearing the red paint off her lips.

She flinches, her cheeks smooshing as I grip her face tightly, causing a spike of pleasure to skitter down my spine. "This suit is cashmere, sweetheart. Don't sully it with three-dollar stains, understand?"

She gulps and nods.

"Good girl." I pat her cheek before lowering her head back to my lap.

My gaze swings to the computer, watching the true object of my desire. And as Moira's hot mouth surrounds my cock, slurping along the shaft and sucking me down her throat, my eyes stay locked on the cameras, imagining the day when I'll have Wendy in her place.

And I'll make her choke on something *truly* filthy.

"Still alive, I see," I deadpan as Ru waltzes through the office door.

"Alive and never better." He grins, walking to the tan globe that houses his brandy and pouring himself a glass.

"I take it that means the meeting went well?" My brows rise, noting the time. It's only been a few hours.

There has been an anxious energy pricking at my insides while I waited on his return. Regardless of Peter Michaels's squeaky-clean image, I know he's a dangerous man. I also know Ru sometimes lets his temper get the best of him, and even though I'm thankful nothing nefarious happened, I still wish he would have let me accompany him, if only to ensure his safety.

I haven't mastered the art of propriety only to lose my composure at the first sight of Peter. I would have remained calm. Shook his hand and looked him in the eye as I imagined all the ways I'll enjoy bringing him a torturous death.

Ru sighs, sinking into the black couch against the wall, sipping from his tumbler and grabbing a cigar. "The prick never showed up. Sent some kid to do his dirty work, like I'd put *everything* on the line for some two-bit punk."

A strange sense of relief floods my chest. "Absurd."

"Disrespectful," Ru spits.

"Does this mean you've changed your mind about working with him?" My head cocks.

I hope he says yes, having Peter embroiled in our business will make it difficult when it comes time to end his life. Not impossible, just *challenging*.

Ru shrugs, staring at his cigar as he rolls it between his fingers. "I told the boy to send a message to Mr. Michaels. Let him know how we do things here and hope he comes to realize it doesn't matter how much money he has if he can't put respect on my *fucking* name." Ru's grip tightens, the cigar crumbling under his fingers. "You know, I think I've had a change of heart, kid. If he wants to meet, it's only fair he gets to meet us both."

Excitement erupts in my stomach. "Excellent news." My eyes stray to the computer screen, noticing that Wendy and her friends are leaving. Standing up, I button my suit jacket. "If you'll excuse me, there are a few loose ends from the night I'm desperate to tie up."

Ru waves me off, drinking from his brandy.

I leave the room, using the back stairwell to exit the club so I'm not seen. Slinking around the side of the building, I watch as Wendy hugs her friends goodbye and clambers into a yellow cab, disgust filling me at her recklessness and the complete disregard her friends have for her safety.

Her father has money, yet he doesn't afford her a driver? *Any protection?*

Sliding into my Audi, I pull onto the busy street to follow close behind and make sure she gets home safe. I have no interest in owning something damaged, even temporarily.

And until I decide otherwise, Wendy Michaels is mine.

CHAPTER 5

Wendy

"WHAT DO YOU MEAN 'HOMESCHOOLING'?" I ASK my brother, Jon.

He shrugs, his dark hair bobbing with the motion, arm waving to the papers strewn out in front of him. "It's exactly what it sounds like. I asked Dad if I could do it this way, and he said okay."

My brows scrunch. *Why wouldn't he tell me about this?*

"Cool. So you and Dad had a good talk then?" I plop next to him at the dining room table.

His lips curl slightly. "Wendy, be real. When's the last time Dad actually talked to me?"

My insides clamp down and I sigh, the excuses for our father rolling off my tongue, so practiced I can barely taste the lies. "He's just busy, Jon, that's all. You know he loves you and wishes he could be here."

Jon scoffs, gripping his pencil so tight his knuckles turn white. "Yeah, sure."

"Besides," I continue, "you have me, and we both know I'm all you need."

He smirks, rolling his eyes behind his large square-framed glasses. "You're right. Who needs parents when they've got you? You mother me enough for the whole damn town."

I force a scowl, amusement weaving through my chest. "Hey, watch your mouth."

"Proving my point." He pushes his glasses up his nose. "It is cool, though…about homeschooling. I'm happier this way."

He's not wrong. I suppose I do mother him more than a normal sibling would, but I'm all he has. Our mother died when Jon was barely one, a fatal car accident from a drunk driver. And although I'll never admit it out loud, my dad definitely doesn't give Jon the time or attention he deserves. It's a sore spot in our relationship, one I don't like to focus on for too long.

"Well, I'm glad he's letting you stay home if it's what you want. You think you'll miss the interaction?"

He huffs out a breath, rolling his eyes again. "No. Kids are assholes."

My heart pangs. Maybe homeschooling *will* be the better option. Hope flares in the middle of my sternum, wondering if my father actually listened all the times I've begged him to intervene with Jon's bullying.

I smile. "Okay, well, I gotta go to work. You want to watch a movie tonight?"

"Why do you work when you don't need the money?" he asks.

I shrug, chewing on my lower lip. "So I don't die of boredom, I guess."

"You could always go to college." He smirks, glancing at me.

"And leave you here? What would you do without me?"

He grins, leaning over his paperwork and effectively dismissing me.

Sighing, I stand up, leaving him to it. I love to be around him, but I miss the days when he would attach himself to my legs or put his sticky toddler hands on my cheeks and tell me I was his favorite person in the world.

As he got older, he shuttered himself, the cruelties of being bullied making him hide behind walls he was forced to build. An ache spreads across my chest, and it stays with me the entire drive to the Vanilla Bean.

It's two hours later—after I've messed up two macchiatos and spilled an entire gallon of caramel on the ground—that I realize today is *not* going to be my day. The other barista called off, so it's just me, and for some reason, I can't do a single task without messing something up.

"Can someone give me some service around here?" A man's voice hollers from the main area.

I stand up from where I'm cleaning the remnants of caramel and brush my hair from my eyes, peering around the corner. I hadn't even heard anyone come in. "Hi! So sorry. Give me just a sec."

The man scowls, crossing his arms, a large watch blinging on his wrist. "Some of us have things to do. I've been standing here for five minutes."

Irritation stabs my gut. I drop the rag on the counter, the water dripping from the fabric and onto the ground, and walk to the front. "So sorry about the wait, sir."

He huffs, his hand tapping the counter in a jittery rhythm. I'm no stranger to rude customers—unfortunately in the service industry, they happen more often than not—but today, my nerves are shot, and I can feel the ball of fire brewing in the center of my stomach, spinning and growing, the flames licking up my insides.

I paste a smile on my face. "What can I get you?"

"Large hot coffee, black."

I nod, blowing out a relieved breath that his drink is something simple. He pays and I spin around, side-eyeing the small puddle that's collected on the floor from where the rag has been steadily dripping. I pour his coffee just as the bell above the front door dings, the sound making me jerk. Before I can turn my head, my foot slips on the water, causing me to tip backward, the burn from the sloshing coffee scalding my skin. My tailbone throbs with a sharp ache as I lie on the cold ground, eyes closed, trying to collect myself enough through the humiliation to stand up and just *finish* this guy's order.

"Jesus *Christ*, is there anyone here who's competent enough to get me a drink?"

The sting from the coffee mixes with the tears collecting behind my lids.

Fuck this guy.

I move to my knees gingerly, blowing out slow and steady breaths to calm my racing heart. Today is definitely *not* my day.

"And here I was thinking men were supposed to know how to treat a lady."

My body freezes, wet coffee-soaked shirt sticking to my skin, my hands getting a purchase on the tiled floor. *That accent.*

The angry customer scoffs, smacking his hand on the counter to punctuate his words, his gaudy watch counting the seconds audibly. "And here *I* was thinking I'd be able to get a cup of coffee without it being a production."

A flush rises to my cheeks, and I get up slowly, wincing at the pain that's throbbing in my lower back. My eyes lock on ocean blue, the mystery man I met the other night standing as if he was plucked straight from my dreams and placed in front of me.

Great. He would show up during my humiliation.

My eyes narrow on the other customer, trying to keep my breathing steady and my temper in check, and the smile on my face stretches from ear to ear. "I'm so sorry about that. I'll make you another one, on the house."

His lips turn down as he glares at me. "I already paid. Just make the damn drink!"

My stomach curls in on itself, visions of making him another cup and then throwing it in his face assaulting my mind.

"Stop." My mystery man's voice makes me falter.

I would be lying if I said I hadn't thought about him over the past two days, but I never in a million years would have expected him to show up here.

He leans against the glass case, his three-piece suit perfectly pressed, giving him an air of sophistication that swallows the guy next to him whole. "Do you have a tendency to let small men speak to you in such a way, darling?"

Shame curdles my insides. "No, I—" I clear my throat. "He's a customer is all."

"Nah, man, this bitch just doesn't know how to do a simple job."

A low chuckle rumbles from my mystery man's chest, the sound vibrating through the café. His frame already towers over the other guy, but like a shape-shifter, he morphs, sucking all the energy from around him and using it to expand his stature. I've never seen anything quite like it, and my gaze is transfixed on the vision.

He leans in close to the customer's ear. "Your watch is rather loud."

The guy scrunches his brows. "Huh?"

My mystery man nods toward the asshole's wrist, the diamond-encrusted watch gleaming like a beacon. "Your watch. It's…*ticking.*"

"Okay, and?"

My mystery man sighs, a hand coming to rub across the bottom of his jaw. My eyes track the movement, taking in how incredibly attractive he is, even more so in the light of day.

The jerk turns toward me, eyes widening as he smacks his palm on the counter *again*, the sound slapping against my insides like nails on a chalkboard.

"Enjoying the show? Make my coffee."

I grit my teeth. If I wasn't at work, I wouldn't be trying so hard to bite my tongue, but I enjoy this job. It's the first one I've ever had, and while I definitely don't *need* it by any stretch of the imagination, it feels good to have something that I've earned. Something that wasn't handed to me because of my last name and the blood that runs through my veins.

As much as I love my father, sometimes it gets heavy living in his shadow.

"*Don't* make his coffee, darling." The pet name flips my stomach, and my eyes volley between the two men.

The customer's face turns ruddy, but he doesn't speak. Doesn't argue. Presumably because even *he* can feel the power radiating from the man standing at his side.

My stranger's tongue swipes along his bottom lip, causing a sharp ache to spread between my legs.

"It's graceful," he says, meeting my eyes. "The way you're acting. Says more about your character than his."

Heat rushes to my cheeks, gratitude lighting me up like Christmas lights. How is it possible that this man was able to take away my humiliation and turn it into something beautiful with a few simple words?

"Fuck you," the jerk spits.

Mystery man's blue eyes harden, a tight smile twisting his lips. He slips a hand into his pocket, leaning in close to the guy, muttering something in his ear.

My ears strain, unable to stop myself from eavesdropping, but he speaks so softly it's impossible to hear. Whatever he says causes the man's eyes to grow large, and he turns and rushes out the door without another word spoken.

I'm frozen in place, my heart beating rapidly in my chest as I glance around. And it's only then I take in that there are other people in the shop. Two young men, standing off to the side, both in black suits and both wearing identical faces. *Twins.*

I was so zoned into what was happening, I didn't even *see* them. Mystery man's eyes glance to them, and he gives a short nod. Without another look, they walk out of the shop and onto the street.

Odd.

He brings his attention back to me, and like a moth to a flame, I'm sucked into his gaze, the questions fading to the back of my mind.

"Are you alright?" he asks.

My heart skips. "Yeah, I'm fine. Thank you, though, for standing up for me."

"He was a cad, darling." His eyes glint. "Not worthy to taste the air you breathe."

My cheeks heat. I had forgotten how forward he is—how absolutely consuming his presence is to be around.

"If you say so." I smile, glancing at my pink nails before raising my eyes back up to him. "What would you like?"

"A date."

My breath stutters, my stomach somersaulting. "A…what?"

He grins, one side of his mouth pulling up. "I think you heard me."

My brow lifts, that same fire I felt two days ago raging back to life. "I did."

"Fantastic." He glances around at the empty tables. "When do you get off work?"

I rest my fingers on the counter. "I appreciate the gesture, but…I have plans tonight."

"That's right," he says. "With me."

Irritation brews in my stomach. "*Not* with you. God, you're cocky as hell, aren't you?"

His eyes flare. "There goes that mouth of yours again."

I smirk, my heart jerking as it slams against my chest.

He leans forward on the counter. "Tell me your name."

"Couldn't find that out when you somehow figured out where I work?" I tilt my head.

He chuckles, standing up straight, his eyes searing through me. "Happy coincidence, I assure you."

"What's *your* name?" I reply.

"I'm James." His hand reaches out across the counter.

My stomach tightens and my teeth sink into my lower lip. Slowly, I lift my arm, placing my palm in his, the warmth of his skin shooting up my arm. "Wendy."

"Wendy." He twists my hand, bringing it to his lips. "It's a *pleasure*."

Heat spikes through my middle.

The bell chimes above the door, a young woman walking in with kids, and I jerk my fingers out of his, straightening my apron.

The left side of his mouth lifts, his eyes never leaving my body. "I'll be seeing you, Wendy, darling."

And then he turns and saunters out the door, the woman who just walked in staring after him with her mouth slightly agape.

I can't say I blame her.

Taking a deep breath to settle my nerves, I ignore the way my insides flush. I've never had attention on me the way he gives it, and I can't help but wonder if this is how he is with everyone— like his world stops spinning, its axis tilting just for you.

Either way, I like it.

It isn't until hours later, when I've closed up shop and settled in for my movie night with Jon, that I realize he never ordered a drink. A small smile lights up my face, butterflies erupting in my stomach at the thought that maybe he was there for me after all.

It should put me on guard, but instead, excitement floods my insides.

And that night, when I go to bed, I dream of cerulean blue.

James.

CHAPTER 6

James

MY SHOE TAPS AGAINST THE STONE TILE OF THE JR's basement floor. I smile, remembering when Ru fought me on installing it, wanting to stick with concrete instead. But I insisted. Concrete is porous, harder to clean. He was thankful for it after realizing that having a cement dungeon in the bottom of a bar would have looked far more suspicious when the feds sniff around.

Which they do every few years.

Even more so after Ru became sloppy—shooting a man in broad daylight and expecting to have no blowback.

If it were anyone else, I would let them rot. The only way to grow from mistakes is by living through the consequences after all. But this is *Roofus*. And if Ru is the sand, I'm the wave that washes away the footprints.

So I handled things. And now we have the feds on our payroll, focusing on our competition, making sure nothing passes their desks with our names. Free rein, as long as it also pads their pockets and keeps their families alive.

The Lost Boys, as the newspapers have affectionately labeled us, run wild and free.

I'm sure it would come as a shock to people who don't understand the game. The majority of Americans live under the illusion that everything works as it should. That government and people who promise an oath actually *do* protect and serve.

They do. Just for me instead of others.

It's one of the reasons I find it *so* lovely to have Peter Michaels and his daughter showing up in the belly of the beast. He's a powerful man. But here, his name is useless, his money nothing more than dyed paper.

People in this city answer to *me*.

Including the pathetic excuse of a human tied to the metal chair in the center of the room. The one who thought he could call Wendy Michaels a bitch and not have to deal with the repercussions. I don't care for disrespect, especially when he was exerting misplaced power over a woman I'm planning to own.

"So," I start, my shoes clacking on the tile as I move to stand in front of him. "Here we are." I grin, my arms raising to the sides.

The man jerks against the zip ties binding him, his eyes wide and red. He mumbles something, but it's difficult to hear behind the duct tape covering his mouth.

My smile grows and I lean forward. "I'm sorry, what was that?"

I look to the twins, two brothers who have been in my employ since I found them panhandling when they were fifteen. They're identical, and I used to confuse them so frequently that I've stopped referring to them by their names at all.

"Did you understand him?" I ask them.

"No, Hook. Couldn't hear a thing," one of them says.

"Hmm." I look back to the bound man in front of me, tapping

my finger to my mouth. "Hard to hear behind the tape. Perhaps we should remove it."

Twin one nods and walks over, ripping the duct tape off. The man's eyes wince, his mouth rubbed raw from the tape being torn roughly off his skin.

"There." I nod. "Now, what is it you'd like to say?"

"Fuck you, man," he spits.

Irritation flickers deep in my chest as I glance down at the saliva pooled on the floor from where it flew out of his disgusting mouth.

"Fuck *me*?" I point to myself, chuckling as I walk toward the metal table lining the wall, unbuttoning my suit jacket. "It's always amusing to me when a man lacks the capability to understand that his life is in danger. I find that it's normally one of two reasons. Would you like to hear them?"

Silence is my only answer.

"It's quite interesting, I assure you." Picking up my black gloves, I slip them over my hands, moving my fingers once they're encased in the leather, admiring the way they feel against my skin. "It's either a matter of pride, or it's a lack of awareness. Both of which are terribly unbecoming traits."

Anticipation simmers low in my gut.

"Do you know which one you are?" I spin around, reaching into my pocket and drawing out my hook knife. Flipping it open, I weave it between my fingers as I walk slowly toward his chair, stopping right in front of him.

He doesn't answer, his eyes following the movement of my blade. I step closer, and his arms jerk against his zip ties, the plastic scraping against the metal backing of his chair.

"No?" I cock my head. "If you ask me"—the tip of my knife

skims across his cheek as I walk behind him—"you lack the type of awareness it takes for one to understand danger. To really *feel* it. You see, if you had"—my gloved hand comes to rest on his shoulder—"you would have known better than to continue disrespecting Wendy Michaels in my presence."

"Look, I don't kn-know who you are, but if this is about the coffee shop, I'm sorry, man." He stutters his words, his voice growing high-pitched and tense.

I *tsk*. "There's that loss of pride. Pity I can't enjoy it."

"Just let me go! I'll do whatever. I'll go apologize to that girl if that's what you want. I just… *Please*." His panic seeps through his words.

My grip tightens, and I bend until my face is next to his ear. "*Stop* speaking, or I'll cut out your tongue and feed it to the dogs while you bleed out all over your cheap polyester suit."

His body tenses under my hand, but he grows silent.

I stand straight, squeezing his shoulder. "Good boy."

Walking around to the front of him, I glance down at his trembling frame, the cast of my shadow creating a haunting aura.

"Where was that self-preservation in the coffee shop, friend?" My grin widens. "We could have saved so much time if you had just recognized your place."

My head tilts when he doesn't respond, my stomach tightening with excitement at the fear swirling through his muddy gaze.

I lean in close, my voice low. "I asked you a question."

"I do-don't kn-know… I just… Sorry. Please let me g-go."

"There, was that so hard?" I twist to face the twins. "Honestly, it's rude how often people don't speak when spoken to." Turning back to the man, I note the wet spot forming on the front of his suit pants, the light gray material growing dark and damp.

Pissing himself no doubt. A smile spreads across my face, and a low chuckle escapes my chest. "Relax, *man*. I was only kidding about cutting out your tongue."

Tick.

Tick.

Tick.

A chill scratches through my insides, causing my head to twitch. I breathe deeply through my nose, trying to calm the nausea rolling through me, growing like a wildfire uncontained.

I lose the battle.

Lunging forward, I grip the man's face between my gloved fingers. He grunts in pain. "I've already told you once how loud that vile piece of machinery is, yet you still wear it in my presence?"

His eyes grow wide, tears dripping down his ruddy cheeks.

Tick.

Tick.

Tick.

The sound causes my insides to shrivel, memories surging forward, reminding me of all the times I had no power. Of all the times I was forced in positions where pride and respect didn't exist. All the nights I lay in bed as an eleven-year-old boy, fresh from England and grieving the death of my family, wondering why on earth God made *me* survive.

What had I ever done that was so wrong?

My stomach rolls and heaves, bile burning up the back of my throat, as my mind spins from the flashbacks. I'm surrounded by the slap of my uncle's crocodile boots on the wooden floorboards. My chest squeezes tight at the sound of his pocket watch, the *tick, tick, tick* bleeding into the still of the night as he closes my bedroom door behind him.

Rage unfurls from the middle of my stomach, thick and heavy, bursting through my insides, blinding me from the explosion until all I see is fire.

My fingers grip the man's jaw until his lips deform, forcing his mouth open in an O. My other hand, holding my knife, reaches into the open orifice and grabs the tip of his tongue, pulling until he screams, his body thrashing against the chair. The feel of my blade slicing into the meaty flesh sends a slither of satisfaction racing down my spine.

"Well," I say as I sever the last of the connective tissue, the *rip* of the muscle making me smirk. "I suppose I lied."

Tossing the useless slab of meat somewhere behind me, I hook my knife in his armpit, thrusting the blade until the edge of the handle meets skin before yanking out, his axillary artery spurting, the liquid hot as it sprays across my face.

Blood drips onto my arm as I raise the edge of my knife behind him, the *snick* of the zip tie being cut lost in the muddled screams of agony that unfurl from his blood-filled, tongueless mouth. I pull his arm to the side of the chair, taking the blunt edge of the handle and slamming it on top of the watch, shards of glass sparkling as they crash to the ground.

"Don't." I repeat the motion. "Disrespect." The bones of his wrist collapse from the impact. "Me." His fingers this time. "Again."

Over and over, I bring down my arms until my sides grow tired from the repetition. My hair is falling on my forehead, a slight sheen of sweat breaking over my brow, and I flip the knife around, the rage burning through my soul urging me to cut off his hand completely. Make sure that he'll never have control of my reaction this way again.

How dare he think he could in the first place.

My knife saws through the tendons and vessels until it meets bone, the useless extremity dangling, skin mutilated and unrecognizable.

I move on, making gashes over his torso, one for every *tick* he's made me endure.

The gurgling screams grow silent, as do the sounds from his timepiece, and as they fade, so does the rage.

Slowly, the nightmares disappear and my eyes blink back into focus. Glancing down, my chest heaving, I take in the blood spatter along my exposed skin and the fabric of my clothes.

I crack my neck, soaking in the blessed sound of *silence*.

My eyes move from the twins, lounging against the far wall, to the man bound in front of me, his eyes vacant and mouth gaping, his corpse soaked in blood from the long, jagged slashes across his frame. His arm is hanging at an odd angle, a pool of dark red formed under the mottled skin. I walk forward, glass from the broken shards of his watch crunching underneath my shoes.

The tightness in my chest eases, and I blow out a satisfied breath. Moving to the metal table, I strip off my gloves and grab my suit jacket before spinning to head out the door. I look at the twins, who have straightened off the wall, and my steps falter as my foot presses on something soft. I look down, amusement flowing through my veins when I see a severed tongue squished beneath the sole of my shoe.

I glance at the twins, running a hand through my hair. "Clean this up, and make sure he wasn't someone important."

They nod, and I leave the room, adrenaline causing every cell to spark under my skin, my blood pumping fast, and my cock hard from the rush of the kill.

There's something strangely gratifying about becoming someone's judge, jury, and executioner. A type of thrill that can't be replicated. One that courses through your insides and makes you feel untouchable. Infallible.

Like a *god.*

Walking up the back stairs and into the office, I grab a plastic bag and unbutton my shirt, followed by my pants, stripping off the blood-soaked fabric to have one of the boys discard.

Changing into the spare clothes I keep hanging in the closet, I sit down in my chair, kicking my feet on the desk, and light up a cigar, basking in the earthy taste. Clicking on the computer screen, I pull up a photo of Peter Michaels and his family, desire cramping my stomach when I zone in on Wendy's face, imagining what it will feel like to have her underneath me. To have her submitting to me fully before I break her and send her back to a fatherless home.

I groan, palming my cock over my pants as it pulses behind the zipper.

Wendy Michaels is a delicious treat, and I can't wait to enjoy every bite.

CHAPTER 7

Wendy

"BUT YOU'LL BE HOME FOR DINNER?" I HATE THE
way my voice sounds—infused with a pleading tone in hopes my
father will actually come home.

The faint sound of paper rustles in the background. "I won't
make it there tonight, honey, but I'll try my best for the weekend."

I chew on my bottom lip, worrying the flesh. My father has
always been a busy man, but he used to make time for me. Over
the years, he's slowly slipped further and further away, and now I
don't know how to reach him. I'm not sure how to convince him
that we need attention too.

"You haven't even been to the new house, Dad. It's like... I
don't know."

He sighs. "What did you expect, Wendy? You know how
things are."

I don't want Jon to have to keep raising himself.

It's on the tip of my tongue to say it, but I swallow it down,
hoping that if I bite my tongue, maybe he'll come home. "What
are you doing anyway?"

He sighs again, and this time there's a distinct feminine voice in the background.

My stomach tightens, my hand white-knuckling the phone. "Are you even in Bloomsburg?"

He clears his throat. "Not at the moment, no."

I scoff, resentment billowing like a storm cloud in the center of my chest. "Dad, you *promised* that when we moved, you'd be around more."

"I am. I *will* be."

My eyes burn. "Then why are you still just…everywhere else?"

Once upon a time, I thought my father hung the moon. I followed him everywhere and did everything with him. So much so, he dubbed me his "little shadow." But as I grew older, things changed. Slowly, I was pushed to the back of the bus until I wasn't even in the same vehicle. Left behind like unnecessary luggage.

Sometimes I wonder if Jon has it easier, not ever having known what it was like. Our father has never given him the attention he's given me. Still, I would do almost anything to have my father's love the way I once had it, and I would do even more to guarantee that Jon could taste it for the first time.

I don't think my father is a bad man. I just think his thirst for adventure overpowered his need for a family until he forgot he had one at all.

"We just miss you is all." I swallow around the lump in my throat, rife with all the things I want to say. "Thank you, by the way, for putting Jon in homeschool."

"Yeah, about that, I've changed my mind. There's a great boarding school outside Bloomsburg I'm sending him to."

My heart seizes in my chest. "*What?*"

"I met with the dean the other day, and they assured me this would be the best place for him."

The breath whooshes from me, realizing he met with a stranger but can't make time for his own children. "Boarding school? Dad, he'll *hate* that. You know how things are for him with other kids."

"Well, these are different kids now."

"*Dad...*"

"*Wendy*," he parrots. "Listen, this isn't up for discussion."

My fingers squeeze tighter around my phone. "Why?"

He hesitates and clears his throat *again*—his tell for when he's trying to avoid the subject. Biding his time, formulating his thoughts before he lets them escape as tangible words in the air. "The dean is a business associate. They've assured me this will be the best fit."

My mind replays the conversation with Jon from the other day, how his shoulders seemed to ease as he talked about getting to stay home. And just like that, a bit of rage seeps into the center of my chest, unfurling like smoke and curling around my edges. The entire reason I moved here was to stay with Jon, to try and bring our broken family back together. My father promised he'd be home more, that Bloomsburg was the perfect spot for him to settle and put down roots and stop living for everyone else.

And now he's going to ship off the only person I have. And I'll be here. Working in a coffee shop and living in a mansion. Alone. *And for what?*

I squeeze my eyes tight and blow out a breath. "When are you going to tell him?"

"He doesn't leave for another week, so I'll be home to tell him then."

"Dad, you *cannot* let me be the one to handle this. He needs to hear it from you. He needs you to explain the reasons why."

My stomach cramps with the realization that I can speak until my throat is sore, but it doesn't change the fact that somewhere along the way, my father stopped listening to what I had to say. And with every day that he's gone—another business trip, or another sight to see that doesn't include us—he slips further from our grasp. Away to somewhere nobody can reach, even if we wanted to.

"I hear you, sweetheart, I do. I'll do it when I come home. Sorry about dinner."

Click.

Swallowing down the irritation, I glance at the fireplace mantle to the photo I placed there of the two of us in hopes it would remind me of better days. In hopes it would remind *him* too. I'm sitting on his shoulders, a big smile splitting both our faces. I wonder when it was that the shift happened. Whether it was me who changed and started to outgrow my naive, fairytale view or if it was he who regressed sometime after our mom's death.

Maybe people *never* change, and it's only our perceptions that alter the view.

My phone dings the second I put it down, and untapped hope spirals through my center, even though I *know* it isn't going to be my father again.

And of course, it isn't. It's Angie.

Angie: The JR tonight, bitch! No saying no. I'll pick you up at seven.

My stomach flips as I read her message, my mind immediately going to the handsome stranger who asked me on a date and then disappeared for days.

Will he be there?

Chewing on my bottom lip, I type out a reply.

Me: Okay. Count me in.

CHAPTER 8

James

"PETER MICHAELS WANTS TO MEET."

My heart clenches the second his name passes Ru's lips. "I'm aware of this already, Roofus. You've talked of nothing else for the past week."

Ru's brows draw in. "Don't be a smart-ass. It's…what do you say? *Unbecoming.*"

My lips tilt up at his attempt at an English accent, although to be fair, even mine isn't as crisp as it once was. The years have muddled it down until it's an odd mix, not quite British yet far from American.

"Do you have a point?" I ask.

"My *point* is that I need you there with me."

I breathe out a sigh, unbuttoning my suit jacket as I sit down opposite his desk. "And why is it I couldn't go in the first place again?"

His eyes narrow. "Because you intimidate people."

My brows shoot to my hairline and I point to myself. "Me?"

He chuckles. "Don't play dumb, kid. We both know you

have this"—his arm waves between us—"thing about you. Other powerful men don't like to be around that."

I bite back my smirk. "*You're* a powerful man, yet here we are."

Ru grins, spinning a cigar between his lips. "I know your loyalty. You work for *me*." He shrugs. "I'm not worried about my place in this world, and I'm not worried about your role in it."

While I appreciate the sentiment behind his words, they cause a cramp to spear the center of my stomach regardless. Ru may think he knows my purpose in this life, but even he doesn't know the truth. He doesn't know that my father moved from America when he was just shy of twenty, becoming the premier businessman in all of England. That I was born into the life of luxury and until his death, there wasn't anyone on earth I looked up to more. Ru doesn't *know* that every second since has been spent focused on vengeance against the man responsible.

A phantom twinge splits my side, and my knuckles tighten against the urge to brush the jagged scar that mars my torso.

Some men are born into this world with purpose; other men are mutilated into it.

An unwelcome emotion threatens to slither its way into the moment, an odd ache attempting to settle heavily in my chest. I clench my jaw as I force it back down. The time for sorrow has long since passed. Now it's simply a thirst for revenge that keeps me going.

Leaning forward in my chair, the fire of my life's goal licks me with its tempting warmth. "So when are we meeting?"

Ru smiles. "Next week."

"Perfect. I have plans the next few nights. It would be a shame for them to fall through."

"Oh?"

I nod, not willing to elaborate—not wanting to give up my prize before I've caught her in my web. I want Wendy to come willingly. To be the bright accent on my arm while I show her off to the world, watch the look on her father's face as she brings me home for dinner.

A grin sneaks along my lips. "A *pet project*, if you will."

He chuckles, running his hand down the front of his face. "Fuck it, kid. If I had your looks, I'd be pussy-deep every single day. I'm surprised you show the restraint you do in the first place."

The muscle in my jaw twitches, and I swallow back the disgust at the vision his words create. As if I'd ever give up control for sexual pleasure. Having the urge is one thing; losing yourself to temptation is quite another. And while yes, I may use Moira to keep my darker urges at bay, I never *need* it. Years of being at the hands of someone who frequently lost their wits have taught me that control is paramount. And while fucking and coming is stress relief, that's all it will ever be. It's never for actual enjoyment.

"You'll be around tonight, though?" Ru asks, his eyes skimming the top of his desk, a vulnerability seeping into the words, so slight you can barely hear it.

Nodding, I stand and make my way to the front of his office. "Of course, Roofus."

I reach into my jacket pocket and grab the box I've brought with me today. Ru isn't much for presents, but he loves his lighters. Has an entire case filled with his collection. This one is special. A custom-made S. T. Dupont, encrusted with red rubies and with an inscription on the front.

Straight on 'til morning.

It's the first piece of advice he gave me and one that's stuck ever since. My thumb swipes across the words, my mind flashing back to that night.

Breathing heavily from exertion, I peer around the building, the brick crumbling under my fingers—evidence of how malnourished the area is as a whole. We aren't in a good part of town, and my mind races, wondering who the man I followed here is. What he must do for a living to be so comfortable in an area that even my uncle has told me to steer clear of.

"Stay away from the town square with the clock tower."

The man's red hair bobs when he moves from the front stoop of the building, the faded green fabric of the awning swaying overhead. He says something and the guys he's with nod before they walk inside, leaving him alone. The stranger twists, the movement sudden, causing my heart to skip. I suck in a breath, whipping around the corner, the brick rough against my back, even through the fabric of my shirt.

Taking a few deep breaths, I peer around the edge again, but this time, he's standing right in front of me, hands in his pockets, gray eyes sparking with amusement.

"Are you following me, kid?"

His accent is thick, his r's sounding like elongated a's, and my eyes widen as I look up at him and nod. I've never been much of a liar.

Maybe I should be afraid, but I'm not. The biggest monster of them all is one who sits at the same table for dinner. Fear has long since marinated in the bottom of my gut like a bubbling cauldron, waiting for me to master the brew so I can use it as poison. So while maybe it's nonsensical, this man doesn't scare me. He inspires hope.

An enemy of my enemy is a friend.

"Well, you've got my attention," he continues. His eyes scan me, lips curling up in the corners. "You Croc's kid?"

My brows scrunch at the name. "I don't know who that is," I reply.

"Croc?" His hand rubs down his face, his head tilting to the sky. "Ah, shit. You are. I saw you watching us from the hallway earlier tonight. What the hell are you doing all the way out here?"

My stomach tightens, shame coursing through my insides at the realization that I wasn't as stealthy as I had hoped. He knew I was there all along. Nausea teases my throat when I think of my uncle also being aware. I run a hand through my hair. "It doesn't matter. It's stupid." I turn to walk away, but a rough grip on my shoulder jostles my frame until I spin back around.

"Don't walk away when someone asks you a question, kid. You've already come this far. Keep going, yeah?"

My forehead scrunches as I take in his words. "Going until when?"

He points to the clock tower that sits in the middle of the town square, the moon and stars shimmering in the background. "Straight on 'til morning."

My head tilts. "What's that mean?"

His arm wraps around my shoulders, bringing me in close. "That means you don't quit until you get what you want. Even if it takes all damn night. Understand?"

I smile at the memory, tossing the present on the desk. "Roofus," I tsk. "Come now. You really think I wouldn't remember?"

Ru grunts, waving me off, but I see the weight slipping from his shoulders and the lift of his lips.

As if I'd ever forget the birthday of the man who saved me.

Jason is a two-bit drug dealer who goes by the nickname Nibs. He's the type who doesn't wash his undershirts and thinks a gold chain makes him tough, but he's always done a decent job at pushing our pixie. Lately, however, he's acquired loose lips, trying to spark an uprising with the other nobody lowlifes who run along *my* streets and think that means they're theirs.

Jason shifts in the booth across from me while I spark up a cigar. The low lighting of the bar casts a shadow across his face, highlighting the beads of sweat forming along his hairline. I'm not entirely sure he knows who I am. Low-level pushers don't normally get the privilege of meeting me.

"Jason, do you know why you're here?" I ask.

"Because I work for you?"

I twirl the cigar between my lips before placing it down on the ashtray, the table sturdy underneath my elbows. "That's correct, Jason. You work for *me*."

His face tightens.

"Have you forgotten?" My head tilts.

"No," he mumbles.

I lean forward. "No, *sir*."

He glances to the twins on either side of him, his Adam's apple bobbing with his harsh swallow.

"Don't look at them," I say. "The time for you to deal with the twins has long since passed." My fingers scratch my chin. "In fact, it was you who decided to turn them away in the first place. So now you get to deal with me. Understand?"

He clears his throat. "Uh…ye-yeah, yes, sir."

"Attaboy." I smirk, relaxing back into the booth. "I've just realized you don't have a drink. You must be thirsty. Would you like one?"

I nod to Moira, who saunters over, hands on her hips. Jason's eyes bounce between me, the twins, Moira, and then back. He opens his mouth to speak, but movement from the front of the bar distracts me from whatever he says.

Like a beacon of light splitting apart the darkened clouds, Wendy Michaels waltzes into the room—straight into the viper's den, like she's waiting to get bit.

Like she belongs.

Sparks tingle at the base of my stomach, my gaze soaking her up like water in the sun. She reaches the bar, followed closely by her friends. Immediately, she's greeted by our bartender Curly, saying something that makes her head toss back in laughter, the lights glinting off her hair as it swishes down her naked back. My shoulders tighten at the restraint it takes to keep from walking over and pulling her away from his attentions.

Tearing my eyes away, I focus again on Jason. I was planning to draw this out, but suddenly I'm desperate to wrap things up. My insides twist with anticipation, and I have to force it down, trying to keep my mind on the task at hand.

"Jason, you seem like a man of…many talents."

His chest puffs out, preening like a peacock.

"I've brought you here today because there seems to be a traitor in our midst. And I need your help." My lips twitch as he nods in agreement, relief visibly coasting across his face. Such a simple, *stupid* creature. "It's come to my attention that somebody has been working against us from the inside."

Jason leans in like he's expecting me to continue, but I don't. I sit back in the booth, picking up my cigar, ignoring the way the smoke suffocates as it swirls around my face.

And I wait.

The seconds stretch into agonizing moments, the only sound the backdrop of patrons in the bar, and my inner voice nags at me to turn my attention back to the pretty girl at the front. But I don't. I keep my focus on Jason, waiting for him to break.

He fidgets the longer I stare, until finally his shoulders tighten. "No, you don't think I—"

I lift a hand, cutting him off midsentence. "It's very interesting to me what happens when you allow the space for people to speak." I chuckle. "You see, silence is often the best way to draw out the *rats.*"

Leaning in, I lower my voice. "There are two ways we can do this, Jason. You can hold on to a modicum of dignity and allow the twins to take you to your new accommodations without causing a scene." I grin. "Or you can do this the hard way." Reaching into my pocket, I grip the leather handle of my knife, gently placing it on the table next to me. "I assure you, picking the latter won't end in your favor."

Jason's head shakes back and forth, his chest heaving with his staccato breath. "Listen, you don't understand. He *made* me. He would have killed me, man. I can't—I didn't have a choice."

My head tilts, filing away his slip of the tongue for later. I'm not surprised he isn't the one behind the whispers. Ru and I both have many enemies, and someone of Jason's stature is more likely to be a bitch boy than a mastermind. My stomach tightens, wondering if he'll be forthcoming with the name or if I'll have to drag it from his throat by force.

I nod, sliding from the booth and running my hand down the front of my suit as I move to his side of the table. I bend down next to his ear. "There's *always* a choice."

And then I walk away, my eyes already locked on the girl at the front of the bar.

CHAPTER 9

Wendy

"OH, *FUCK*, HE'S COMING OVER," MARIA WHISPERS, practically vibrating on the barstool next to me. She zoned in on him the first moment we walked in the bar, nudging me in the ribs until they ached, letting me know her man was in the house.

He's just like she described—surrounded by suits, sitting in the back booth under lighting so dim you can barely make out his shadow.

But I can feel him.

Being raised around a man similar in stature has fine-tuned my ability to know what it feels like when someone bleeds power. And as much as I don't want to admit it, I understand the appeal.

I smile and wink at Maria, twisting in my seat to see, but her nails dig into my arm, clamping down like a vise. *"Don't* look," she whispers. "What are you thinking? This is my moment. We can't act too eager."

Angie snorts into her drink. "As if he hasn't seen you staring over there every two seconds. How do you even know he's coming for *you?* He's probably just going to the bar."

Maria's eyebrow quirks. "When have you ever seen him do that?"

Angie shrugs, and I take a sip from my wine, the dry red liquid making me cringe as it hits my lips.

"I bet he is," I say. "You and he had a connection or whatever, right? He's probably just been busy until now."

"You think?" Maria asks.

I nod, desperate to get on her good side even though she's been nothing but a bitch since the second we met. "Seizing the moment!" I giggle as I fist pump the air.

Her ruby-red lips split into a smile, her gaze widening the slightest bit as they slide past me.

"Fancy seeing you here, darling."

My breath whooshes out of me, dread snaking its way through my insides, because I would know that voice anywhere. And from the way Maria is staring, I have a sneaking suspicion that *her man* is also *my stranger.*

I ignore him, hoping that maybe if I don't react, he'll just go away. But lately, it feels as though nothing I wish for comes true, so of course, he doesn't.

Maria draws her shoulders back, pushing out her chest, and whether I like it or not, my stomach twists, because even though I don't want his attention, I'm not sure I want her to have it either.

I choke down another sip of wine.

Heat prickles along my back, making my hair stand on end. I peer from the corner of my eye and see Maria's face change, her lips drooping ever so slightly. Glancing the other way, I notice Angie's gaze flickering between the man at my back and me.

"Ignoring me in my own bar?" His breath coasts across my ear, and I close my eyes, fighting back a shiver. "That's not very nice of you."

I look one more time toward Maria, trying to convey an apology through my expression, before exhaling a heavy breath and giving my attention to the man who wants it. "I didn't know it was *your* bar."

Spinning around, I expect him to back up, but he doesn't, and my knees brush against his thighs as he crowds my space. My chest squeezes as my eyes meet his ice-blue gaze.

"There are a lot of things you don't know about me." His head tilts. "Let's change that."

My mind replays all our encounters. "Was it you who let us in the first time?"

The right side of his mouth lifts.

"And the secret admirer sending drinks?"

He watches me, his hands slipping effortlessly into his pockets, so similar to the first time we met. "Would you like me to say yes?"

"I'd like you to tell the truth."

"Where's the fun in that?"

"*Wendy*." Maria's voice cuts across the air, snapping me out of the moment. "Are you going to introduce us to your...friend?"

"I wouldn't call him my *friend*." I grimace. "Maria, Angie, this is James. James, this is Maria." I wave my hand toward her, ignoring the slight churning of my stomach. "And Angie."

"Hello, ladies," he greets, his eyes never leaving mine. "Pleasure."

"Oh, believe me, the *pleasure* is all mine," Maria pipes in.

I resist the urge to cringe at her tacky line but wait for him to shift his focus. To realize there's a woman here who's ripe and ready for the picking. I've always assumed men like easy targets, and while I won't lie to myself and say I haven't enjoyed his attention, I am most definitely *not* a sure thing.

Still, his eyes stay locked on mine.

And I don't drop his stare either, feeling somehow like if I do, I'll have lost something I didn't even know to keep.

The air grows thick, and my tongue swipes out to lick my dry lips. His eyes darken as they drop to my mouth.

Angie clears her throat. "So," she says. "You own this place?"

His gaze lingers before he finally, *finally*, breaks away and turns to Angie. My chest expands as I take my first full breath in what feels like a century, and I glance over at Maria, but she's avoiding my stare, her lips pursed and back rigid.

Great.

"Something like that," he responds. "I hope you're finding everything satisfactory?"

Angie's cheeks grow rosy, and she grins. "Drinks could use some work."

"Oh?" He steps in closer, the heat of his body racing up my side and blanketing me in its warmth, his arm resting on the back of my chair. A simple nod from him, and the bartender rushes over, the white towel on his shoulder contrasting against his dark brown skin.

"Sir?"

"It would seem as if the ladies aren't satisfied with their drinks, Curly."

I watch as Curly's broad shoulders stiffen, and for some reason, a prickling sense of urgency comes over me. Like it's important he knows the drinks are fine, that Angie was just making a joke, most likely to ease the tension that's still radiating off an eerily silent Maria.

"The drinks are incredible," I say reassuringly. "They're perfect, James. Angie was just teasing."

His gaze moves from the bartender to me. "You're sure?" I nod, and he turns back to Curly. "These ladies are the most important people here, understand? Their money's no good, and you give them *anything* they ask for."

Curly nods. "You got it, boss."

"In that case, I'll take another." Angie giggles. "You guys want?"

James is already locked back on me, his stare so intense it splits me in half and burrows in my chest.

"You don't have to do that," I say.

He smiles. "I don't *have* to do anything." His hand moves up and brushes a strand of hair from my cheek. The gesture is soft, *gentle*, and butterflies erupt in my stomach. "I want to make sure you're taken care of, darling."

Heat flares deep in my abdomen, and I resist the urge to rub my thighs together, not wanting to show how much he affects me. How this virtual stranger can say something like that and instead of being repulsed or disgusted, I'm *turned on*.

His palm slips into mine, my stomach somersaulting at his touch, and he raises it to his mouth, lips grazing the back of my hand. "Go on a date with me."

Goose bumps sprout along my arm. Vaguely, I hear a gasp to my left, but I can't focus on that, because everything about this man sucks me in like a vortex. An alternate dimension where everything is muted apart from him.

Excitement swirls in the pit of my stomach. "Okay."

He grins, and my breath stutters at how disarming he is when he smiles. Before he can say anything else, a young man—the same one who let us in the bar the other week—rushes up behind him, whispering in his ear. And just like that, James's entire demeanor shifts, the sparkle dropping from his face. He nods before turning back. "Unfortunately, I have to handle some business." He brings our tangled palms up, pressing them into his chest. "You won't leave without saying goodbye?"

I shake my head no, unable to form the words on my tongue, and he brings his other hand forward, his thumb swiping across my cheek. "Good." He glances toward Angie and Maria, tipping his head. "Ladies."

And then he walks away, leaving me to gaze after him, my heart in my throat, weighted stares burning holes through me from both sides.

CHAPTER 10

Wendy

DIPPING MY MOUTH TO MY GLASS, I FORCE THE bitter liquid down my throat. I don't even like red wine, but I wanted to fit in—be *sophisticated*—instead of admitting I didn't really want a drink at all. My chest pulls tight, not sure why I bothered when everything has gone to shit anyway since *he* walked over.

James.

Apparently, the same guy who Maria's been obsessed with, which means he's also…

Hook.

Reality smashes into me like a sledgehammer, throwing everything I thought I knew to bits. He's the one they spent hours waxing poetic about. The man they'd let "split them apart with his monster cock."

I snort into my drink, a giggle bubbling from the center of my chest, unsure if it's the wine that's gone to my head or the remnants of how dazed James makes me feel.

He's elusive. *Dangerous.*

A thrill sparks in the base of my stomach.

I shouldn't be excited by the possibility. I should be on edge with how he has no qualms letting underage girls into his bar. How he always has men surrounding him, seeming to be at his beck and call. I should be wary at how quickly he spins me off-balance until I become so wrapped in his presence I can barely breathe.

But I'm not.

And maybe it's because in the deepest parts of me, I already knew he was different. The hint of danger stretches out like tentacles and suctions to my skin like a dark caress. It's *exciting*, even if I know it shouldn't be. Even if I know my father wouldn't approve.

But my father stopped listening to me a long time ago, so maybe it's time I return the favor.

"What was *that*?" Angie asks.

I shrug, trying to stem the blush that's rushing through my bloodstream and heating my cheeks. I hadn't meant to give in. Had definitely not meant to agree to a freaking *date*, especially not in front of Maria, who's been consoling herself for months with the knowledge that he's "untouchable."

But he isn't.

He'd let me touch him.

Nerves erupt in my stomach, and as much as I try to ignore it, I like the way it feels to be the one who's getting his attention. Like I'm *special*.

Maria downs her drink, placing it gingerly on the counter before she turns her eyes on me, her stare stinging as it rips through my skin.

"Look," I start. "I didn't know he was the guy you were talking about."

She scoffs.

"I'm really sorry, Maria. He's been...persistent." I cringe, knowing I'm only making a bad situation worse.

"It's fine. I'm *fine*." She pauses. "I'm just surprised is all. I can't imagine him being into someone like you."

My nose crinkles, her judgment drizzling on my body like rain. There's never been a moment in her presence where she hasn't found some way to cut me down, and I'm sick of it.

"Maria, don't—" Angie starts.

"What's that supposed to mean?" I cut in.

She shrugs. "It just doesn't make sense. He's a powerful man. One who could have any woman he wanted, and he's stuck on *you?*"

My body instinctively curls in on itself. "Ouch," I whisper.

She smiles, reaching over and patting my forearm. "No offense, of course."

Her words hit their mark, bruising my insides and cutting me open just enough to let my anger bleed. It whips through me like a windstorm, but I push it back down with a few deep breaths.

It doesn't matter what she thinks.

"I won't lie, girl. He was pretty intense," Angie pipes in. "How do you even know him? You've been holding out."

My fingers play with a napkin, shredding the fragile paper to pieces. "I didn't know who he was." I look at Maria. "I *swear*. I literally ran into him last time we were here, and then he showed up to the coffee shop."

Angie's eyes widen. "He *did?* I've never seen him there before."

Shrugging, I look down at the bar top, nausea churning my stomach from how badly I want to change the conversation.

"It's no big deal." Maria waves her arm. "There're a million fish in the sea and all that. Besides, maybe he'll come around more. You don't mind if I snatch him up once he's done with you, right?" She smirks.

She's probably right and I'm just a passing thrill. Something unattainable that he's eager to catch, but the vision that forms in my mind of them together makes my gut twist, green whooshing through my chest.

The feeling stays there for the rest of the night, long after I've switched to sparkling water and watched as the girls get wasted.

It's there as we walk out the front door and flag down a cab, my insides sinking in disappointment because James never made another appearance.

One of my legs is halfway into the cab when a voice calls from behind us.

"Miss."

I spin around, my heart soaring.

"You." He points at me. "I was told to make sure you didn't leave."

When I turn back around, I come face-to-face with Maria and Angie, their eyes wide as they look up at me from inside the car.

It's irritating that I waited all night, like he asked me to, and it's only now he's bothered to stop me. Well, not even *him*.

He begged me for a date and then just as easily pawned me off to his employees.

My jaw locks into place, and I move to slide into the car with the girls, but the icy, drunken daggers of Maria's gaze make me falter, and I find myself replaying all the words she said through the night—the thinly veiled insults striking harder with every lash.

The whisper of anger that's been brewing in my gut finally boils over, and if I have to choose between being irritated with James or verbally assaulted by Maria, the choice is pretty simple. I lean into the car. "Go on without me, ladies. Thanks for a fun night."

Maria's eyes narrow to slits.

Angie laughs. "You sure, girl?"

I nod and spin back around, walking toward the nameless man and waving my arm toward the entrance. "Well? Take me to your master."

His grin drops into a sneer, but he doesn't say a word. His hand pushes on my lower back to propel me toward the front door.

CHAPTER 11

James

MY OFFICE AT THE JR IS THE LARGEST OF ALL THE back rooms. It used to be Ru's, but I convinced him to switch, citing the need for the en suite shower. He doesn't necessarily do any *dirty* deeds, so he didn't put up a fight, but there *are* certain occasions that call for stains to be washed from my skin.

Tonight was no exception.

My hair is still damp as I sit behind my desk, reminiscing over the knowledge I ripped from that idiot Jason's brain. He deteriorated into sobs as soon as I walked into the room, my knife glinting under the fluorescent lights. The sight of my hooked blade twirling through my fingers was all it took for him to tell me everything he knew. Not that his version of truth does me much good. He'd never *actually* known the man whom he decided was worth crossing me for. Not even a name.

But Jason is a pathetic excuse of a boy. And boys are fickle.

Real men have loyalty.

That being said, I'm no idiot. It doesn't take a rocket scientist to put two and two together. There's a new player in town, one with power and money to fly under the radar. To not expose his evil to the world while he parades around like some type of king.

Peter Michaels.

It's smart, truly. After all, it's easier to do misdeeds when you hide them in plain sight. People don't *expect* to see darkness in the daylight.

A knock on the office door snaps me from my thoughts.

"Come in."

A scowl mars Starkey's boyish face as he pushes Wendy into the room.

The pink of her cheeks darken as she glances around the office, her gaze locking on me behind the desk. Her hands twist together, and I bite back the satisfaction at seeing her nerves play so visibly.

"Leave," I say to Starkey, my eyes never moving from Wendy.

The air is thick—the same way it always is when she's here—the energy crackling between us. It would make things easier for me personally if I wasn't attracted to her, but having this type of chemistry will undoubtedly help my plan unfold.

Help make it *believable.*

She moves closer, her pale blue dress swishing around her knees, dark hair framing her cherry cheeks. Her tongue swipes out to lick her bottom lip.

"Hi," she says.

My stomach flips. "Hi back."

"Do you normally send lackeys to do your dirty work?"

I tilt my head. "That depends. Are you planning on getting… dirty?"

She laughs. "You don't ever turn it off, huh?"

"Turn what off?"

"The charm. You must have had lots of practice, as good as you wield it."

I stand up from my chair, walking around to the front of my desk and leaning against it. "Do you find me charming?"

Her face flushes a deeper shade of crimson, making a thrill zip through my chest. "You don't need me to inflate your ego."

I reach out and grasp her palm, gazing at the pink nail polish on her dainty fingers. My thumb swipes across the back of her hand. "On the contrary, darling. I believe I need you for a lot of things."

Her mouth parts on an inhale.

"My turn for questions." I step into her. "Do I make you nervous?"

"No," she mutters. Her chest grazes against my torso with each breath, sending a shiver up my spine.

My free hand brushes a strand of hair behind her ear. "Don't lie to me."

"Or what?" she whispers.

The corner of my mouth tilts. "Better you don't find out."

Our eyes lock again, and my chest spasms. She looks at me as though she's trying to see the colors of my soul, and the feeling makes me *itch*, so I break our stare, knowing the only thing she'll find is its absence.

Her hand reaches up and turns my face, my stomach jolting when she does.

"Why did you bring me back here?"

My gaze bounces from her eyes to her mouth, suddenly desperate to know if she tastes as good as she feels. I lean closer, her breath skating across my lips. "To say good night," I rasp.

She pushes farther into me, her curves pressing against the

length of my body, and even through the fabric of my shirt, I can feel the heat.

This girl is liable to make me lose my mind.

"So are you going to?" she asks. "Say good night, I mean."

My brows shoot to my hairline, surprise flickering through me at how forward she's being. Blood rushes to my cock, making it stiffen, and my arm wraps around her waist, pulling her flush against me, my fingertips skimming up her sides. "Would you like me to?"

"Y-yes," she stutters.

Her hands press against my chest, and I dip down, my lips *so* close to brushing hers.

Knock. Knock.

Wendy jumps back, and my jaw tightens, frustration flowing through my veins at whoever is interrupting. "What?" I hiss.

Ru opens the door and waltzes inside. "Kid, I—oh, shit." His footsteps falter as he takes in the scene. "Am I interrupting?"

I stifle the urge to tell him to get out and instead paste a smirk on my face. "If you're asking, then you already know the answer."

He sits down on the couch against the far wall and spreads his legs wide. "You gonna introduce us?" He nods to Wendy.

My heart skips. *No.* I hadn't intended for Ru to meet her yet. The last thing I want is for him to put two and two together and realize she's the daughter of the man who's trying to dip his hand into our business.

"I'm Wendy."

My head snaps to her, then to Ru, and then the strangest thing happens.

A surge of something hot whips through my insides and slices up my middle until I have to physically stop myself from pulling her into my arms and making sure Ru knows that she's *mine*.

"Wendy." He smiles. "I'm Ru. Nice to meet you."

"You too." Her hand rises in a small wave. "I'll leave you to it. Good night." She smiles, but it's strained, and my chest pulls when she moves toward the door.

I grab her wrist as she walks past. "Let me take you home."

She shakes her head. "No, that's fine, really. I'll grab a cab."

My teeth grind, wanting to argue but knowing I may scare her away if I come across too strong. "At least let me walk you out."

She bites on her bottom lip and nods, turning toward the door.

My palm goes to her lower back, my eyes narrowing at Ru when I see the giant grin on his face. "You." I point. "Stay there."

He raises his hands in the air, chuckling. "Go handle your business, kid. We've got all night."

I walk Wendy out front, ignoring the few patrons left in the bar and Moira and Curly in the corner cleaning up for the night. When we make it to the street, a cab is already there and waiting.

She moves to open the door, but I stop her, my arms caging her in, the metal of the car's roof cool under my fingers. "You're sure you won't allow me to drive you?"

She spins, smiling up at me. "Thank you, but I'll be fine."

I cup her cheek, my thumb brushing across her bottom lip. Her pupils dilate under the yellow glare of the streetlights. "When will I get my date, darling?"

"When do you want it?"

"Yesterday." I press into her. "Now." She stumbles into the cab's door. "Tomorrow."

Her hands push against my chest. "Tomorrow works."

I lean down, my lips brushing against her ear. "And how will I find you?"

"You can pick me up from the coffee shop at seven." She rises on her tiptoes to brush her lips across my cheek. "Good night, James."

And then she slips into the cab, closing the door behind her.

I move to the front, knocking on the passenger window until it's rolled down, taking in the nameplate of the driver, and lowering my voice so Wendy doesn't hear. "*Anything* happens to her and there will be no corner of the earth that can hide you from me. Understand?"

The cabbie's eyes widen as he takes the fold of bills from my hand and nods.

"Good man." I tap the top of the cab and stand at the curb until they turn the corner, wondering what the warm sensation is in my chest and why I feel as though tomorrow can't come soon enough.

CHAPTER 12

Wendy

MY CLOSET IS DESTROYED, MOUNDS OF OUTFITS covering the floor. I groan, glaring at the piles. How is it possible to own a million pieces of clothing but not have a single solitary thing to wear?

Nerves race down my spine as I look at the clock and realize I have half an hour before I'm supposed to meet James at the Vanilla Bean.

Crap.

I could have had him pick me up here, but the thought of him seeing where I live has my stomach churning. If he sees the mansion, he'll wonder how I'm living in it, and considering he's the first person in my life who seems to like me for *me*—instead of who my father is—I'm hoping to avoid that as long as possible.

Plenty of men have tried to woo their way into my heart, all with an agenda in their smile. Their gazes were sweet, but it was only a matter of time before their eyes lit up for my father in a way they never did for me. Not that I fell for them in the first place. I learned at a young age—six, to be exact—that people were more interested in how I could serve their well-being instead of them caring about mine. Even children understand the sting of loneliness, and when my mother died, everyone I had grown to depend on slipped away. As if *I* were the problem. As if my grief was too much of a burden for them to bear.

And maybe that's why I feel such a pull to James. Because for the first time in my life, there's someone who wants me for *me*, not all the other bullshit that comes along with it.

Sighing, I settle on a black dress, tight enough to show off my curves but simple enough where it doesn't look like I'm trying too hard, and I finish getting ready before heading down the stairs.

Jon is sitting in the family room, a hundred pieces of a model airplane deconstructed and taking up the entire coffee table. I plop down in the chair across from him.

He glances up, eyes widening as he takes me in. "You look nice. Big date?"

I smile, my chest warming at his compliment. "Thanks. Yeah, actually, I do have a date."

"Cool." He smiles. "I'm gonna get a head start on the homeschooling stuff."

His words smack my insides, making my chest heavy with indecision. I haven't told him about the boarding school. It doesn't feel right to know and not tell him, but Dad said he would come home. *He* should be the one to see the look on Jon's face when he realizes he's being sent away.

I glance around, noting the finished model airplanes set up in various spots. It's something Jon's always been into, but since we moved, he can fill up the whole house with them. "How you doing with everything?" I ask.

He tilts his head, eyes narrowed on the pieces he's gluing together. "Vague question, Wendy."

"I mean...*everything*. Like, the move and stuff? You okay?"

He shrugs. "I'm fine. Prefer it this way, actually. If I could stay here in this house forever and never leave again, it would be too soon."

Guilt weaves its way through me, wrapping tightly until it bursts. Maybe there's still time to talk Dad out of this stupid boarding school idea. But then again, how healthy can it really be for a kid Jon's age to stay holed up in a house all day with only his big sister for company?

He rubs his nose. "Seriously, Wendy. I'm *fine*. You worry too much."

I grin. "Someone's got to."

"Go enjoy your date." He waves me off.

I chew on the inside of my cheek, my fingers twisting in my lap. "Maybe I could cancel and we could hang out instead?"

Jon's gaze finally leaves his airplane, his eyes wide as he stares at me.

I huff out a breath. "*Fine.* You don't have to look so mortified by the thought."

He smiles at that, the dimples in his cheeks making my heart ache from how identical they are to our mother's.

"Alright then. I'll see you later, I guess." I stand up to leave.

"Don't do anything I wouldn't do."

My eyes narrow. "You don't do *anything*."

He chuckles. "Exactly."

For half a second, I think about canceling with James anyway. He's intimidating—all-consuming in the type of way that makes your insides quake and your mind go muddy. But even as the thought crosses my mind, I toss it to the side, knowing I won't.

James's attention is an ember, flickering through my middle and lighting up everything in its path. And in the darkest parts of my mind, I hope that if my dad hears I'm gallivanting around with a man like James—one who's a little bit older and a lot more powerful—he'll finally come home.

My anxiety rises like a storm surge on the way to the coffee shop. I walk toward the front door, my clammy hands skimming down the front of my dress, breathing deep to calm my nerves.

What was I thinking saying yes to this?

I got here a little early specifically so I'd have some time, but when I walk inside, he's already here, chatting with Angie like they're old friends, his suit cut perfectly to his frame. Idly, I wonder what he'd look like in jeans or an old, stained shirt. It seems like he's never anything less than perfectly put together.

My gaze flicks around the shop. It's busy tonight, and James hasn't noticed that I'm here yet. My heart slams against my ribs. Walking toward him feels like diving in the deep end without knowing how to swim, but it doesn't make my steps falter. If anything, I pick up the pace, an odd sense of excitement making me want to find out how far down the water goes.

Angie sees me first, her eyes sparkling as she takes me in. "Hey, girl, look who's here. Tall, dark, and handsome showed up *early*."

James turns toward me, and like a power surge, my body sparks, the electricity from his stare making my hair stand on end.

"Hi." I smile.

He straightens and moves toward me, close enough to dust a kiss across my cheek. I suck in a breath, the heat of his body sending a shiver down my side. His fingertips trail down my arm as he backs up, and his stare is heavy, stripping me naked with a simple look. A heady sensation grows deep in my belly and settles between my legs.

"Beautiful," he says.

It's one word, but it caresses me like velvet, my insides purring at his approval.

"You too."

He smirks. "You think I'm beautiful?"

His tone is playful, and it ignites that same foreign fire from the first night we met, when I wondered what it would feel like to be a different type of Wendy.

My eyebrow quirks. "What, you think a man can't have beauty?"

"A man can have many things, darling." He steps in closer. "But the only beauty I hope to have tonight is yours."

My stomach flips, butterflies bursting like from a cannon. "Your mouth should be illegal," I mutter. "So where are you taking me?"

Angie laughs. "Who *cares* where he's taking you, girl? Just go." She makes a shooing motion with her hands.

James glances her way before resting his palm on my lower back. "She's right, you know. You should relax, let me wine and dine you properly." He leans in, his lips skimming the top of my ear. "And if you're a good girl, maybe I'll show you the *real* reason why my mouth should be illegal."

Heat floods my body, swirling through my insides and pulsing between my legs. I huff out a surprised breath, my fingers pushing against his chest. "That's extremely presumptuous."

His eyes sparkle, his hand never leaving my back as he moves me toward the door. "Just letting you know what's on the menu."

He leads me outside to a blacked-out Audi. My hand reaches

to grasp the handle, but before I can, he's there, opening the door and helping me in.

My heart skips. Such a simple gesture, but one that makes me feel special. *Taken care of.*

"I feel like I should be offended," I say as he slides into the driver's seat.

He grins, starting the car but leaving it idle as he twists to look at me. "Why?"

"You just told me to be a good girl, and you'd…you know."

His brow rises. "I'm not sure I do."

He moves quickly, leaning over the console, his body crowding me until I press back against the seat. He skims his nose up my neck, and my stomach cramps so tight I lose my breath.

"Because I want to put my mouth on you?" His lips dance from my ear down my jaw until they're hovering above mine.

My heart slams against my chest. *I am so out of my element.*

"I promise you'd like it," he whispers.

And just like that, his body heat disappears as he moves to his side of the car and reverses out of the lot.

CHAPTER 13

James

I'M TAKING HER TO THE MARINA, TO MY HOME. I considered a more public outing, but I've decided against it, not wanting to take the chance of her father finding out before I'm ready.

I'd like him to know exactly who I am before I pull the rug out from under him.

Luckily, Ru didn't ask questions, most likely assuming she was something quick for me to enjoy. If he thought about it long enough, he'd realize I've never had a random girl in the office, only Moira, and only when I need the release. But people see the world through a personal lens, and sometimes it's easier to believe what *you* think is true instead of having to figure out others. Generally, this works in my favor.

Our meeting with Peter is tomorrow, and I'm practically giddy at the thought of meeting him face-to-face and watching the look in his eyes as we tell him no. He can be a dirty businessman all he wants—in fact, I'm quite sure he's excelled at the role for many years—but he won't come into *this* territory and stake ownership. He's taken enough from me. I won't allow him to have this too.

A whiff of vanilla spirals through my nose.

Wendy.

I force a grin, refocusing my attention on her, not wanting to show the violent thoughts running through my head. Surprisingly, I feel no resentment, despite the fact that she's the child of my enemy. In fact, if I think on it long enough, there's a tendril of something sickly and sweet that winds through my insides, regretful she has to be used this way—as a pawn in a goal much larger than she'll ever be.

But I'm never one to pass up a golden opportunity, and that's exactly what she is. A way for me to play with my prey before I end him.

Peter Michaels doesn't deserve a quick death. He deserves a reckoning.

A realization that he has no friends. No family. No pride. That *everything* was taken from him, his choices stripped away, and his reality molded into nightmares.

And *then* I'll kill him.

We pull into the marina, and before I even have the key out of the ignition, Wendy is reaching for the door. My hand shoots out, wrapping around her wrist. "What's the rush? Stay still."

Her eyes widen as she pauses. "Oh, I—"

Releasing her, I slide from the car, walking around to open the passenger door. A spike of arousal flares through me as I gaze down, her chocolate eyes sparkling as she grins up at me, her face level with my groin. Such a pretty position we're in. I reach my hand out, and she places her palm in mine, my fingers squeezing slightly as I pull her from her spot. As soon as she's standing, I jerk her forward, her breath whooshing as she stumbles into my frame. "Allow a man to be chivalrous, won't you?"

Her head dips slightly to rest against my chest before she clears her throat and backs away. She glances around. "Are we going on a boat?"

I smile. "Is that alright?"

Nodding, her fingers twist in front of her. "It's fine. I just... I don't do the best on water."

My hand rests on her lower back as I guide her toward the walkway, past the other boats, where at the last slip, my forty-three-meter sailing yacht sits. The *Tiger Lily*.

"We aren't taking it anywhere. I just thought we could have dinner somewhere private."

Sliding my palm around her waist, I help her step from the walkway onto the side deck. I don't normally bring people to where I live, and definitely never a woman, but I want her to feel special. *Different.*

"This is yours?" she asks.

Nodding, I follow behind her, the feel of her black dress soft underneath my hand. "It is."

Sailing yachts are wonderful for a number of reasons. Luxurious, comfortable, and most importantly, they're extremely mobile, allowing me to escape to one of the many slips I own around the world if needed.

She looks around the living room, the cream furniture setting nicely against the cherrywood floors. "Do you live here?"

My stomach tightens as I watch her take it in. "I do."

"It's beautiful."

Warmth trickles through my chest. I walk up behind her. "You're beautiful." She spins and I step closer, enjoying the way her body flushes crimson every time I do. "Would you like a tour now or later?"

"Hmm." She tilts her head to one side, and I resist the urge to lean down and skim my lips across her skin. "I think dinner first, and then a tour."

Nodding, I lead her to the sun deck where I had my live-in crew member, Smee, set up dinner. I smile, pleased with the result of his work. Patio lights are strung, casting a romantic glow, and white linen and plates are set on the round table surrounded by the U-shaped cushioned benches, champagne cooling in the center.

"Wow, this is gorgeous up here," she breathes. "Is that a *hot tub?*"

I pull out her chair as she sits before walking to my side of the table. "Yes. We can get in it if you like."

Sitting across from her, I uncork the champagne and pour us both a glass, ignoring the way my chest pulls at the sight of her surrounded by the pinks and purples of the sunset. I wasn't lying when I told her she was beautiful. She is.

Achingly so.

"I hope salmon is alright?" I ask.

Glancing at the food, she nods, picking up her fork. "It's perfect."

She's quiet while she eats, and I take her in, my cock growing with every small bite she slips into her mouth, her eyes closing as she moans at the taste. We both clear our plates, small talk and the breeze off the water the only things to keep us company.

Smee comes by silently to clear our plates, making Wendy jump in her chair. "Oh my *god*, I didn't know anyone else was here."

I smirk. "That's Smee. My first mate, if you will."

He smiles, his brown hair bouncing under his ridiculous red beanie as he inclines his head. "Pleasure, miss."

"First mate." She giggles. "Like a pirate? Does that make you the captain?"

Amusement trickles through my chest and I sit forward. "Why yes, actually. I commandeer *every* vessel I'm in. I'd be more than happy to show you."

Her mouth drops, her cheeks splotching with pink.

The sun has long since set, the moon casting a haunting glow off the water, and I wait until Smee clears our plates and walks inside before I speak. "You look wonderful in the moonlight, darling."

Taking a sip of her drink, she laughs. "You're really something else, you know that?"

I lift the champagne flute to my lips, letting a bit of the bubbly liquid fizz on my tongue before I swallow. "Compared to what?"

She tilts her head. "Well, I'm not sure. To all other men, I guess."

"And that's a bad thing?"

"No, not at all." She grins.

It's a gorgeous smile, but it doesn't light up her face, and irritation smarts at my insides knowing that she's suddenly putting on an act. I may be using her as a prop—a temporary toy—but I don't enjoy when things I consider mine aren't taken care of in my presence. And that's what she is until I decide otherwise: mine.

"Don't do that."

"Do what?"

"Put on a show. Not here. Not with me."

She shakes her head. "Then can I be honest?"

"I hope you'd never be anything less."

"I don't really know how to act around you. I can't tell if you're really trying to get to know me, or if you're trying to impress me, or what."

My brows lift. "And what if I *am* trying to impress you?"

Her lip twitches. "Then it isn't working."

"Oh?" My brows lift and I set down the champagne flute, leaning in. "Well then, what *would* impress you?"

She smirks. "If I have to tell you, then it's not very impressive, is it?"

A laugh bubbles in my chest, but I bite it back, my hand coming up to rub at the scruff on my chin.

"I want to know about *you*," she says.

My stomach turns at her words. I open my arms and glance around. "Sorry to disappoint, but this *is* me, darling."

She shakes her head, placing her napkin on the table before standing and coming around in front of me. And then she plops down right in my lap. My hands shoot immediately to rest on her thighs, surprise flickering through me at her boldness. *This* I did not expect.

"No," she whispers, her face inches from mine. My abdomen tightens, noticing for the first time how amber flecks scatter within the dark brown of her eyes. "This is what you have," she continues. "I want to know what's in here." Her hand presses against my chest.

My heart thumps against its cage, hoping she can't feel it through my skin—not wanting to admit, even to myself, that what she's doing is affecting me.

But it is.

Moving my hand to cup her cheek, my thumb presses into her bottom lip. Her breaths are heavy, her chest brushing against mine with every exhale. Our eyes are locked, and there's this unsettling feeling brewing in my gut. It's new and *unwelcome*, and I don't know how to control it, so I do the only thing I can think of to drown it out.

I lean in and I kiss her.

CHAPTER 14

Wendy

HIS LIPS ARE SURPRISINGLY SOFT WHEN THEY MEET mine, not that I'm complaining.

I give in, sinking farther into his hold, his arm wrapping around my waist and pulling me tighter as his hand cups my cheek.

My heart soars with his sweet caress, but soon enough, as if the fire licking my veins is reflected in his actions, he deepens the kiss, his tongue prying my mouth open. I moan at his taste, my stomach somersaulting at the way he completely consumes me. Heat shoots through my middle and throbs between my thighs, and I fling my leg over his to straddle him, my center coming to rest directly on top of his lap.

He groans when I settle my weight, his hips pushing into me. I suck in a gasp at the movement, my lips breaking away at the feel of him hard and thick beneath me. His hand drags my face back to his.

I press down, rocking forward, the friction of his length along my slit causing tingles to race through me, my clit swelling as a rush of wetness seeps from my core.

Moving his hand from my cheek, he settles both palms on

my hips, guiding my movement as we work up a rhythm, his lips breaking from mine to move down the length of my neck. He bites, sucks, and kisses, and while I'm sure he's leaving marks, I can't find it in me to care, too lost in the way he seems to mold me to fit perfectly to every single piece of him.

"You taste so much better than I imagined," he groans into my skin.

My head falls back, allowing him more access to the expanse of my throat.

"Do me a favor, pet."

"A—anything," I stutter out.

"Grind that sweet little pussy on me until you make a mess all over my lap."

I moan, even though his filthy words send a rush of embarrassment through me. I've *never* had someone speak to me that way. Still, there's such an enticing command in his tone, one that reaches out and wraps around my body, urging me to comply.

My wetness is soaking through the fabric of my underwear as I chase my high. His length pulses against me, growing more rigid with every roll of my hips. The thought that I'm the one doing that to him, that *I'm* the one causing him to become so hard, sends a burst of confidence through me, and I double my efforts, something hot coiling in the base of my stomach.

His gaze soaks me up like a sponge, and I close my eyes, imagining what it will feel like with him inside me. My core clenches, aching for something to fill it, even though nothing has been there before.

He leans forward, his lips brushing up the side of my neck, causing goose bumps to sprout along my body. "When you're all alone in your room, how do you make yourself come?"

I can barely focus on his words, my mind foggy from pleasure, but I get what he's asking. And for some reason, I trust him to know. So instead of speaking—something I'm not sure I'm even capable of right now—I show him.

Moving his hand from where it's resting on my waist, I place it back on my neck. And then I press his fingers in, because I want him to squeeze.

His eyes flare, his arm wrapping fully around my waist and jerking my body flush against him. "Do you like to be choked, darling?" His fingers grip tighter with a thrust of his hips. "Want me to squeeze your throat until you're on the edge of oblivion and seeing stars?" The pressure increases.

I moan, my eyes rolling as my head tilts back. Pleasure skitters along my skin and rushes through my bloodstream. The truth is that even with my inexperience, I have urges. Nights where I lie in bed, playing out my fantasies in the shadows of the moon. And there's only been one way I've been able to make myself come: by holding my breath until my lungs seize and my mind goes dark.

Maybe it's stupid of me to allow this virtual stranger to control something as vital as the air I breathe, but for some reason, I trust him.

"Please," I force out.

He flips us, my body pliable and willing beneath him as he lays me on the cushioned bench. His body looms over me like danger in human form, his eyes dark as he applies the perfect amount of pressure against my windpipe. His other hand glides down my body, lighting up my insides with sparks, his touch like gasoline to the fire in my veins. His palm skims along the hem of my skirt and he slips underneath, running the pads of his fingers right along the crease of my drenched underwear. My hips push against his hand, desperate to feel him touch my skin.

His grasp tightens on my neck at the same moment as he sneaks beneath the seam of my panties. "So wet for me," he says, his fingers coming up and smearing my arousal along the seam of my lips.

My heart skips, my stomach screwing up so tight it may shatter at any second.

"Such a delicious temptation." He licks the juices from my mouth.

My legs tremble.

And then his hand is back at my core, two fingers spreading me open and slipping easily inside from how soaked I am. I gasp, my back arching at the intrusion.

His face is still next to mine, his mouth laving kisses along my jaw. "So tight. Has anyone touched you here before?"

I'm not sure if he wants me to say no, but the thought of him assuming I'm some untouched flower with *zero* experience is so unappealing, I can't find it in me to lie. "Yes," I rasp.

His eyes darken, fingers twitching against my esophagus. His breath coasts along my ear and down my neck, sending a chill racing along my spine. "No one is allowed to touch you here again." His fingers pump in and out while his thumb circles slowly against my swollen clit. "I'm a very possessive man, Wendy. And I want you for myself."

His words should set alarm bells ringing, but all they do is stoke the flames of my passion, making it hard to breathe.

Or maybe that's his hand slowly increasing the pressure against my neck.

I suck in as deep a breath as I can with his iron vice grip, feeling like I might die if I don't get to come. My head grows light as my lungs beg for air, my mind screaming for me to claw at him to try and relieve the pressure. My hand flies up, fingers wrapping around his wrist, the veins of his forearm tensing under my palm. My center contracts.

His grip on my throat tightens as the pressure in my clit pulses and throbs, spreading a tingling sensation through my body. A burn grows through my chest, radiating outward, and darkness rims my vision. And then I explode, my mouth opening on a silent scream, inner walls milking his fingers as if they want to suck him up and never let him leave. His hand immediately loosens, turning into soft, soothing strokes as I suck in mouthfuls of air, my chest heaving against his.

"Such a good girl," he purrs.

Satisfaction courses through my veins and burrows deep into my chest, warm and fluffy and everything good. He moves, lifting my body so he can settle in behind me, and I curl up on him, his large hand stroking my hair and whispering words of praise.

I don't try to speak, don't try to think too hard over what I just let happen. How he's treating me like some type of pet that he's proud of—or how it makes me feel when he does. I just close my eyes and let this moment be what it is.

And when I wake up, I'm no longer on the deck, and I'm all alone.

CHAPTER 15

James

THE TEAKETTLE BOILS ON THE STOVE, AND I STARE at the backs of my hands as they grip the counter. That—what happened earlier with Wendy was unexpected. But *Christ*, the way she came apart under my fingers, the way she *begged* me to cut off her air supply and trembled beneath my touch, had me dangerously close to losing control.

And that is unacceptable.

I'd love to deny it, but unfortunately knowing one's own weaknesses is paramount to overcoming them, and *Wendy* becoming a weakness is painstakingly obvious. Especially after I carried her off the sundeck to my personal quarters and then proceeded to watch her sleep, enjoying the way her dark hair contrasted against the cream of my sheets.

I glare at the teakettle, irritated that she affects me so strongly. That she calls to my base urges and brings them to the forefront, making me wrestle for control. With a scoff, I push the kettle off the burner, running a hand through my hair.

"I can do that for you, you know," Smee says as he walks into the room with the remaining dishes from dinner.

"That won't be necessary, thank you."

He nods, heading to the sink, placing the glasses next to the basin. "She's a beautiful girl."

"Hmm?" I ask, my thumb and forefinger rubbing against my chin.

"I said she's a nice girl."

I turn, taking him in. Smee is close to my age and has been working on my boat since I found him on the streets next to the JR when I was eighteen—the weekend after I killed my uncle. He was homeless, begging for change, but there was a look in his eye. Something that told me he was dealt a bad hand in life and just needed a way to regain control after it had been stripped away.

And that's something I can relate to.

For weeks, I would visit him, taking small rations of money and warm food and clothes, watching from the sidelines to see if he was a by-product of the drugs I funnel onto the streets or if he was something else. Someone worthy of a second chance.

Luckily for him, it was the latter.

When I bought the *Tiger Lily* with my parents' inheritance, the one that was kept from me by my uncle, I went straight to Smee and offered him room and board. A new chance. A fresh start. So long as he swore his loyalty and only worked for me. Outside of Ru, he's been the most constant thing in my life.

Still, I keep him at arm's length, not allowing him to know about the darkest parts of my life. Anyone can flip if given the right incentive, and while I know Smee would follow me to the ends of the earth, I'm not willing to risk him being snatched up and spilling secrets that aren't his to tell. It would be a shame to have to end his life.

"I don't need you to approve of my conquests, Smee. Wash

the dishes and keep my yacht in check. *That* is what I pay you for," I snap.

"Apologies, boss man." He nods and turns his back, focusing on the dishes in the sink. But his words have filtered through my already frayed edges. I *know* what a nice girl Wendy is, her purehearted innocence bleeding from her pores like oil, shiny and impossible to look away from. Maybe that's why she calls to me the way she does—the pitch-black parts of my soul aching for her light.

Heading back to my personal quarters, I remind myself of what's at stake. She's a *tool*. Something to be used and broken, a means to an end and nothing more. And while I'm quite looking forward to enjoying myself with her, allowing these *feelings* to muddle up my insides will do me no good.

My purpose reinforced, I slide open the door, steps faltering when I see her sitting up in the center of my bed, hair a mess on her head and eyes still heavy with sleep.

A grin lights up her face, making my stomach tighten.

"Hi. I was worried when I woke up all alone."

I sit on the edge of the bed. "My apologies. I thought you might be thirsty but then realized I'm not sure what you'd like."

"Oh." Her cheeks grow round with her smile. "That's nice of you. For a moment, I was worried I'd been kidnapped. Waking up in a strange room was a little disorienting."

"Wonderful kidnappers to keep you in such high-quality sheets."

"Well, you never know. They could have been trying to trick me into submission."

My lips twitch, amusement bubbling in my chest. "Trick you?"

"Yeah, you know." She moves a strand of hair from her forehead. "Stockholm syndrome or whatever."

My brows raise. "And you think you're susceptible to such a thing?"

She nods. "I think we're all susceptible to strange things when our emotional and physical states are under duress."

"Very astute, darling." Nausea churns in my gut.

The backs of her hands come up to rest against her cheeks. "I'm so sorry I fell asleep after...you know. I didn't mean to."

She shakes her head and a faint dusting of color catches my eye. My arm moves forward to brush my fingertips along the pink marks gracing her neck. "Don't ever apologize for finding comfort with me." I remove my hand, blood rushing to my groin as I realize she bears my prints around her throat like a collar. "Is your neck okay?"

Her hand moves from her cheek to her windpipe. "It's fine."

"You're sure?"

"It doesn't hurt." Her lips turn up. "It feels perfect."

"It looks as though it may bruise."

She shrugs.

I lean in, tilting her head to the side and pressing a soft kiss to the prints. "I rather like the idea of you having a reminder of me on your skin." Her mouth parts as she sucks in a breath. I tip her chin and close her lips with my fingertips. "You can stay here if you like, or I can take you back to your car."

"What time is it?"

"Late," I reply.

Her fingers twist in her lap. "I think I should probably head home. I have to work in the morning."

I nod. "I understand, although I do wish you'd spoil me and stay."

The car ride back to the Vanilla Bean is quiet, soft classical music playing through the speakers while she gazes out the window. Again, I find myself appreciating all the ways she doesn't push for conversation, instead choosing to find comfort in our silence. There are not many people who can do that, and it makes my respect for her grow.

I park next to her car, and this time, she doesn't even attempt to open her door. Pleasure trickles through me, knowing she's already doing as I ask. Once I open the door, she takes my hand and lifts herself out before resting her palms on my chest. "Thank you for a wonderful date," she says.

"You can thank me again after our next one." My arms wrap around her waist and pull her closer.

"You're so sure there will be one?"

I grin, walking her back until she's flush to the side of the car. My hand leaves her waist, gently wrapping around her neck, my fingertips ghosting on top of the bruises. I tip her head back. "I've told you once before that I want you for myself." My lips brush against her jaw. "I think you'll find I can be very *persistent*."

Her breath stutters and a visceral want slams into me, my insides quaking with the need to dive inside her. To feel her body mold around me as I destroy her from the inside out.

I force myself to pull back, my fingers squeezing slightly before releasing.

"What's your last name?" she asks.

"Barrie," I respond without thought. My heart kick-starts, lungs squeezing. I didn't mean to tell her that. It's too risky; our fathers worked together for years, and I can't be sure she's never heard it. Luckily, she doesn't even flinch.

The reminder of who she is filters through my veins like poison, anger slicing through the fog of her presence, and I regain the control I felt slipping away.

Her hand rises to my face, fingers splaying under my eyes. "What was that?"

"What was what, darling?"

She shakes her head. "Something…your eyes…they changed."

"Did they?" I rock back on my heels, ignoring the way my stomach is knotting up tight. "Just hoping you'll put me out of my misery and agree to be mine."

She glances at the ground before peering back at me. "If I'm yours, then what are you to me?"

Your worst nightmare. "I'm whatever you'll allow me to be."

Her teeth sink into her bottom lip, and my thumb reaches up to release it. "Tell me you're mine, Wendy darling."

"I'm yours," she breathes.

Satisfaction races through my bloodstream and I smile, leaning in and pressing my lips to hers, then helping her into her car.

As soon as she turns the corner, my smile drops, cheeks aching from the show. But satisfaction flows freely through my veins, the taste of vengeance fresh on my tongue.

CHAPTER 16

James

GIDDINESS FLOWS THROUGH MY VEINS LIKE PIXIE dust flows through a junkie, my mind racing a thousand miles a minute. I've been waiting for years to see Peter Michaels face-to-face, and the moment is finally here. Sooner than I originally anticipated, but welcome nonetheless.

I wonder if he'll recognize me. I was often told growing up that I was the spitting image of my father, but I'm not sure how much truth there is to that statement anymore.

Right after my parents' deaths, I remember sitting in our empty home, strangers attempting to comfort me as they asked what I'd like to pack. What I'd like to *keep*. As if my entire life could be summed up and shipped off with a few cases of clothing. I stayed silent, choosing to only take a small box of mementos. An old book of fables my mother read to me every night and a single photo of the three of us: my mother, my father, and I. I kept them hidden underneath the bed at my uncle's, and at night, when the grief would wind its way through my insides and wrap around my throat, making me feel as though I couldn't breathe, I'd take them out. I'd grip their still faces in my hand as I cried into my pillow, imagining my mother's voice reading me fairy tales with happy endings.

But one night, shortly after my arrival, my uncle found them. I begged and pleaded on my knees like a pathetic *dog*, willing to do anything to keep what small pieces of them I had. But he didn't care about that. He didn't care for much of anything other than obedience and pain. And that night, he made sure I learned the meaning of both. He kept me on my knees as he promised to give me back my things, his thin knife nicking along my torso, causing beads of blood to spill—the sight making fear clamp down on my soul. He told me how he hated my father, how my face made him sick. And after he stripped away any innocence I had left, he burned every single item and laughed as I cried, shame and agonizing grief mixing together with the aftertaste of his vile pleasure.

But my tears dried quick, and I vowed to never let them fall again.

Over the years, I tried to hold on to their faces, the sound of their voices, and the smell of their hair. But like all things, memories fade. The mind is far too easy to manipulate, even by our own subconscious. Fact becomes fiction, or at the very least a warped version of the truth. And the past grows distorted and blurred.

"We're meeting him at Cannibal's Cave." Ru's voice snaps me out of my thoughts.

My brows rise, surprised that's where Peter wants to meet.

Cannibal's Cave is an abandoned cavern deep in the forest about half an hour outside the city. The rumor is that it was used by the government back in the fifties to hold military equipment, but it's long since been abandoned. The random hiker goes by now and again, but for the most part, it's an empty space, too hidden behind dense trees for even the homeless to seek shelter.

Ru grins, sitting back in his chair and lighting a cigar. "So where were you last night? I had the twins collect the new shipment, thought you'd be there to inspect the product."

My insides twist. "I was indisposed. The twins can handle it."

"But they don't know weapons like you."

"Was there an issue?"

"Not that I know of."

I nod. "Well, if there's an issue, I'll see to it."

Ru scowls, lifting the back of his hand up like he's ready to smack the air. "The amount of disrespect that comes outta your mouth, kid. I swear to God."

"Oh, come now, Roofus. You're one of the only people alive that I *do* respect."

He puffs on his cigar. "Yeah, well... I didn't say it the other day, but thank you for the gift."

I cringe, my stomach twisting.

"Now don't go getting all weird on me, kid," he continues. "Just let me say what I need to say."

Sighing, I stand, walking to the globe in the corner of his office that houses the brandy, pouring myself two fingers and spinning around. The ice clinks against the edges of the glass.

"You're the closest thing I've ever had to a son," he says.

My heart twists violently in my chest, my fingers gripping my drink so hard the ridges of the crystal imprint onto my skin.

"And I know you don't like the sentimental garbage, so I'll make it quick. We have a lotta enemies. And I'm just saying..." He clears his throat. "I'm glad you've got my six, kid."

The tendons in my jaw tighten as I clench my teeth, pushing down the knot of emotion lodging itself in my throat. I tip my drink toward him. "Every night."

"And straight on 'til morning." He winks.

The first and only time I met Peter was on a "family vacation," which was actually code for my father, Arthur, having business in America. I never knew exactly what he did for a living other than he was powerful and everyone in London seemed to know and revere him. I knew he had a business partner here in the States, one whom he visited often, usually without us. However, this time, it was my parents' anniversary, and my mother insisted we come along for the trip.

It was the next morning at brunch where I met Peter and his picture-perfect family. At the time, I didn't think anything of it. After all, I had parents who loved me, and I never wanted for anything. Still, for some reason, the strongest sense of urgency filled me when I saw him for the first time. I wrote it off as hating the Florida weather. It was too muggy and hot. Too *bright* after a lifetime in the overcast skies of London.

And then his beautiful wife walked in carrying a baby, couldn't be older than a year, and holding the hand of a young girl with brown hair and a smile that reached out and struck you with its glow. Their mother was pretty, but she paled in comparison to mine.

Peter smiled and shook my hand, the soft skin of his palm making me feel important. *Respected.* Stupidly, I looked up to him in the same way I did my father. And two days later when we flew home on a NevAirLand private jet, courtesy of Peter Michaels, it went down in flames, crashing into trees and killing everyone on board. Everyone except me.

I'll never forget the look on my father's face as he read the handwritten note minutes before—the one passed off by Peter himself. I had never known a living man could go as sickly white as a ghost.

It's that image that haunts me now as we drive up the darkened pathway to the entrance of Cannibal's Cave. The crunch of the gravel underneath the tires echoes the feeling of my insides, knowing I'll have to hold myself together and not kill Peter where he stands.

Starkey parks the car and leaves the headlights on—the only way to light up the black of the night.

And there he is, leaning against a Rolls-Royce in a green button-down shirt and dark slacks. His men stand slightly ahead, and a stunning blond woman is by his side.

"You ready, kid?" Ru looks over to me. "Keep it cordial, yeah?"

I lift my brows. "Of course, Roofus."

"And *don't* call me Roofus in front of him, for Christ's sake."

Ru steps out of the car first, and I follow shortly after, allowing the limelight to land on him as I slink behind in the shadows, not wanting Peter to see me just yet.

"Ru, I presume?" Peter's voice sails across the air, making my stomach churn.

Ru grins. "That's me. You would know that if you had shown up the first time."

Peter inclines his head, his graying hair bobbing with the motion. "I apologize. I'm sure you can understand why I sent one of my men first. Privacy and discretion are of the utmost importance."

I place my hands in my pockets, my thumb rubbing harshly against the wood of my knife, trying to drown out the thumping of my heart.

"And who is this?" Ru asks, his hand waving toward the woman standing behind Peter.

Peter glances back at her. "This is Tina Belle. My assistant."

Her blond hair is pulled back tightly, and she smiles and waves.

"Tina, nice to meet you," Ru says. "Well, we're here. Talk to us."

Peter's head cocks to the side, his eyes floating from Ru to Starkey and finally to me, standing in the shadows. "You have me introduce my people, but you don't give me the same courtesy?" He points to his chest. "If you're planning on us working together, respect goes both ways. There needs to be a level of trust."

Anger burns deep in my gut. *Trust.* Laughable, really.

I step out of the shadows and into the light, my hands in my pockets.

"Trust *is* a funny word, isn't it?" I ask.

Ru turns to me, narrowing his eyes. I grin at him and wink.

Peter gazes at me for long moments, as if he's soaking in every single feature. And then his cheeks pale the slightest bit.

Excellent.

"After all," I continue, "we *trusted* that when someone of your caliber comes into our territory and requests a meeting, he would do us the courtesy of actually showing up." I step forward until I'm shoulder to shoulder with Ru, my hand white-knuckling my knife, trying to filter all my rage into my grip so it doesn't show on my face.

I've waited on this for fifteen years, and I'm going to see my plan through, no matter how much my blood is scratching at my insides, screaming to end him here and now.

Peter licks his lips. "And you are?"

I chuckle, glancing at the ground before meeting his stare. "You can call me Hook."

"Ah, yes. *Hook*." Peter sneers. "Your reputation precedes you." He tilts his head. "Didn't know you were British, though."

I smirk, resting against the front of our car.

Peter's men come closer, but he shakes his head. "Relax, everyone. We're all just businessmen having a conversation." His eyes sear into mine. "Isn't that right?"

"I suggest you get to your point," Ru snaps. "You've already wasted enough of our time, and I'm liable to get *impatient* quick."

Peter's brows lift to his hairline. "Do you know who I am?"

Ru cocks his head. "Are you suggesting I'm stupid? You come into *my* territory and think because your name is Peter Michaels that you can ask us to jump and we'll say how high, then thank you for the favor?" He shakes his head. "That isn't how it works here. You want to run for me with your planes and your ships, we can talk. I'm more than willing to strike up an amicable agreement. But don't think for one second that because you're a golden boy in the eyes of the world, I'll give a damn here in my home." He points to his chest. "These are *my* streets. And everyone in them pays their dues. You get me?"

My insides splinter at Ru's words, shock spearing my stomach like an arrow. He's considering working with him. After we agreed he'd say no.

Peter's silent for long moments before he rubs his chin and nods. "I'll run your pixie and your weapons, but I want fifty percent."

My teeth grind, and Ru huffs a laugh. "Ten."

Peter smiles. "Forty."

Ru's lips thin, his eyes growing dark. "I think you got me confused, huh? I don't *need* you."

"That may be true." Peter nods. "But you'd be a fool to turn me away. You may have runners, but none with my expertise and none with a globally known carrier service that can enter any country at *any* time." He walks closer to Ru, and my spine straightens. "All you have to do is say the word, and I'll pack your pixie and fly it to places you've only seen in your dreams."

A ring interrupts the moment, and Peter pulls his phone from his pocket, glancing at the screen. Sighing, his body slumps. "Unfortunately, gentlemen, I have to cut this meeting short." He looks up, his eyes crinkling in the corners with his smile. "I promised my daughter I'd be home for dinner."

My stomach somersaults at the mention of Wendy. I wonder how he would feel knowing that his daughter's cum was covering my fingers just the night before. That I held her life in my hands while she begged me to edge her to the brink of death.

Peter walks forward, putting his hand out for Ru to shake. "We'll finalize plans sometime this next week. Make the right decision, yeah?"

And then he comes to me. His charming mask slips slightly as he cranes his neck to look me in the eyes. Bile burns the back of my throat as I place my palm in his.

His gaze is cold. Calculating. "Maybe one day you'll tell me your name?"

Anticipation slams into me like a battering ram, and a smile stretches across my face. "I look forward to it."

CHAPTER 17

Wendy

MY FATHER ACTUALLY CAME HOME. TWO HOURS later than he said he'd be and with a mystery woman attached to his side, but I'll overlook the details, because having him here outweighs any of the negatives.

Even though he missed dinner.

"So what is it you do for my dad again?" I ask Tina, following them into the unused home office.

She grins, grasping a folder under her arm as she makes herself comfortable on the dark leather couch. She's beautiful in a spritely sort of way. Slim and petite, with a button nose and wispy bangs. But I can't help the envy that swirls deep in my gut, knowing she gets untapped access to my father's attention while the rest of us pray for a drop.

"I'm his right-hand woman. Your father would be lost without me." She turns to him, smiling, and he winks back.

Gag me. Sucking my bottom lip into my mouth, I nod. "Oh."

"She's my assistant," Dad chimes in.

"Is she the voice I always hear right before you rush me off our calls?" I lift my brows. Lines form between his eyes, his lips turning down, and the little girl in me, still desperate for his approval, cowers at the stare. "I'm sorry, that was rude," I rush out. "I just... It's hard with you gone so much. Especially in this new place."

He sighs, glancing at Tina and then back at me. "Leave, Tina."

Her eyes widen, and she shifts in her seat. "Peter, we need to—"

"I need to speak with my daughter. Alone. Leave."

She sucks in a breath and nods, setting down the folder that's on her lap and slowly making her way out the office door, her eyes narrowing as they land on me.

Bitch.

I watch her close the door behind her before spinning to face my father.

"So..." He smiles, walking to the front of his desk and leaning against it. "What's new with you, little shadow?"

The term of endearment strikes out like a lasso, wrapping around my middle and tugging, nostalgia clawing at my insides. It's on the tip of my tongue to tell him. *I'm seeing someone. You'd hate him.*

But I don't want to wade those waters yet, still want to keep James to myself before I introduce him to family.

I force a smile on my face, an ache settling heavy in my chest. "Just working at the coffee shop and settling into the new place. Did you look around yet?"

His face softens, his eyes warming the way they used to, and with that simple look, my insides turn to mush, all my anger and resentment being drowned by the hope that flows through me.

"Not yet, but you've done a nice job setting the place up," he says.

I wave him off. "That was easy. Jon and I have just been trying to acclimate to the weather, to be honest. It's so different from Florida." Pausing, my fingers twist together, palms growing clammy because this is a nice moment, and the last thing I want to do is ruin it with questions and nagging. Still, the words flow from my mouth before I can stop them. "When are you gonna tell him?"

His hands rest in his pockets. "Tell him what?"

I roll my eyes to the ceiling, blowing out a breath. "You know what, Dad. Tell Jon about the fact that you're shipping him to boarding school."

He shifts, his palm coming up to rub at his chin. "Wendy, it's been five minutes since I've been home. I haven't even seen him yet. I'll tell him. Don't worry."

"When?" I repeat.

"When *what?*"

Frustration boils in my veins, my anger rising like lava, the pressure building in the center of my chest until it explodes out of me like a geyser.

My fists clench at my sides. "*When* are you going to stop by for more than a single night?" I hiss. "*When* are you going to realize that your children are here?" My hand slaps my chest. "We're right here, Dad. And you're"—I wave my arm around the room—"everywhere else. You and *Tina Belle.*"

"Wendy, I—"

I raise my palm. "Don't. Please, just…don't. I am so *sick* of placating words and empty promises. I am so *tired* of feeling like I'm failing Jon when it's really you who is. That's not fair to me, and you know it." A knot lodges in my throat. "And I know you're busy, I get that. But damn it, just *be* here, Dad. Like you used to."

His nostrils flare as he straightens off his desk, walking slowly toward me.

I lean back against the wall, sliding until I'm on the floor, pressing my palms into my eye sockets to try and stem the burn. I've *never* spoken to him that way before.

Shoes come into my line of vision, and my dad crouches at my side. "Little shadow." He sighs, slipping down next to me, his elbows resting on his knees. "I don't know what you want me to say, Wendy."

"Just say you'll be here." The words stick in my throat, the hole in my chest throbbing. "Say you'll start to make us a priority."

He's quiet for long moments before his arm comes around my shoulders and brings me into his side. I bite my lip and swallow harshly to keep the sobs at bay. The last thing I want is to look weak in front of the man who's always so strong.

"You're the most important thing in the world to me," he says.

"Doesn't feel like it," I mutter.

"You are. You always have been."

"And Jon," I add, irritation slicing through the haze of his attention.

"What?" His body tenses.

"You said *I'm* the most important thing in the world to you. But I'm not your only kid. You forgot to mention Jon."

He clears his throat. "Right, of course. Jon too."

"Sometimes," I whisper, seizing my newfound confidence and running with it. "Sometimes it feels like you've forgotten we exist at all." There's a tingling sensation on the top of my head as he presses a kiss to my hair, and I curl into him farther. "*Please* tell him," I beg again. "I don't want to be the one who does."

He nods against me. "I'll tell him in the morning."

Blowing out a breath, I allow his words to wrap around me like a blanket, relief swallowing up the sadness—at least temporarily.

But in the morning, he's gone. And Jon still doesn't know.

CHAPTER 18

James

MEETING WITH PETER PUT EVERYTHING BACK IN focus, his death so close I can smell it in the air. Now I just have to convince Ru that striking a business deal with him won't work in our favor. I will be extremely *irritated* if my plans become more difficult because our business starts depending heavily on his.

Even if Peter's days weren't severely numbered, I would be wary of using him. Years of dreaming up ways to kill the man responsible for every trauma of your life gives you ample time to learn about his weaknesses. About his past. And I've learned more about Peter than even his closest confidantes. I know that he grew up in South Florida, his parents so poor they could barely afford the rice they put on the table. I know that he was a common drug pusher by the age of fourteen, running through the streets, going by the name of Pan, whispering ideas of grandeur in people's ears. Promising a life of *adventure* if only they followed his lead. I know that while he rose to power slowly through the ranks, he left others behind, most of whom ended up disappearing without a trace.

And I know that when he bought a failing airplane company,

it was for pennies on the dollar, and somehow, the original owner was never heard from again.

I know Michaels is not his original last name. And I know the only thing he cares about in this world besides his money and his stature is his daughter.

Wendy.

But I can't tell Ru all that without admitting there is a huge piece of my life he's never been privy to. And while Ru isn't a nosy type of man, I can't imagine he would take it well knowing that he's allowed me into his fold and I've kept the majority of myself a secret.

But I'll deal with that tonight when I get back to the JR.

Right now, my focus is on a new bakery that opened on Maize Street. Normally, it's the twins who make the rounds, collecting protection tax and the like, but after having issues with the new shop, I figured I'd pay them a *personal* visit.

Sighing, I sit down in the seat across from George, the owner, my stomach twisting with unease from the way flour sticks to all the surfaces in the kitchen. I take out my gloves, the black leather encasing my hands in warmth, and I flex my fingers slowly as I speak. "Now, George." I smile, crossing my foot on my opposite knee. "Tell me one more time what happened."

George wipes his brow with a white towel, his potbelly expanding with each of his heavy breaths. "I told you, someone already came three days ago. I already *paid.*"

"Impossible," I snap, irritation at this man's blatant lies tearing up my insides. Taking in a deep breath, I lean my neck to the side, allowing the crack of my bones to settle my anger. "I do apologize," I chuckle, closing my eyes. "I didn't mean to lose my temper. It's just…that's *impossible.*"

He puts his hands up. "I'm telling you the truth."

"I certainly hope so." Uncrossing my legs, I pull out my knife, flipping it open and running my gloved thumb across the blade, reveling in the way the metal shines as it presses against the leather. "Tell me, do you know who I am?"

The man shakes his head no.

"Your neighbors didn't mention me?" I press my free hand to my chest. "I'm hurt."

"Listen, I told you what I know." The man starts to stand up, throwing the towel over his shoulder. "There are customers ab—"

"Sit. Down," I hiss.

The twins—who up until this point have been standing to the side—straighten and move closer. His eyes widen, but he plops back into the chair.

"Now, I'm a reasonable man. And I understand how upsetting it must be to learn that you were taken for a fool by some common *beggar*. I'm willing to overlook your mistake, since you didn't know better."

His shoulders slump. "So what, I'm just supposed to pay some bullshit twice?"

I tilt my head. "I said I was reasonable, not weak. And as much as I'd like to let it slide, you know how it goes." I stand, rolling my eyes as I twirl my blade in the air. "If you do it for one, then you end up doing it for all. And honestly, if you're good at something, you should never do it for free." I stop when I'm standing in front of him, my blade sliding underneath his chin, tilting his head until his eyes meet mine. "And while our protection is courtesy, it *is* the best chance your business has at survival."

His lips thin, beads of sweat trickling down his face. "And if I refuse?"

My hand presses the knife deeper into his skin. "We can find out if you'd like."

"I don—I don't *have* it," he stutters.

Leaning in, I allow the hooked edge to angle up, slicing into the meat under his chin, blood trickling down the blade and onto my glove. "Then I suggest you *get* it."

"Fine," he wheezes. "Please."

I remove the knife, standing straight. "Wonderful, Georgie." I pause. "May I call you that? Georgie?"

His Adam's apple bobs.

"Let me explain to you how this is going to go." I reach into my breast pocket, withdrawing a handkerchief as I wipe the red from the hooked edge of my knife. "First, you're going to tell me *everything* you know about the person who came in three days ago. And then you're going to pay my friends here"—I tilt my head toward the twins—"what you owe us."

"But I just said I—"

I lift my hand. "I understand, I do. And like I said, I'm a reasonable man. If you can't pay today, we'll be back tomorrow. But I feel I must warn you, I don't like to be kept waiting, Georgie. I'd hate to see what becomes of our friendship if you test my patience." I tsk, shaking my head.

"I'll get it."

"Smashing." I grin. "Now, tell me about this person."

"It…it was a woman. Said there was a new boss in town, and she was doing a courtesy by allowing me to show my loyalty up front."

Rage clamps on my insides. Of course.

"A woman," I repeat. "What else?"

"Th-that's it," he says. "That's all I know. I was warned by my neighbors not to fight when y'all came asking for your dues, and I didn't want to start off on the wrong foot."

I rub my chin with one hand, blade twirling through my fingers with the other.

"I'm telling you the *truth!*" he pleads.

Sighing, I place the knife back into my pocket. "I believe you. Be good to my boys, understand?" The twins smile in tandem, stepping forward to take my place.

They'll rough him up a bit, do the dirty work I don't care to do. Send a message.

A ball lodges in the center of my chest, twisting until all I can see is red. Whispers aren't good for business, and that's what this *annoyance* will cause. Whispers.

A woman.

There's only one woman I know in business with a powerful man, and they both just came to town.

My gloves are spackled with drops of blood, so I remove them, placing them in my pockets as I push through the front door. Suddenly, I'm jolted backward, a small frame crashing into mine. Clenching my jaw, my arms reach out. A whiff of vanilla hits my senses.

"James?" Wendy's voice flows through my ears, and just like that, my irritation drains away, a smile taking over my face.

"Darling," I purr. "What a pleasant surprise."

"You're telling me." She grins. "What are you doing here?"

I twist around to look at the shop, George's wife standing behind the front counter, flicking her eyes to the sidewalk every few seconds.

"Just paying my respects. I know the owners."

"Do you?" Angie asks. "I've heard their scones are to *die* for."

I glance at Wendy's friend, my smile tightening. "I'm sure they are."

"Do you want to come in with us and grab a snack?" Wendy asks.

"Unfortunately, I can't stay, no matter how much the view has suddenly improved." My thumb runs along her jaw, a warmth expanding in my chest when the apples of her cheeks redden. "Go out with me tomorrow."

"I work until three."

"Perfect. I'll pick you up there." Leaning down, I press my lips to hers. I meant it as just a peck, but her tongue slips out and tangles with mine, and I force back a groan, the noise from the sidewalk fading away as I get lost in her taste.

It will truly be a shame when I have to break her.

I'll move on, of course, without a second thought, the joy of having finally accomplished my life's desire washing away any of the empathy I have from knowing *she* isn't the one who did anything wrong. But sometimes you must make sacrifices for a greater purpose.

"We might stop by the bar tonight," her friend says once we break the kiss. "Will you be there?"

"I wasn't planning on going," Wendy tells me.

"You should," I reply. "I'll be busy, but I quite like the idea that you'll be close."

She grins, her eyes softening as she leans into my touch. "Okay."

"Good girl." I press a kiss on her forehead and step back just as the twins exit the building. "Tell Georgie to put anything you want on my tab."

Wendy's eyes widen. "You have a tab here?"

I brush a strand of hair behind her ear. "Darling, drop my name anywhere in this town, and you'll never pay for a thing again."

"Which name?" her friend pipes in.

I glance at her, my jaw clenching. "Pardon?"

She sucks on her bottom lip. "I'm just asking...which name? James? Or..."

The corner of my mouth twitches. "I believe you know the answer to that."

Wendy sucks in a breath. "Hook?"

I incline my head. "That's what they call me."

"Why?" she asks.

"Just an unfortunate nickname, I'm afraid." I wink and turn to the twins, nodding at them to head to the Escalade idling at the curb. "Do me a favor, darling?"

She lifts a brow.

"When you come to the JR tonight, wear something blue." I lean in, my breath ghosting along her ear. "It's *such* a lovely color, and I want to spend all night imagining the way it will look shredded on my bedroom floor."

She sucks in a breath, and I press my lips to her cheek before stepping away and into the car, my cock stiff and my heart pounding.

CHAPTER 19

Wendy

I'M SITTING IN THE FORMAL LIVING ROOM OF MY home, waiting for Angie to pick me up. *Wearing something blue.* Jon's across from me, working on yet another model plane.

"Dad called this morning," he says, his voice cutting through the silence.

My heart jumps to my throat. I highly doubt it was a personal call just to say hello, and disappointment settles in my gut like a brick, knowing without Jon saying the words that he told him. *Over the phone.*

Jon's fist tightens around his paintbrush, pausing from where he's filling in a black line down the side of his plane. "Look, he told me, okay? So you can stop looking at me like that."

I inhale a slow breath. "Told you what?"

"That I'm going to that stupid boarding school. It's *fine.*"

Sighing, I lean back into the chair, resting my arms on the cushioned sides. "It is?"

His eyes flick to me over the rim of his glasses. "Would it matter if it wasn't?"

"Of course it would."

He tosses his paintbrush down, running a hand through his jet-black hair, so similar to our mother's. "There's nothing you can do to change it, Wendy. It is what it is, and you sitting there looking like you're about to burst into tears isn't helping the situation."

My chest pulls tight. "I'm not—"

His eyes narrow. "You *are*."

"I just want you to be happy. That's all." I raise my hands.

He doesn't respond, his attention going back to his craft. The silence is suffocating as it wraps its way around my throat and stuffs into my ears, allowing room for my thoughts to grow wild and uninterrupted.

This is the *only* thing I've asked my father for, and yet somehow, he still couldn't follow through, choosing to take the easy road, to cast Jon's feelings aside as if something as huge as this doesn't really matter. Another charred and heavy log is thrown on the fire of my anger, simmering at the base of my gut.

"He said I'm going tomorrow."

The words are soft and short, but they pummel me in the chest anyway. "*Tomorrow?*" I gasp. "Is he coming home to take you there?"

Jon's lips curve into a small smile, but it isn't happiness I feel vibrating through the air. "Wendy, be real. The driver will take me."

Flames lick up my insides, heating my veins. "I'll take you."

He shakes his head. "You don't have to do that."

"I *want* to." I force a smile. "I've gotta see it for myself if I plan on visiting every week."

Jon groans. "You are *not* allowed to visit every week."

My grin grows. "Well, you better let me take you tomorrow then. Otherwise, I'll come *all the time*, and I'll make sure to be extra embarrassing."

Jon chuckles, his eyes sparking the tiniest bit. "Wendy, you're never embarrassing. Just…overbearing."

My hand flies to my heart. "Should I be offended by that?"

"No, it's…" He shakes his head. "It's nice."

The knot in my stomach unravels at our banter, the familiarity bursting through me like a long-lost friend. But it's quickly swiped away by the knowledge that after tomorrow, it will really just be me all alone.

We've been at the JR for two hours, and I've yet to see James.

Maria—who isn't with us tonight—said he owned the bar, but the longer I sit here without his overbearing presence to muddle my thoughts, the more I realize I don't actually know anything about him.

Well, that's not true. I know *some* things, like he has a ridiculous nickname, and he apparently has so much clout in this town that said nickname is as good as gold. But for someone who says I'm his, I feel like he's nothing more than a stranger.

How could I be stupid enough not to ask?

"Thanks for saying you'll cover my shift tomorrow," I tell Angie, sipping from my sparkling water.

She waves me off, smiling. "No worries. I could use the extra hours anyway." Her eyes move past me. "Besides, you're dating a dude who wears three-piece suits by *choice*, so I think it's safe to say I need the money more than you. Oh, and you live in a mansion." She cackles. "You hussy. God, it isn't fair."

The chuckle I force out feels like razor blades, slicing through the sudden tightness of my throat.

She tosses back the remainder of her drink and sighs. "Ugh, where's your man, girl? Since I've gotta work in the morning for your ass, I need to head home. Beauty sleep and all that."

My insides clench and I glance around, looking for a sign of James anywhere. The bar is thinning out, we've been here for hours, yet there's still no sign of him. My fingers twist in my lap. "He's probably busy. You go ahead. I can just catch a cab."

I cringe as the words leave my lips, hoping they don't sound as pathetic as they feel.

"You sure?" Her eyes scan the room.

"Yeah, he said he would be here." I nod.

She bites her lip. "Well, yeah, but he hasn't even shown his face. I don't want to leave you here without a ride."

Reaching out, I pat her arm. "I appreciate the concern, but you really don't need to worry."

She sighs, standing up. "Okay, but text me if he doesn't show up. I can come back."

I stay at the bar long after she leaves, watching the bubbles pop and fizz in my drink. I could probably get something besides sparkling water—I haven't been carded since that first night, and my birthday is in three days—but the truth is that I'm not a big drinker. I don't like the way it makes me feel.

"And then there was one." A voice filters through my daze, and I look up, meeting the amber eyes of Curly. "You want a drink, sunshine?"

"Aren't you guys closing soon? I'll probably just go... He's not here, is he?" I ask, breaking eye contact.

"You're gonna have to be more specific." He leans his elbow on the bar. "There's a lot of 'hes' around this place."

"Ja—Hook." Unease swims through me as I realize I'm not sure what to call him when I'm talking to other people. Yet another thing that shows I know absolutely nothing about this man.

But I *do* know it won't stop me from leaving with him tonight if he shows up.

It may be stupid. It's definitely reckless. But it's also exhilarating having someone like him shower his attention on me. Makes me feel less like the picture of innocence and more like a woman.

Something about the way he stares makes me feel *alive*.

A laugh to my left cuts off whatever Curly was about to say. My head turns and my eyes take in the curvy, raven-haired beauty who's polishing wineglasses and hanging them on the bar rack.

Curly scowls in her direction. "Cut it out, Moira."

"I'm sorry." She smirks, her eyes locking on mine. "You're really waiting around here for *Hook*?"

Another dose of doubt creeps into my consciousness, pouring through my body like sludge. There's a smile on her face, yet her tone is anything but friendly, and my hackles rise. A retort is on the tip of my tongue, but I swallow it back and nod, my knuckles turning white from how tightly my fingers tangle around each other.

She huffs out another laugh.

"Moira," Curly hisses.

"What?" she asks, her eyes widening as she looks at him. "You can't seriously be entertaining this?" Her hand shoots out toward me. "Another groupie showing up who knows *nothing* about the man, thinking the little innocent act will work? It's honestly pathetic. You shouldn't encourage it."

My jaw clenches, her words battering against my wall of confidence—already shaken from my own twisted thoughts.

"Yeah, well, he knows this one at least," Curly replies.

Moira's hand pauses on the rim of the wineglass, her eyes flicking back toward me.

I chance a look at Curly, warmth filling my chest from the way he defended me. From the way his simple words made me feel a little less stupid, a little less like just another dumb girl with a crush.

"Hmm," she hums. "Well, you'll be waiting a long time tonight, *sunshine*, because Hook isn't even here."

Curly tilts his head. "He was earlier."

"Well, that was earlier." A grin sneaks across her face, her white teeth gleaming. "He had me give him a *proper* goodbye before he left for the night."

I can tell she's trying to get a reaction, so I don't give her one, but it doesn't stop her words from slamming into my middle, planting roots and spreading their seeds.

"Moira." A shadow appears behind her, James stepping into the light of the bar. His eyes glint, his black hair tousled like his hands have tugged at the roots. *Or maybe Moira's.* "You should know better than to lie to my special guests."

Her frame stiffens, the polishing rag and wineglass frozen in the air.

"Hook," she says slowly. "You're back."

A bolt of satisfaction splits through the cloud of doubt. *She called him Hook.* Not James.

His head tilts as he stops next to her. "Never left."

He grabs the wineglass from her hand, holding it up to the light as if he's checking for smudges. The air grows thick, a few voices from the remaining patrons splicing through the tension and soft music floating through the speakers. But none of us move. None of us speak.

"Hmm." He tsks, setting the glass down on the bar top. "Your job is lackluster, I'm afraid."

"Hook, I—" she starts.

He spins toward her, the move so sudden it makes my breath stall in my lungs. I've never seen this side of him before, and while it should put me on edge, I realize the heat brewing deep in my belly is *arousal.*

"Did I give you the assumption that I would enjoy you speaking of me when I'm not around?" he asks.

Her eyes widen, lips parting. "No, I—"

"No," he snaps. His eyes flick toward me, the harshness of his gaze softening. He cracks his neck, running a hand down the front of his suit and gesturing toward the glasses. "These look terrible. Start again, and if there are any spots at the end, don't bother coming back tomorrow."

"*What?*" she scoffs.

But it doesn't matter, because she's already lost his attention, his eyes zoned in on me as he strides over, a smile breaking across his face.

My mind whirls with the scene I just witnessed, lost between what I should feel and how I actually do. His hand touches the open back of my dress, chills skating down my skin at the warmth of his palm.

Breath coasts across my face, James's lips pressing softly against my cheek. "Darling, you look edible. I regret wasting my night in meetings instead of showing you how thoroughly I enjoy you in that color."

Blood rushes to my face, heating me from the inside out.

Call me petty, call me vengeful, but I can't stop the way my eyes glance to Moira, satisfaction burrowing in my chest at the way she's watching him touch *me* and whisper in *my* ear.

"Hi." I grin up at him.

"Are you ready to go?" His thumb presses into my bottom lip.

"With you?"

"As if I'd allow you to leave with anyone else."

His hand encases mine, pulling me from my seat and into his arms.

And regardless of all the things left unsaid between us, all the ways I still need to get to know him, I let him lead me out the door.

CHAPTER 20

James

PEOPLE DO WHAT I TELL THEM. IT ISN'T A NOVEL concept. In fact, it's when they *don't* that is the rarity. However, it's normally either fear or respect that has them bowing to my whims.

So seeing Wendy walk into my bar wearing the exact baby-blue dress from the first night I saw her, it does things to me. Sends pleasure skating through my insides, knowing that she did it for no other reason than to please me. *Like a good pet.*

It was more difficult than I expected to sit in my office, watching her on the security feed, testing to see if she'd wait for as long as I needed. But once I saw her interact with Moira, I knew I needed to end my experiment. Can't have a silly waitress messing up my plans by scaring the girl away.

Although I do think she might be rather difficult to get rid of. While the media has always painted her as Peter's pride and joy, she's succumbing to me so easily. Almost like she's desperate for the attention.

If I could still feel things the way a normal person does, her attachment would cause sympathy to swell in my chest. I assume, after all, it's trauma of some type that has her clinging so quickly. But my heart no longer pumps the way it should. And while my blood still runs red, any soul I once had has been eaten by the acid that runs through my veins.

Even as a boy, there was something about me that attracted the darkness in even the lightest of souls, drawing it to the surface until it cascaded from their bodies and drenched my skin, burning like black tar on a sunny day.

And maybe that's why I find Wendy so refreshing. Why it's so easy to get lost inside her. Because she's the only person who hasn't been swallowed whole by my sickness.

Not yet anyway.

"Where's Smee?" she asks, sprawling out on the couch in my living room.

I settle in close, offering her a glass of water and crossing my foot over my opposite leg. "I'm not sure." I glance around. "His time is his time. I try to stay out of his personal life and expect him to do the same. I'm sure he'll turn up at some point."

She nods, taking a sip of water before setting it down. "That's nice. You seem like a good boss."

I grin, my hand reaching out and running up the bare skin of her thigh. "I think you'll find I'm *phenomenal* at giving direction."

She giggles. "And so humble too."

Smirking, my fingers tease the hem of her dress. She trembles under my palm, and my cock hardens at how responsive she is to my touch.

"I—" She swallows, shaking her head. "I have some questions."

Annoyance flickers in my chest, but I pull back, raising a brow. "Alright."

Her fingers twist together as she stares down at her lap—something I've realized she does whenever she's nervous.

"What do you do for a living?"

The question surprises me. I foolishly assumed that if she hadn't asked by now, she wouldn't. I lean back, my arms spanning the length of the couch. "I'm a businessman."

She rolls her eyes. "Yeah, so is my father. But I mean, what do you *do*?"

The mention of her father sparks a blaze inside me, and I'm suddenly desperate to know everything about him from her point of view. "Your father?"

"Ugh." She palms her face. "I wasn't actually planning on talking about him. But yeah. He's a *businessman*."

"Oh." I run my tongue over my teeth. "Maybe I've worked with him."

She shrugs. "Maybe. He's pretty well known."

"Who is he?" I put great effort into keeping my voice low and steady, my nerves dancing like Pop Rocks under my skin.

"Peter Michaels."

Pushing a hand through my hair, I sigh. "Never heard of him."

Her eyes widen, but I don't miss the way her shoulders drop, as if she's been relieved of a weight. "Really? That's kind of... surprising."

My fingers rub at my jawline. "Is it? I'm sorry I'm not as versed as I should be then."

Her grin grows, her upper body leaning toward me. "I like that you don't know. I was so worried about telling you, to be honest. I didn't want your opinion of me to change."

I snap forward, my arms wrapping around her waist, pulling her the rest of the way into me. She whooshes out a breath as her body lands on mine, her ample breasts pressing deliciously into my chest. "Darling, no one on this earth could change my opinion of you. I'm afraid it's already set in stone."

She lifts her head, her lips centimeters from mine. "What is it then?"

"My opinion?" My mouth dips down to skim across her neck, my hand reaching behind her head to tangle in the strands of her silky hair. "I can show you if you'd like."

Her breathing stutters as I tighten my grip and tug, the expanse of her neck elongating. I press kisses up the column of her throat, making my way back to her lips. The taste of her invades my senses, need spiraling through my center and heating my blood.

She moans, her hips pressing against my shaft through the thin material of my pants, creating a friction that has pinpricks of pleasure skittering up my spine. I release her mouth and lie back, allowing her to start up a rhythm. She's teasing me. *Torturing* me, but *god*, does she look a vision. Her blue dress is bunched at her hips, lips rosy red to match her cheeks, and eyes half-lidded as they look down on me.

My fingers release the strands of her hair, my arm wrapping around her as I sit up, our bodies suddenly flush against each other.

Our noses brush as I thrust into her panty-covered center. I suck in her breath and take it as my own, pressing my lips to hers. She moans, her arms curling around my neck, a sharp sting radiating through my mouth as the taste of copper floods my taste buds. I jerk back, my thumb brushing across my bottom lip, coming away with red. *She bit me.*

Normally, the sight of my own blood makes me retch, but for

some reason, arousal floods my system. My arm tightens around her waist as I slide forward, my lips molding to hers, the taste of my blood mixing with her saliva. She sucks on my tongue as if she wants to swallow me whole, and I groan, pushing her down on the couch, my hips settling between her thighs.

I break away from her lips, moving my mouth to her ear. My palm wraps around her throat and squeezes. "Are you going to let me see that pretty pussy?"

Her teeth sink into her bottom lip, hips pressing up to meet mine. My fingers drift from her neck, down her torso to meet her core, my hand wrapping around the center of her cotton panties and pulling until they snap off her frame. Her inhale is audible, and it makes my cock throb, desperate to feel her from the inside.

Tossing the torn fabric behind me, I push her thighs apart, my nose running up her glistening slit. A groan rumbles in my throat. She smells *delectable*. Like musk and woman and everything pure, as if her pheromones were bred just for me. My mouth waters with the need to taste her while she comes apart underneath me.

I move toward her opening, lapping at the wetness that's seeping from her center, coating my tongue with her taste.

She giggles, her fingers wrapping around the strands of my hair. "That tickles, James."

I grin against her, my arm pressing down across her stomach firmly. "Stop moving, pet."

My fingers slip into her at the same time as I suck her swollen clit into my mouth, feeling it pulse on my tongue. Her body jerks under my arm, and I pin her down tighter, my hips pressing into the couch cushion to relieve the ache throbbing in my cock.

She's *tight*, and precum leaks from my tip as I imagine how it will feel when her walls are hugging the thickness of my shaft instead of sucking on my fingers. I have a sneaking suspicion she's a virgin, and the thought of being the first man to have her—the one who will ruin her for all others—makes me ravenous to destroy her body, mind, and soul.

I continue to pump my digits, wetness coating my hand from her dripping pussy. My arm lifts from her torso, moving up until it wraps around her neck, my fingers tapping against the pulse of her heart.

Releasing her clit from my mouth, I look up, noting her flushed cheeks and the way her breasts heave underneath the beautiful blue of her dress. "Take a deep breath for me, pet, and don't let it out until you see stars."

She does—immediately—her throat tightening as she inhales and holds. My hand wraps around the sides of her neck, and I dive back into her pussy, slowly increasing the pressure around her windpipe and my suction on her clit.

Her hands grapple in my hair, thighs trembling as they close around my head. My fingers curl inside her, rubbing the spongy spot of her inner walls, and my gaze locks on her from my place between her legs. Her eyes are rolling in the back of her head, her lips parted as I ensure she can't take in air even if she wished.

My cock throbs as I think of her lips turning blue, her body on the verge of giving in, of giving up, right before I allow her to come, letting the sweet air expand in her lungs and bring her back to life.

Her back bows off the couch as she explodes, her fingers nearly ripping my hair from the roots, the sting of pain making my balls tighten and heat coil at the base of my spine.

I release her throat, reveling in her deep gasps of air, and continue to lap at her while she soars from the high.

Finally, I release her clit, my fingers making an audible noise as they withdraw from her sopping cunt. My gaze locks on hers as my tongue swipes across my lips, cleaning her taste from my mouth.

My chest pulls, insides reeling as I stare down at her, realizing that I've never held such beauty in my hands.

And in this moment, I'm not sure how I'll let her go.

CHAPTER 21

Wendy

NO ONE HAS EVER DONE THAT TO ME BEFORE, and as my body floats back down to earth, the aftershocks of my orgasm give way to a tightening in my muscles—a need to please him back. To give him what he's just given me.

I've never felt so wanted. So sexual. So...*free.*

And sure, we haven't talked yet, haven't had the meaningful conversations I've always imagined I'd have with the person who I give my firsts, but for some reason, this feels like enough. Like he already knows me without needing to speak. It's possible I'm making a mistake. Maybe I'll wake up in the morning and regret my choice, but right now, I've never been so sure of anything in my life.

I just want, for one second, to be able to *let go.*

If I'm honest with myself, in the deepest parts of my mind and the darkest chambers of my heart, there're pieces of me hoping that maybe once my virginity is gone, the coat of innocence I can't seem to shed will disappear too.

It's exhausting having everyone treat you as though you're something fragile. Breakable. Less than.

Moira's words from earlier flash through my mind, and so do Maria's sharp jabs. Everyone sees me as a child, a young girl with no experience in the world, and for so long, I've let them speak their thinly veiled insults and backhanded compliments. I've let them assume that because I have soft features and don't speak out of turn, it means they're right.

But I'm *tired*.

And James, he makes me feel like a woman. Like his equal. Like I have a choice, and he respects me to make it.

He rises from his spot between my legs, his pink tongue licking along the seam of his lips as he gazes at me. Arousal swirls through my middle, my stomach flipping from his stare.

I sit up, leaning on my elbows, my insides warm and my head floating. James made me ride the edge of consciousness, blackness rimming my vision and euphoria flooding through my veins, the pressure winding through my core combined with the press of his palm making endorphins explode like fireworks. And now I'm still riding the high. I crawl toward him, the couch cushions soft under my knees, praying that I don't look ridiculous. I have no clue what I'm doing, but for the first time, I unlock the clasp that latches my urges down deep, and I just do what feels good.

My hand runs up his leg, the fabric of his pants soft under my palms. His gaze tracks my every move, his nostrils flaring as he stares down at me.

I continue my trek upward, my stomach soaring and falling like a roller coaster as my palm meets the thick length between his legs. It's surprisingly stiff, different than I expected, and heat builds in my center, desperate to know what it feels like in the palm of my hand.

"Can I touch you?" I ask.

His blue eyes flash, his fingers moving to cup my cheek. His touch is so tender my heart skips, warmth spreading like molasses through my chest, and I lean into his hand, wanting to bask in the comfort it provides.

"You never need permission to touch me, darling." He sits forward, pressing his mouth to mine, suckling my bottom lip before pulling back. "I'm yours just as much as you're mine."

His words spread through my body like a wildfire, and I push him back on the couch, my hands going to his belt and unzipping his pants. His hips lift, allowing me to strip him from the waist down until his cock bobs free, standing straight in the air.

I sit back on my legs, heart ramming against my rib cage, nerves sizzling beneath my skin and making my hands clammy.

It's bigger than I thought it would be. And thick, a large vein running up the underside and disappearing underneath the head. My tongue sneaks out to run along my lips, my insides tightening.

James reaches down, the veins on his hand flexing as he wraps his fingers around the shaft, stroking lewdly. My stomach cramps, an ache settling between my thighs, my already sensitive clit swelling from watching him pleasure himself.

His free hand runs through his hair, mussing the already tousled strands, and I'm transfixed at the sight of him so disheveled—so opposite to how everyone else gets to see him.

It's intoxicating to know that *I'm* the one who makes him this way.

"Strip." His voice scrapes across my insides like gravel.

A shiver shoots through me, and I sink into the comfort his direction provides, anxiety melting away because I know he'll tell me what he needs.

"Okay." I trail my fingertips from the top of my throat, slowly running them down the length of my sore neck and over my collarbone, slipping underneath the strap of my dress, allowing the material to loosen from where it's resting on my shoulder.

My eyes never stray from James's, his hand slowly working his length, his gaze zoned in on where my fingers are toying with the thin material of my dress.

"I said strip, pet, not torture me to death."

His words sink into my skin and meld with the marrow of my bones, making me feel powerful. Making me feel like if I can bring *this* man to his knees, then I can do anything.

I let the strap fall off my shoulder. First one side, then the other. He bites his lip, his fingers squeezing the tip of his cock. His balls visibly tighten, and the sight makes my stomach flip.

My arm splays across my chest, holding the fabric in place, a small grin sneaking onto my face. "Say please."

His nostrils flare. "You're playing a very dangerous game."

I lift a shoulder. "I'm just making sure you don't forget your manners, *darling*."

Quick as lightning, he bolts off the couch, my body forced back onto my elbows. I gulp down air, my eyes roaming from his face to his hand that's still wrapped around his erection. It sticks straight out, liquid seeping from the tip as he moves his palm up and down, jerking off *right* in front of me. My legs squeeze together to ease the heavy ache throbbing between them.

"Do you like watching me?" he purrs. "Like knowing it's you I'm *desperate* for?" His hand releases his length, moving to my waist. Butterflies burst in my stomach as he skims his fingers up my torso until they rest on the swell of my breasts.

He slips under the sweetheart neckline of my dress, gliding

back and forth in a teasing caress, sparks of arousal ricocheting off my insides and settling deep in my core.

He pauses, his hand curling beneath the fabric. "I don't beg," he says. "*Ever.*" My breath sticks in my lungs as a small smile graces his lips.

And then he pulls.

Hard.

My body flings forward as he rips the dress from my frame, the fabric tearing, creating a burn against my skin. I exhale harshly, adrenaline and arousal mixing in my veins like a lethal cocktail, making me dizzy with want.

His palm cups my breast in his hand, manipulating the flesh beneath his fingers. "Beautiful."

He releases me and moves back to the opposite end of the couch, settling back into his reclined position. "Now *strip.*"

I stand on shaky legs, my palms trailing a line from the top of my chest down to my nipples, grasping them between my fingers and twisting. Tingles trickle through me with every pull, so I continue the motion, my eyes closing as I get lost in the way it makes me feel.

"*Fuck,*" he whispers.

My gaze springs open at the word. It's the first time he's cursed, and hearing it now makes my core throb.

His hand glides down his abdomen, wrapping around his thick cock. "You are always a vision, darling, but you look absolutely *devastating* while you touch yourself."

I feel like a goddess under his stare, and as I remove the tattered remains of my dress and walk to him, I allow my newfound confidence to coast along my skin and fill up every pore. Climbing on the couch, I slide between his legs. My hands go back to their spot on his thighs, tracing up the muscles until I surround the base of his groin, my face inches from his length.

Nerves trickle through me, and I blow out a shaky breath. Slowly, I slide my palm up until my fingers wrap around his shaft. For a moment, I just hold my hand there, taking in the feel of him. It's more malleable than I expected, and when I squeeze my fingers, it jumps. A giggle bursts out of me.

A low chuckle rumbles through his body, his teeth gleaming from his grin. "I can assure you, laughter is not something a man wants to hear when you're facedown in his lap."

I shake my head. "No, I'm sorry. It's just... I've never—" I move my hand experimentally, sliding it up the length and running my fingers over the tip. "Will you show me how you like it?"

His palm wraps around mine, making my grip tighter before moving us in tandem, stroking him up, twisting at the top, and then moving back down. I breathe deep, my core contracting.

He sits up, his free hand cupping my cheek, like he knows I need the comfort. "I *like* that you've never done this before. There's nothing you can do to me that I won't enjoy. Understand?"

I nod.

"Good girl." He lies back. "Now put your mouth on it."

My chest expands at his praise, the urge to please him filling me from the inside out. I lean in, my mouth parting as I suck him between my lips, my jaw stretching to accommodate him.

His hand shoots down to tangle in my hair.

My tongue swirls around the flesh, surprise flowing through me at the taste, and when the tip of my tongue finds the ridge on his head and flicks, he groans, his palm pushing me farther onto him.

My eyes widen, but I don't resist, allowing him to push me down.

One of his hands trails from my hair to my jaw, his fingers massaging the muscles as though he's urging them to relax. "Such a perfect girl," he coos.

Pride shoots through me like a bullet, and I double my efforts, his length filling my mouth until he hits the back of my throat. My eyes water from the sting, a slight ache radiating through my jaw.

How am I supposed to keep doing this?

The vein on the underside of his shaft pulses on my tongue, and I moan, a rush of desire surging through me. I've never felt as powerful as I do in this moment, bending over a man who bleeds dominance and making him come apart at the seams.

He jerks my head back, his cock literally popping out of my mouth. The rush of air makes me gasp, and tears well in my eyes from the sudden shift.

"Was it..." I suck in a breath. "Was it not okay?"

He smiles but doesn't speak, moving forward until his arms wrap around my body so he can lift me up. He carries me through the hallway and into his room, tossing me on his bed, my body bouncing off the soft mattress and silky sheets.

"You did wonderful, pet." His lips trail up my legs, laving kisses along every inch of my body. "*Too* wonderful."

He rises above me, his knees placed between my thighs, his frame casting a shadow over my body. I reach forward, my fingers grasping for the buttons on his shirt, but his hand comes down and stops me, his jaw tensing as he shakes his head no.

The rejection burns its way through my insides, and I snap my hand back, heat flooding my cheeks. I wait for an explanation, but it never comes, and I don't want to ruin the moment by asking.

His touch runs up the length of my body as he lowers himself on top of me, his teeth scraping along my jaw. A gush of wetness seeps from my core, pooling underneath me on the sheets.

He thrusts his hips forward, the tip of his cock sliding against my swollen clit, pleasure swirling deep in my abdomen.

"Tell me you're mine."

My center clenches around air, stomach tensing as the coil wraps tighter. "I'm yours."

"Prove it." He moves his tip to my opening, his cock glistening from sliding between my lips. But he doesn't move. He simply waits.

"Take it, James." His eyes lock on mine for long moments, and I reach up, stroking his jaw with my fingers. "I trust you."

A flash of *something* coasts across his eyes. "You shouldn't."

I don't have time to think about his words before he glides inside me, a sharp sting splicing through my body. I inhale quickly, my body tensing around him, immediately wanting to fight against the intrusion.

He grits his teeth. "You have to relax, or I'll never fit inside you."

I bite my lip and nod, the fear of disappointing him worse than the fear of the pain.

His hand grips the nape of my neck, dragging my face to his. "I'll take care of you, darling. Breathe through the pain."

He blows out a breath and I suck it in, a tear escaping from the corner of my eye. *Stupid.* I try to move my hand to wipe it from my cheek, but he bats it away, his mouth pressing kisses along my jaw until he reaches the path of wetness, licking it up.

His hips move forward but stall as he hits resistance, and then with a single thrust, he pushes through. My arms fly around his shoulders, my fingernails pressing into him so tightly I'm sure they draw blood.

Our breaths mingle in the space between us, and when he starts to slowly move, his lips skim mine with every thrust. The sting is now accompanied by a deep throbbing, like a bruise that's settling in deep, but I focus on the fullness instead of the pain.

"Does it feel good?" I ask.

His hips press deeper. "You feel *incredible*."

As he continues to move inside me, the sting gives way to a blissful numbness, allowing me to focus on the sharp angles of his face. On the way that his eyes soak me in like I'm sunshine, and he's desperate for the rays.

The discomfort is still there, but there's also a tendril of pleasure unfurling through my middle simply from feeling him inside me. From the knowledge that I'm the one making him feel this way. That he's letting down his guard *for me*.

I lift my upper body off the bed, my breasts mashing into the fabric of his shirt. "Are you going to come inside me?" I whisper into his ear, my body flushing from the filthy words leaving my lips.

I'm not sure what gives me the courage to say it, but somehow, whenever I'm with him, I do things I never knew I could.

His hips falter, his hands grabbing my arms from around him and pinning them above my head, his palms wrapping around my wrists.

"Is that what you want?" he asks. "Want me to split you apart and come so deep you'll feel me for days?"

I moan, my abs tensing and legs shaking. "Yes."

His hips push faster, his balls slapping against me on every thrust, his palms pressing so deep on my wrists that my hands tingle. And then he tenses, his movements turning choppy as he presses in as deep as he can go.

I can feel him pulse, spurt after spurt, shooting deep inside me, his low groan making my inner walls clench, trying to milk it out.

He collapses on top of me, his fingers loosening from my wrists, and I swear to God in this moment, I've never felt closer to anyone than I do to him.

This man I've only known for days, yet he treats me like I'm precious.

Like I'm *his*.

His breathing is ragged, his face resting in the crook of my neck, and my hands come up to his head, stroking down his hair and over the tops of his shoulders. He shivers under my touch, and I smile, my heart swelling.

I was worried I'd regret allowing him to take my virginity, but all I feel is relief that it's gone.

James took that fragile girl and threw her somewhere I can't find, and at least for now, I'm basking in her absence.

CHAPTER 22

James

IT'S BEEN YEARS SINCE MY MIND HAS BEEN QUIET. Even longer since I've been able to relax, even in the comfort of my own home. But last night, I fell deep into a dreamless sleep and woke up wrapped around Wendy's curves.

I hadn't planned to come inside her. But the thought of her swelling with my child right in front of her father's eyes—right before I slit his throat—had my balls tightening and cum shooting out of my tip before I could even finish the fantasy.

She *unhinges* me in a way I don't quite understand. But I enjoy the dreamless nights and the comfort she provides upon waking.

I lean down, breathing in her scent, my cock thickening against her backside. She stirs in my arms, murmuring something as her eyes flutter open.

My chest pulls. "Good morning, darling."

She grins, her face still slack from sleep, and raises her arms above her head, stretching. The movement pushes her body into mine, causing blood to rush to my groin.

I want to take her again.

Harder this time. But I resist, knowing she must be sore. Surprisingly, the thought of her in pain does nothing to excite me.

"Morning?" She shoots up in bed, running a hand through her tangled hair. "What time is it?"

"I'm not sure."

"You don't have a clock?" Her forehead scrunches.

My jaw clenches. "I haven't been too worried about the time since there's something much more important in my bed."

Her frantic movements stall, pink flooding her cheeks. "Oh," she whispers.

I lean in, pressing my lips to hers. "Yes. Oh."

Her body melts into mine as she peers at me through her lashes. "I have to go. I promised my brother I'd take him to his new school today."

Brother.

I've known about him, of course, but it occurs to me that *Wendy* doesn't realize that, so I lift my brows in what I hope is a surprised expression, tilting my head the slightest amount. "Brother?"

"Yeah." She laughs, shaking her head. "Sometimes it's easy to forget we don't actually know each other well."

My arms wrap around her waist, pulling her into my chest. "I feel as though we got to know each other fairly well last night." My teeth nip her ear.

She giggles. "You know what I mean." She turns in my arms, looking up at me. "Do you have any siblings?"

Ice trickles through my veins, freezing out any lingering warmth. "No family, I'm afraid. Just me."

Her gaze bounces from my eyes to my lips and back. "Oh, I'm sorry."

I brush off her concern. "Don't be, darling. Family couldn't handle the likes of me anyway."

Her mouth turns down, but she doesn't push. I'm thankful for it, not wanting to come up with an elaborate story of how I loved and lost when the reality is it was *her* family who took mine away.

"My brother is sixteen, and he's starting a new school today," she says.

"Which school?"

Her face pinches. "Some boarding school outside the city. He says he's fine with it, but…" She sighs, running a hand through her hair. "He doesn't have the best experience with other kids. And I don't want him to be stuck *living* at a place where he can't get away from the torment."

Her eyes grow glassy, and I reach out, wiping away a stray tear.

"Ugh, I'm sorry. I'm crying so much around you." She wipes her cheeks. "I promise I'm not like this all the time."

"Don't apologize. I *want* to be the one you turn to when life gets hard."

Her eyes gain a curious sheen, and she leans in, kissing me softly. Small, simple pecks, but they make my stomach tighten all the same.

"Okay."

"Do you want me to go with you?" The words are out of my mouth before I can think them through, and I bite back the cringe that wants to work its way onto my face. *Why would I offer that?*

Her eyes light up like the Fourth of July, her fingers grasping the fabric of my shirt. "Would you? I—" She swallows. "That would be really nice. Plus, then you'd get to meet Jon."

I force a smile, mentally berating myself for offering something I truly don't have time to give. But I can't pull out now, and if it provides her with a modicum of extra support and comfort—the type that her father is so clearly not providing—I'll do it.

I'm standing in the middle of Peter Michaels's home.

Wendy has gone upstairs to change, having worn my clothing on the trip back, since I tore hers in two.

And she has left me alone.

Because she *trusts* me.

I walk around the living area, rage simmering in my veins as I take in the smiling faces within the picture frames—a happy family making memories while I was living nightmares.

Moving down the long hallway, I peer in a few different rooms until I finally come to the office.

My stomach tightens as I step inside, my heart beating in my throat. The room itself is warm, full of cedar and oak, but it feels unused. Empty. I doubt he's been here often.

Still, having untapped access like this is…*thrilling.*

"Who the fuck are you?"

I spin around, coming face-to-face with a tall, lanky boy wearing wire-frame glasses and a pressed maroon polo with a mermaid on the front.

I'd know that logo anywhere. *Rockford Prep.*

A memory flies into my brain of the first time I saw it: on the front of a brochure that was sitting on my uncle's desk. I was fourteen at the time, and as I flipped through the pages, anticipation filled me to the brim, wondering if my uncle was finally tired of abusing me. Of reminding me of all the ways he hated my father, preaching in my ears that I was to pay for his sins.

I shoved the brochure in my pocket and took it straight to Ru.

"Do you think Uncle will send me there?" I can't help the way my words lift, hope springing into my voice.

Ru hums, puffing on a cigar. "What ya wanna go to Marooner's Rock for?"

"To where?"

He points to the brochure. "Rockford Prep. It's a boarding school, kept out on Marooner's Rock—an island off the coast. You have to take a boat to get there, and they have a reputation for..." He hesitates.

My eyes narrow. "For what?"

"For fixing troubled youth, kid. And their methods aren't known to be friendly."

My stomach churns, but I stiffen my jaw. "Well, I still want to go."

Ru huffs out a laugh, looking at me with a smirk. "Yeah? Think you could use a few good beatings to whip the Brit outta ya?"

Irritation at his brush-off mixes with the shame that lives in the fabric of my soul until it explodes out of me. "I've had worse, and for far longer." I stand up, stalking toward Ru, my suit hanging slightly loose on my fourteen-year-old frame. "I'd do anything to get away from him." My voice is low.

Ru's grin drops, his chair creaking as he snaps forward, meeting my eyes. "What the fuck is he doing to you, kid?"

I never ended up going to Rockford Prep. I confessed to Ru some of my darkest secrets that day, desperation making my tongue loose, hoping that somebody would act in my favor. That someone would finally *see* me and understand.

And he did.

I'm not sure of the details, but after that night, the worst of it stopped. The beatings continued, of course, until I was old and strong enough to fight back, but my uncle never snuck into my room again.

And even though Ru hasn't said a word since, I know he was the reason why.

Smiling, I force my mind back to the present, placing my hands in my pockets and rocking back on my heels. "You must be Jon."

Surprise flickers in my chest at how different he looks from Wendy.

His chin juts out. "Who's asking?"

I smile. I think I'll quite like this kid. "I'm James, a friend of your sister's. She asked me to be here."

His eyes narrow before he finally nods, walking over to me and sticking out his hand. "Good. She needs a friend."

My palm connects with his, and a small admiration grows for the boy, his loyalty to his sister something I respect. He doesn't drop eye contact for a second, and his grip is strong and sure.

"Oh." Wendy's voice comes from the entry to the office. "You guys have met. Great." She glances around. "What are you two doing in here?"

I open my mouth to answer, but before I can, Jon intervenes. "I was just showing him around," he says.

My brows lift in surprise.

She grins. "That's nice. You ready to go?"

His eyes dim, his finger pushing the glasses up his face. "Yeah. Let's go."

As we make our way to my Audi, my phone vibrates in my pocket. I pull it out, glancing at the caller ID, Ru's name flashing across the screen.

I brush my hand down Wendy's hair, reaching around her to open the passenger door. "I have to take this call. I'll only be a moment."

She nods, she and Jon settling in as I walk a few paces away. "Roofus."

"Kid, where are you? We've got a business meeting tonight. I'm gonna tell him that we're out. Another one of our investments didn't come through, and I don't trust this new guy as far as I can throw him."

My stomach cramps as I glance back at Wendy and Jon, her head thrown back in laughter. "I'm rather tied up at the moment, but I should be done by this evening. Where are we meeting?"

"Same as before. I'm heading there in a few hours, but I'll take one of the boys, don't worry."

My teeth grind so hard I fear they'll break, my mind warring with indecision. I don't want Ru to go without me, but I gave Wendy my word, and if I back out now, I'll lose all the ground I've gained.

Huffing out a breath, nausea churns in my gut. "I'll meet you there as soon as I can."

"Alright, kid. And don't make plans tonight. I'm done playing games. We've got work to do."

He hangs up, and I'm stuck staring at the phone, my mind going over all the possible scenarios that can get me there in time. Rockford Prep is an hour drive both ways, and Cannibal's Cave is another thirty minutes, but if I hurry, I can make it.

Slipping my phone back in my pocket, I head to the car, unease swirling like a shark in my gut.

First, I'll deal with Wendy.

And then I'll deal with her father.

CHAPTER 23

Wendy

I HADN'T REALIZED THE SCHOOL WAS ON AN island. For all the worrying I've done the past few days, it didn't even cross my mind to Google the actual building.

As our car was loaded on the ferry, my nerves ramped up to the point where I could barely focus on the small talk between James and Jon—the two of them taking to each other like ducks to water. But once we're back on land, I'm able to focus in, and my chest warms as I listen to James give attention to my brother the way I always wished our father would. And at some point, I know I'll need to give up my naive view of him. I'll have to stop remembering him as the dad who lifted me on his shoulders and told me I could help him run the world and start seeing him as the stranger who likes to keep me small and useless.

It's just hard to let go of someone, to let them drift away until they only exist in your memories. Once I do, I'll have to admit that maybe he never really existed at all.

"Are you alright, darling?" James's voice snaps me from my thoughts, our car pulling into the lot of Rockford Prep.

I force a grin, not wanting to focus on the absence of my father, choosing instead to think about how it's *James* here now, making sure Jon and I don't do this alone.

The school itself is large, looming over us like a castle with steepled towers and arched windows, but the air surrounding it is heavy, suffocating. I brush off the feeling, hoping it's just my volatile emotions giving me a skewed view.

Maybe he'll love it here.

"Looks nice," I say, trying to infuse a lighthearted tone into my voice.

Jon stands next to me, his eyes taking in the building.

James's hand rests on my lower back. "It looks rather dim, doesn't it?"

Jon grins at him. "I looked it up before I came. I knew what to expect."

Surprise flows through me, my heart pinching at the fact that he so easily shared with James what he hasn't shared with me.

We move inside, a melancholy grip squeezing my lungs. I don't want to leave Jon here, if for no other reason than I'll miss him. Family has always been the most important thing in my world, and now it feels as though I'm in the middle of a riptide, watching as everything gets washed away, and I'm left struggling against the current.

The air in the main office presses around me with every step, and it's only when I feel James's hand on my back that I straighten my spine, allowing him to infuse some of his confidence into my bones. I lean into him for the support.

There's a woman sitting behind the front desk, her gray hair pulled into a tight bun, glasses pinned to her shirt with beaded straps.

"Hi," I start. "I'm here to drop off my brother. He's supposed to move in today."

Her lips pinch as she takes me in, then moves her gaze to Jon before finally resting on the man at my side. "Headmaster Dixon will be available shortly," she says. "Until then, you can sit down. I'll let you know when he's ready."

"Okay, thank you." I turn to go, but James's strong grip at my back keeps me in place.

"I do apologize, Miss…" He leans in over the top of the desk.

The woman's eyes grow round, her lips turning up in the corners. "Mrs. Henderson."

"Right. Of course, you're a Mrs.," he purrs. "Pity."

"Oh, now." She glances down, her cheeks gaining a rosy hue, and amusement dances through my chest at the fact that he seems to be *flirting*.

"I understand you and Headmaster Dixon must be extremely busy people," he continues. "But we *are* rather in a hurry."

My brows pull in. *We are?*

"You'd be doing me a great favor if you would let him know we're ready *now*."

Her grin drops, and it's no surprise, because while he sounds nothing less than a gentleman, there's an undercurrent of command in his tone, one that leaves no room for argument.

She nods slowly, reaching out and picking up the phone before speaking a few words and hanging back up. "I'll take you back." She smiles.

"Wonderful." James claps his hands together.

Jon and I share a look, and James's palm comes back to rest on my lower back, propelling me into the hallway.

Headmaster Dixon is a short, stocky man who sticks out

his chest and smiles so wide you can see his wisdom teeth. He goes through the curriculum and promises Jon will be in good hands, especially being *Peter Michaels's* kid, reminding us no less than thirty times that he's friends with my dad. But for as much posturing as he exudes, he can't command a room the way James does just by existing within it, and for every question that James asks, Headmaster Dixon's voice grows tighter.

"Do you have any other questions before we say goodbye?" Dixon says. "I'll have one of the head boys come down and show Jon to his room."

My throat starts to close, not wanting to say goodbye, and I reach out, my fingers tangling with James's.

He squeezes my palm in his, bringing our joined hands to his mouth and pressing a kiss to the back. My stomach flutters.

"You and Jon go wait in the lobby, yeah?" he says. "I'm going to have a quick word with the headmaster."

My head cocks. "For what?"

"Darling." He brushes my hair behind my ear. "I want to take care of you, and that extends to your brother. I'm simply ensuring we're all on the same page."

Warm, gooey gratitude drizzles through my insides. Because he's here. Because he's going to make sure Jon has what he needs. Because he *cares*. I rise on my tiptoes, pressing a kiss to his lips. "Thank you."

He winks and spins me around, lightly pushing me into the hallway. I twist one last time to see him closing the door, the headmaster's eyes widening the slightest bit.

"What do you think he's doing in there?" Jon asks once we're back in the front.

I shrug. "I don't know. Business type stuff, I guess."

Jon hums. "I like him."

Smiling, I look over at him. "I like him too."

"It's okay, you know?" he says.

"What is?"

"To be sad that I'm gone."

My throat tightens, and my eyes look to the ceiling, trying to stem the tears. I swear I've cried more in the past two days than I have since my mother's death, and I'm sick of it. I *hate* feeling so weak.

"I *am* sad." I smile at him. "But you're not too far, and I'm only a phone call away."

He nods. "I'll miss you too."

His arms wrap around me, and I close my eyes, the knot in my throat expanding until it burns.

"I love you, Wendy."

The sting moves to rest behind my eyes, and my arms tighten around him. "I love you too. I'm sorry Dad isn't here."

He pulls back, his jaw stiffening. "We don't need him."

James walks into the hallway a few moments later, heading straight to Jon and handing him a piece of paper. "I'd like you to take this number and put it in your phone. If you ever need *anything*, you call me."

My heart skips at his gesture.

The muscle in Jon's jaw twitches, his nostrils flaring. "I'll be fine."

"Of that I have no doubt," James replies. His hand squeezes Jon's shoulder as he bends down to speak in his ear.

I lean in close, straining to hear what he says.

"Just remember that whenever things feel bleak, all situations are temporary. It's not your circumstance that determines your worth, it's how you rise from the ashes after everything burns."

CHAPTER 24

James

I LEAVE WENDY AT HER HOUSE WITH BARELY MORE than a goodbye, impatience snapping at my insides like a rubber band with every wasted second.

The trip to Rockford Prep took longer than anticipated, but I felt it important to let the headmaster know what I expect of his staff when it comes to Jonathan Michaels. I'm not sure why I feel such a kinship with him. Maybe because he's Wendy's brother, and since she's mine, by proxy he is as well. Or maybe it's because I see so much of myself in him. I notice the way his muscles tense, defending against an offense he knows he can't control.

In either case, I could tell from simply looking in Wendy's eyes that today was a struggle. She would have been able to do it on her own of course. In the short time I've been with her, it's easy to tell that while she's docile and well-mannered around the majority of the world, she's also strong-willed and loyal to a fault. She loves her brother, and for some reason, that type of familial bond resonates, making me want to ensure her happiness when it comes to the people whom she loves.

It's another thirty minutes before my tires are crunching on the gravel path leading to Cannibal's Cave. The sun has barely set, bathing the landscape in a pinkish hue, not light enough to see clearly yet not dark enough to be blind.

I draw close to our normal meeting spot, my chest squeezing at the realization that there are no other cars here. I'm running behind, but I'm not *that* late, and a shiver skates up my spine, my gut telling me to stay alert. I park the car, leaving it running as I take in my surroundings.

Emptiness.

The weight of my knife is heavy in my pocket, and I reach across the console, opening the glove box, retrieving my gloves and my HK USP .40-caliber pistol. Normally, I like to stick to my blades, preferring a more *intimate* touch, but my intuition has never steered me wrong, and it would be remiss of me to bring my knife to what could very well be a gunfight.

I slip on my gloves, one finger at a time, and lean my head to the side, a deep crack reverberating down my spine. Stepping out of the car, I reach behind me, slipping my pistol in the waist of my pants before moving forward. I walk slowly, not wanting to disturb the quiet of the air. My ears are wide open, waiting to hear Ru's boisterous laugh or maybe his cutting words. But it's silent, nothing but the sound of cicadas in the trees and the breeze as it rustles through the leaves. The sky darkens as the sun continues to slip beneath the horizon, making my vision skew as I walk toward the cave entrance. We normally meet just outside it, but perhaps, for some reason, they moved things farther in.

My heart beats a slow and steady rhythm inside my chest, having learned how to control its tempo long ago, back when my uncle used to tell me how much it pleased him to feel it quicken under his hands.

Something is off.

It's too quiet. My foot slips on something hard, and I pause, glancing down as I lift the sole of my shoe.

A glint of color catches my eye.

I suck in a breath, my heart faltering from its steady pace.

Crouching down, I brush away the debris of fallen twigs and crispy leaves, revealing a blinding sparkle of red.

Rubies, to be exact.

My stomach churns.

No.

Straightening, I reach behind me to grab my gun, my stomach tense as I grip Ru's custom lighter in my hands. I move closer to the edge of the cave, and then I come to a crashing halt.

The *thunk* of my pistol as it hits the ground is barely audible through the heavy whooshing in my ears.

Because right in front of me is Ru. Bound to a tree, nails protruding from his hands and feet, his middle split open from the inside out.

Ice runs through my veins, shocking my nervous system until it buzzes like a staticky TV. I move forward with caution, my feet like lead, wanting to run the opposite way—to rewind time so I can undo this mistake.

Breathing deeply through my nose, I swallow around the thick knot in my throat, my chin lifting as I take in the extent of damage done to his person.

His eyes are open and bloodshot—the same eyes that showed me kindness when I was a young boy only used to seeing hate.

His mouth hangs lax—the same mouth that taught me to

never give up. To never give in. The one that told me I was like a son.

My chest twists so violently I retch, my body folding in half as I rest my hands on my knees, trying to control the heaving.

Slowly, I straighten, my gaze moving to the ripped apart flesh of his hands—the same hands that taught me how to wield a knife, how to shoot a gun. The ones that saved me years of torment from an evil even *I* can't comprehend.

My stomach heaves again, and I glance away, nostrils flaring as I try and shove down the tidal wave of memories threatening to come to the surface. But it's too late. The surge of grief rises up and hits me like a hurricane, my mind not able to connect the mangled corpse in front of me with the man who taught me everything I know.

The man who defended me against my nightmares.

I walk closer still, my feet stumbling over the ground, hands shaky as I reach the tree. My shoe slips in a puddle, the liquid splashing onto the hem of my pants. I freeze, staring down at the pool of blood, the life force of the only man on this earth who cared enough to take me in. The burn in my middle flares, scratching up my throat and pouring from my eyes. Tears track down my face and drip off my chin, the gaping hole in my chest cracking and shaking until my insides feel like they'll rip in half from the quake.

Bile burns the back of my throat from the smell of his insides, but I ignore the stench, my fingers reaching up and gripping the nail embedded in his left hand. It's slippery, caked with blood that's starting to dry, and as I tense my arm and pull, the sick pop of metal releasing from flesh is enough to make even the strongest of stomachs churn.

I stare at the nail in my palm, feeling as though it's being hammered through *me*, until something dark and heavy breaks through the cracks, slithering up my middle and wrapping around my neck like a noose.

And as I force myself to finish his other limbs, his body slumping down the tree and dropping on the ground, I realize that even the most fractured of hearts have further to break.

Because mine was just decimated to ash.

They didn't just kill him.

They *gutted* him and strung him up for the animals to feed.

But I'm worse than any of the wild things that live in these woods, and I'll hunt down everyone involved like prey, bathing in their blood and dancing to their screams until they repent for their sins.

My teeth grind so hard my jaw pops, my vision going blurry as a deep ache settles heavy in my chest.

I could have prevented this.

But I was with...

Wendy.

My head looks to the sky, my mind shattering into a million pieces as I wonder if somehow she was in on this plan. If she knew that by distracting me, her father could sneak in and once again take away the only thing that matters.

His little shadow.

Words from George the baker flow through my head, only this time, I see them from a different angle. My head is clear, no longer clouded with the lust for a woman who has the same DNA as the man responsible for so much of my pain.

"It was a woman. Said there was a new boss in town."

Shock rushes through me like an electrical current, clashing with the simmer of my rage until they combust into an explosion of heat, wrath singeing through my veins and bursting from my pores.

Acid teases the back of my throat.

I had assumed it was Tina, Peter's assistant. But Wendy was there that day. *She was there.* I blow out a deep breath.

My gloved hand runs over my mouth, the leather rough against my dry lips. "They won't get away with it." My voice catches. "I will make them suffer for every moment of pain you endured."

My thumb brushes over the inscription on the lighter, still held tightly in my palm.

Straight on 'til morning.

With a deep breath, I flick it open, the clink of the lid and spark of the flame the only sound other than the silent screams clawing at my soul.

"Rest easy, friend."

Pain splinters through my stomach as I toss the lighter onto fallen leaves, watching as they catch fire and spread, Ru's body slowly being engulfed in the flames.

CHAPTER 25

Wendy

THERE'S A SINGLE, SAD CUPCAKE IN THE CENTER of my kitchen island, with gloppy white icing and sprinkles that look out of place, so colorful in a gray and empty house. It's been three days since Jon has gone, leaving me entirely alone and, quite frankly, depressed.

I've always spent my time focused on family, not willing to let our brittle roots break after the death of my mother.

But now I don't really see the point.

"Happy birthday to me." I sigh, blowing out the flame.

Glancing at my phone, my chest pinches tight. It's almost seven in the evening, and other than a quick birthday text from Angie, no one has called all day.

Not my father.

Not Jon.

Not James.

Although, in James's defense, I've never told him when my birthday was. But he's been MIA since Monday, when he helped me take Jon to Rockford Prep.

I took the day off from the Vanilla Bean, but now I'm regretting the decision, the hollow ring of loneliness echoing through the high ceilings and marble floors of my house.

Suddenly, my phone rings, and anticipation lights up my insides. But when I look at the ID and see it's my dad, disappointment casts a shadow like a storm cloud.

I wanted it to be James.

And that revelation in itself sends a shock wave through me, because somewhere along the line, in these past few weeks, my dad has slipped off his pedestal, the ache of missing him muted and dulled.

"Hey, Dad."

"Little shadow, happy birthday."

My stomach twists. "Thank you. Wish you were here to celebrate."

"Me too."

My stomach drops, and I feel stupid once again for hoping that maybe he was calling to say he was on his way.

"Listen," he continues. "I'm sending out some new security for the house tomorrow."

My nose scrunches. "What? Why?"

My father has always had security for himself, but we've always kept our private home *private*.

"I've had some idiots trying to blackmail me, and I need to make sure you're safe. That the house is safe."

I chew my lip. *Blackmail?* "What? No, Dad… I… I don't need a freaking *bodyguard*. That's ridiculous," I laugh. "I'll be fine."

"This is not up for discussion, Wendy." His voice is stern, and it cuts through me, making my lungs cramp in my chest. He speaks as though I'm a child, unable to care for myself. As if I'm not intelligent enough to handle the truth of whatever's going on.

Blackmail. Give me a break.

"Dad, I'm not a kid anymore. Just tell me what's going on. Maybe I can help."

He chuckles. "Wendy, you can't help. You just need to listen and do as I say."

Anger swims through my veins, and my jaw tenses. Maybe a few weeks ago, I would have *just listened*, but after being with James—after being treated as a woman whose voice is heard and whose opinions are valid—crawling back into the role my father expects me to play feels like steel bars clamping down on my soul.

And I won't do it.

But fighting with my father is as good as talking in circles, so I stay silent on the line, thinking about how I can handle things once I hang up.

Maybe James can help.

"Okay, Dad. I hear you."

"Good," he responds. "I'll be home in the next few weeks, and we can have dinner. A night for just the two of us, okay?"

My throat burns. "Mm-hmm," I force out.

A female voice cuts through the phone. "Pete, where are you taking me tonight? I want to know if I should look fancy or if we're ordering in."

My lungs cramp, realizing that he isn't working, he's just choosing to take Tina out on *my* birthday instead of making sure he's home to spend it with me. And that's fine. It's absolutely *fine*.

I hang up the phone without saying goodbye, not sure I'll be able to stop the cutting words from flying off my tongue, and I don't want to say something I can't take back.

There's a throbbing ache in the middle of my stomach, a sickly, green feeling that weighs me down and makes me want to crack.

But I don't.

Heading up the stairs and to my room, I decide to pack a bag and leave. I have a few thousand dollars in my bank account, and while I'm sure my father won't be happy, there's really nothing he can do. He can't *make* me stay after all.

My bedroom is pitch-black, the sun having set while I was staring at my cupcake, and I flick on the lamp by my bedside, my eyes snagging on the picture of my mother and me from when I was young.

I wonder if she's somewhere looking down on us, feeling sad over the fact that she couldn't stick around. Maybe if she were still here, my dad would be too.

Shaking my head, I ignore the burn radiating from the middle of my chest as I walk to my full-length mirror. My hands run over my pale-green dress, smoothing out the wrinkles as I gaze into the glass.

I pick up my hairbrush from the vanity next to me and point to my reflection. "You aren't a child, Wendy. You are a *bad bitch*." Giggling at the phrase, I run the bristles over my hair, repeating the affirmation in my mind.

"I agree. You are most definitely not a child."

My stomach jumps into my throat, hairbrush dropping to the floor as I meet an ice-blue gaze in the mirror. My mouth opens on a sharp inhale, shock at seeing him in my room freezing me in place. He moves quickly, his body pushing against mine until I'm flat against the glass, a knife glinting as he presses it to my face, his gloved palm smacking over my lips and muffling my scream before it can even think of escaping.

"Now, now, Wendy darling," he tsks. "None of that."

My heart slams against my chest, confusion spinning around me like a spider's web. I'd like to think this is some big, elaborate joke, but the pressure of his hold has dread sneaking up my spine. I watch him in the mirror, strands of his dark hair falling on his forehead, his black trench coat and leather gloves making him look like the angel of death. His blade gleams in the mirror's reflection, the metal cold as its hooked edge presses into my skin.

Hooked.

My stomach flips and twists, realizing where his nickname comes from.

His free hand wraps around my hair, wrenching my head to the side, his nose skimming along the pale expanse of my neck. "Did you know fear has a scent?"

My nostrils flare as I attempt to breathe, terror pulsing in time to the rapid pace of my heart. There's a sting from where he pulled my roots, and I focus on the pain to ground me.

"No, I don't suppose you would." His mouth turns down. "It's all to do with pheromones, really. The scent of fear triggers a reaction in the amygdala and hypothalamus. A type of warning, as it were, that humans have long since become numb to recognizing." He leans back in, inhaling deeply, the tips of his hair tickling my skin.

I try to keep my gaze steady, my body trembling from the adrenaline that's pumping through my veins, my mind racing as I try to think of a way out of this situation.

Is he going to kill me?

My insides pull tight, eyes burning at the realization that everything I thought I knew about him was a lie. Panic seizes my lungs, my hands shaking as they press against the mirror.

"*Your* fear smells sweet," he whispers.

His palm trails down the front of my body, slipping under my dress and cupping between my legs. The fabric of his glove is rough against my sensitive skin, and horror trickles through my veins like a poison, freezing my blood and stalling my heart.

"Tell me, darling…" His voice rumbles in his chest, vibrating through my back and making my hair stand on end. "Was deceiving me always your plan?"

My stomach tenses, tears slipping down my cheeks and trailing over the back of his hand, melting into the leather before it can drip to the floor. I shake my head, my hair matting against his coat. I struggle for breath, wishing he'd release my mouth so I could ask him what the *hell* he's talking about.

"I don't think I believe you." His palm pushes against my center, and my traitorous clit swells against him. "After all, you've always been such a *good girl*. So incredibly adept at following direction." He places a light kiss on my throat before resting his chin at the juncture between my neck and shoulder, smiling at our reflection. "So beautiful," he says, sliding the flat edge of his knife across my cheek until the tip rests against the bow of my lips. It's oddly sensual, and my breath stutters as I try to maintain a facade of calm against the dichotomy of his actions and his tender touch.

Who is this man?

"Such a shame." He sighs, dropping the knife from my face, his eyes locking on mine in the mirror. "This will only hurt for a second."

My brows furrow, my chest seizing when I see a syringe being pulled from his pocket. My body surges into fight-or-flight mode, my heart crashing against my sternum as my hands reach up to grapple against his arms, and then…

Nothing.

CHAPTER 26

Wendy

IT'S THE POUNDING IN MY HEAD THAT WAKES ME. My lashes flutter, a sharp ache stabbing between my eyes. I try to press my palm against the pain, but my movement is stilted, something clanking when I move.

I pull again, and my body jerks forward before falling back against something hard. My brain is sluggish, like driving out of a storm only to end up in thick fog, but as I start to wake, I realize that I am *definitely* not lying down. And my arms are stuck.

The thought of opening my eyes fully makes my stomach churn, but still I pry my lids apart one at a time, my face scrunched in preparation for the light.

When my gaze focuses, I realize it's dark.

Really dark.

Awareness trickles back in, and my heart picks up speed, kicking against my ribs.

I squint my eyes, trying to get my bearings, but it's hard to focus. Hard to think.

Swallowing, I wince against the scratch of my throat and peel my dry tongue from the roof of my mouth. I try to move my hands again, but they don't go far, that same clanking noise from earlier reverberating in my ears and off the walls. Glancing down, I can barely make out thick metal shackles clamped around my wrists. My stomach twists, a dose of panic flooding through my veins. I splay my fingers, feeling something cold and hard underneath me.

Okay, Wendy. Everything is okay.

My heart pounds a staccato rhythm as I blink quickly, trying to adjust my vision to see in the dark. But it's no use. The icy tendrils of fear snake up my spine, coiling like vines around my body and squeezing tighter with every breath. I yank my arms against the chains again, harder this time, causing a sharp ache to shoot down my arm and a sting to slice through my wrists. Closing my eyes, my head smacks against the cold wall as I try to steady my breathing.

Being in a panic won't help.

What happened?

My birthday.

Then James.

Hook.

The memory comes rushing through like a stampede, flooding over the mental barrier of my drowsiness and cracking my chest in two.

A click sounds from the opposite side of the room, and my head turns toward the noise, my eyes squeezing when a door opens and light floods in from a hallway.

"Good. You're awake."

My body trembles as I watch Curly step into the room. He shuts the door, leaving it wedged open a crack to allow the brightness to filter through.

"Wh—" I wince, the scratch in my throat making talking difficult.

His steps are audible on the floor as he comes near, and I attempt to curl in on myself, to hide from this man as much as possible, even though there's nowhere for me to go.

Curly stops in front of me, the right side of his lips pulling up. "Hiya, sunshine."

I stare at him for long seconds, disgust weaving through my insides and rolling around in my gut. He was always so sweet. I actually thought maybe we could become friends, but here he is, looking at me chained to a wall and *smirking*.

"Fuck." My voice catches, but I swallow around the sting and continue. "You."

He crouches down in front of me, a plastic plate in his hands. "Now, that's not very nice. It's not like *I* put you down here."

Anger simmers deep in my gut.

"I brought you some food." He reaches over, picking up a piece of what looks like bread. "Open up."

I press my lips together, turning my head.

He sighs. "Don't make this more difficult than it needs to be."

Something inside me snaps, and my eyes narrow, my face whipping back toward him. A small amount of saliva pools in my mouth as I take in the smell of the bread being held in front of me. I collect it at the tip of my tongue and spit in his face.

The sound of the plate clattering to the floor is the only noise in the room other than the beats of my heart and the sound of our breathing.

His grin drops, his warm eyes icing over as he wipes the wetness from his cheek. "Fine." He leans in. "You can fucking starve."

He grabs the plate from the floor and walks away. The door clicks open and closed, and I'm alone again in the dark.

My stomach cramps, a ball of something heavy and sharp expanding in my middle, tearing through my calm until I'm gasping for air, my heart beating so fast I think I may have a heart attack.

———

Time moves differently when you're chained in an empty room. My mind is still woozy and my body trembles with a shiver so deep I feel it in my bones. I go in and out of restless sleep no matter how much I try to stay awake—to formulate some type of plan.

My eyes peel open after another bout of losing consciousness. *I must have been drugged.*

I'm not sure how many hours it's been, or maybe it's been days, but my vision has long since adjusted to the darkness, and I'm able to clearly make out a long table pushed against the far edge of the room, a small mound of what looks like packaged powder stacked at one end.

I squint my eyes, trying to see clearer, to figure out if it's something I can somehow get to and use to my advantage.

But I know it's fruitless. There's nothing I can do. No weapons at my disposal, not that I'd know how to use them even if there were. No chance of getting to them even if I did, what with me being stuck to a wall.

All I have now is my faith.

Trust.

"Pixie dust."

My heart stutters at the silky accent, my stomach rising and falling like a roller coaster. My head snaps to the right, noticing for the first time since waking that there's a chair only a few feet away. And James is sitting in it, legs spread wide as he watches me, his gloved hands relaxing comfortably with a knife in his lap.

He tilts his head toward the table I was staring at. "What you're looking at. It's *pixie* dust."

My stomach cramps as he stands up and walks toward me, his beauty making my nerves light up. Nausea follows close behind at the way my body reacts to him. At the way I *gave him everything* only for him to be the villain in disguise.

The sound of his steps bounces off the walls, the vibration splitting open my chest, my blood pumping heartache on the floor. He stops in front of me, his perfectly polished black shoes resting at the tips of my bare feet.

I grind my teeth, a sharp stab of pain vibrating up my jaw.

"You should eat."

"Get fucked," I spit out.

He tsks. "What did I tell you about that filthy mouth?"

My head tilts as I glare up at him. "You've said a lot of things, *Hook*. Turns out I really, *really* don't give a damn about a single one." The curse words feel strange as they fall from my lips, but right now, they're all I have. I know they bother him, and since I can't break free and scratch his eyes out with my nails, I have to settle for what I've got.

His lips curve into a thin smile. It sends shivers down my spine. He points at me with his knife. "I'm not the liar here, darling. Let's not cast stones from glass houses."

"I don't even know what's going on!" My body jerks as I pull at the chains, my hands smacking uselessly against the floor.

His eyes flick from my face to where I'm bound to the wall,

the grin dropping from his face. "Playing the victim is a terribly unbecoming trait." His voice is flat, and the hollow tone makes my chest compress, realizing the warm charm I was used to has disappeared entirely.

I huff out a breath, disbelief squeezing my middle. "You have me chained to a wall," I state.

He nods. "A temporary tactic, I assure you."

My eyes narrow, anger bubbling in my gut. "You drugged me."

He flips his knife through his fingers, the move so practiced and smooth it sends a spike of fear bolting through my chest.

"Would you have come willingly?" His brow lifts.

A ball lodges in my throat, my insides fracturing from the strength it takes to keep from letting tears escape. "I would have gone *anywhere* with you." My voice breaks. "Please, I—"

I lose the battle to my emotions, and wetness coasts down my face, the tears hot against my chilled skin.

He crouches down, blade hanging between his legs, his gaze stripping me bare and burning me alive. "Your father took something." He pauses, his eyes briefly closing. "Something irreplaceable from me."

My heart stalls, and I sniff, trying to stop my nose from running with my tears. "My father? I don't—"

He shoots up from his position, pacing across the room until he meets the chair, his hand wrapping around the back and flinging it toward me. My lungs seize, stomach dropping to the floor as the wood splinters next to my head, my hair blowing from the force of it smashing against the wall. He stalks back to me, lunging forward and gripping my jaw tightly in his hands. "Don't play innocent, you vapid, *stupid* girl."

My heart claws at my chest, hiccups stuttering my breath as

his insults and small pieces of wood slice like paper cuts along my skin. Looking straight into his eyes, I search for a sliver of the man I thought I knew. The man who I gave everything to.

But he's long gone.

Or maybe he never existed at all.

He's right. I *am* a stupid girl.

My tongue swipes out, getting caught on the rough, chapped edges of my lips, and I speak slowly, trepidation filling me from the inside out. This man—Hook—is a stranger. And something whispers in the back of my head to tread carefully. To do whatever it takes to just stay alive.

My father will come for me. *He has to.*

"James," I say slowly. "If my father...if he did something."

His sharp laugh soars through the air, his grip tightening until my teeth cut into skin. "You showed up at my bar," he hisses. "And then you distracted me when others needed me most."

I attempt to shake my head, but his grasp is strong, his eyes wild as they stare into mine before flicking to the chains at my side.

My insides are twisted in tight coils, nerve endings frazzled and frayed, and I watch this stranger as he rages at me with the fire of a thousand suns. He looks like he wants to kill me.

My fingers press into the ground at my sides, my heart beating in my throat.

Leaning his head to the side, his eyes close in a slow blink. And when they open, the fire has been doused.

He's a blank slate, his gaze just two vacant holes, rimmed in blue.

The grip on my jaw loosens, his gloved fingers caressing my skin like a lover, before his focus flicks to the bindings on the wall.

I inhale, holding it in my lungs, afraid to even breathe, worried that it might set him off again.

He stands, pulling something out of his pocket.

My body cowers, chest squeezing as he nears. He hovers above me, his spicy scent invading my nostrils and making me *hate* myself for the way my heart skips at the smell. A jostling sensation on my wrist, and then a click, followed by pinpricks of pain lancing down my arm as blood flows freely back into my hand.

He's unlocking my chains.

"I find it's rather erotic having you cuffed to my walls," he says as he moves to the other side. "But you're no use to me damaged."

I pull my arms to my chest, my fingers rubbing against the raw skin of my wrist.

"At least not at the moment."

His face comes within inches of mine, my stomach compressing at the sudden movement.

"If you act out, I *will* retaliate."

Heartbreak sits heavy in my gut, rising up and coating my throat like bile. "What could you possibly do that you haven't already done?"

His eyes dance over my face, almost as if he's memorizing the lines. The sudden switch of his demeanor makes unease weave through my every cell. He leans in, pressing his lips to mine. My body freezes in place, eyes widening.

His thumb caresses my cheek. "You will eat. You will drink the water we provide." His fingers reach around to the nape of my neck, squeezing slightly. "And you will not do anything *reckless*, or I will chain you to the ceiling and rain your blood onto the floor."

Betrayal lodges deeper with each word he says until it fills up every pore and marinates in my blood. "I *hate* you," I whisper.

He smirks before he forcefully tosses my head away, my hands catching my body as I tumble sideways, my elbows cracking as they hit the ground.

Standing up, he runs his gloved palms down the front of his suit. "Do not make the mistake of thinking I'm someone you can disrespect."

Nausea sloshes through my gut.

I watch from my spot on the floor as he moves to the end table, collecting the stack of pixie dust and heading toward the door. He pauses at the threshold, turning to look at me. "Do try to behave, darling. I'd hate to have to punish you."

And then he turns, and once again, I'm all alone.

CHAPTER 27

James

IT'S BEEN THREE DAYS SINCE I TOOK WENDY FROM her home and stashed her in the basement of the JR. In that time, I've felt more emotion than the previous fifteen years combined. My nights are restless in a way they've never been before. Dreams of Ru rising from the grave and telling me how I've failed him keep me wide awake and frazzled.

Funny how he once stopped my nightmares, only to become them in the end. Life is always full circle, I suppose.

That combined with the continual disappearance of our crates, and my insides are wound tight, a live wire waiting to be tripped.

And Wendy... *Wendy*.

Well, it's a shame it's gotten to this point, but there's nothing to be done for it now. I'll still use her for the same purpose, only in the end, instead of allowing her to go free, I'll make her watch as I drain the life from her father's eyes.

And then I'll do the same to her.

There's a sharp ache in my chest at the thought, but I take

another sip of brandy and let the burn of liquor numb the pain. The glass clinks on the table as I set it down and settle into my chair, watching Wendy on the cameras and twirling an invitation to tonight's charity gala.

She's cross-legged in the middle of the room, her eyes closed and hands on her legs, almost as if she's in deep meditation.

Starkey sits across from me, and I lean forward, placing my elbows on the desk.

"Tell me again," I say slowly. "Who went with Ru to his meeting?"

Starkey's jaw is set, his light brown hair ruffling against his fingers as he combs through the strands. "Nobody."

"Nobody," I repeat.

He lifts a shoulder. "Didn't even tell anyone he was going."

Irritation snaps in my veins, paper crumpling under my fingers. "You're sure?"

Starkey's leg bounces against the floor, and my eyes dip down, tracking the movement. Annoyance flows through me like an untapped faucet, and I bite my cheek so hard copper floods my mouth.

"Ye—yeah, boss, I'm sure."

A pounding forms between my eyes and I sigh, pinching the bridge of my nose. "Get out of my sight."

"But we still have to—"

I shoot from my chair, picking up my knife and flinging it toward him, lodging it into the far wall. "I said *leave*." My knuckles ache as they press into the wood of my desk, and I look down, breathing deeply to keep my temper at bay. "Before my aim improves."

He leaves within seconds, the soft click of the door making my shoulders drop.

The heartbeat in my ears combined with the grinding of my teeth is a symphony of sound, accompanying the tornado of white-hot frustration whipping through my insides, so potent I can't drown it out.

It's been almost a week since Ru's murder, and still I'm no closer to answers.

Shipments are going missing, Peter Michaels is doing *everything* to control my streets, and now I'm supposed to step into Ru's shoes and take over officially as the boss.

A title I've never been interested in having.

Add on top of that the infuriating woman in my basement, and I feel like a blank jigsaw puzzle with a thousand scattered pieces.

Someone knocks on the office door, and I heave a breath. "Come in."

Curly walks through, his chin dipping in acknowledgment.

"Any new developments?" I ask.

He shakes his head, walking over to where Wendy sits in silence on the screen. "Nope. She pretty much just does that all the time."

Glancing down at the invitation in my palm, an idea forms in my mind. After all, I know Peter will be there—he's their guest of honor—and it's the first time he'll be in Massachusetts since the night of Ru's death.

It's time to show him what happens when you underestimate a monster. A thrill zips through me, lighting up my stomach and electrifying my veins at the thought of *finally* putting my plan into action.

And Wendy is going to help me do it. Whether she wants to or not.

"Miss me, darling?" I ask as I walk into the darkened room.

Wendy still sits in the center, her eyes closed and legs crossed. "Like a hole in the head," she replies.

A chuckle bubbles up my throat, but I bite it back. Leaning against the wall, I watch her, my chest pulling tight as I take in the bruising on her wrists and the matted strands of her hair.

She peeks open an eye, then snaps it shut when she meets my gaze. "People are going to notice I'm gone, you know."

I nod, placing my hands in my pockets. "I'm counting on it."

Both of her eyes open at this, her stare locking on mine, sending a flash of heat through my abdomen.

"My father will come for me."

I tilt my head. "Are you quite sure?"

She hesitates, her jaw tightening as she looks away. "Of course."

"Right." I straighten off the wall, walking toward her. "In any case, he won't need to. We're going to him."

Her head snaps in my direction, and she scrambles to her feet.

I continue my slow steps in her direction, and she stiffens, her feet moving backward as if she can break away. Her back hits the stone wall, and I walk into her body, my hips pressing against her, arms reaching up to cage her in. "Where do you think you could run to, Wendy darling?" I move my palm from the wall, my fingers wrapping lightly around her neck. "Even if you were to escape this room, there's nowhere you could go that I wouldn't find you."

She bares her teeth, her breathing shaky. "Get your hands *off* me."

Her arm moves quickly, palm open and swinging toward my

face. My stomach jumps as I grab her wrist before it hits, twisting until her body spins. She grunts as my torso pushes into her forcefully, my free hand pressing against the back of her head until her cheek is flush against the wall, her arm locked behind her, wedged between us.

I lean in, my chin resting on her shoulder. "I'm not a fan of repeating myself, so I suggest you listen close." She jerks her arm, her elbow grazing my stomach, and I tighten my grip. "I'm going to take you to my home, where I'll allow you to shower and make yourself presentable."

"You're *disgusting*."

My stomach twists. "That may be. But until I decide otherwise, I'm also your *master*."

She scoffs, her body writhing against mine, causing blood to flow to my groin, my cock twitching.

I smirk. "Do continue, sweetheart. I love it when you fight."

Her body stiffens.

I release her, and she spins around, her eyes narrowed as she grips her wrist, her fingers massaging the red marks. A flare of concern trickles through my mind, but I bat it away. A little bruising won't hurt near as bad as the wounds she's caused. And in the end, it won't matter once she's dead.

"I have an event tonight," I say. "And I'd like you to accompany me."

She huffs out a laugh, but after a few seconds, it quiets, her eyes widening. "You're serious?"

"I am."

"Go to hell," she spits.

"Alright." I pull my phone from my pocket, bringing it up to my ear.

"What are you—"

I hold up a finger, silencing her. "Hi, yes, Mrs. Henderson. It's so nice to hear your voice. This is James Barrie."

Wendy's gasp sends a rush of satisfaction through my veins.

A grin breaks across my face and I wink. "Can you please let Headmaster Dixon know that I'll be coming to pick up Jonathan Michaels?"

"You *bastard*." Her voice is pinched, and my eyes glance to hers, a spike of *something* coasting through my chest.

I cover the mouthpiece with my hand, my brows raising. "Come again, darling? I couldn't quite hear you." I point to my phone. "Important *business*, you know."

"I called you a *bastard*," she hisses. Her palms press into her eyes, her head shaking. "I'll do whatever you want. Just, please—"

The knot in my stomach loosens at her agreement, and I nod. "You know? Never mind, Mrs. Henderson. It appears my plans have changed. I *do* hope you have a wonderful day."

I hang up, sliding the phone back in my pocket, and walk toward her. I stop when the tips of my shoes press against the bare skin of her toes. My fingers tilt her chin up. "I do regret that it's come to this. It didn't have to be this way. But we all have times in our lives when we must pick a side."

Her brows furrow. "What? I—"

I run a finger down her jaw. "Unfortunately, you picked wrong." I drop my hand from her face and turn toward the door. "I'll be back soon. And it would do you well to remember what's at stake."

CHAPTER 28

Wendy

MY WRISTS ARE BOUND AGAIN, ONLY THIS TIME, they're *actual* handcuffs instead of heavy shackles. I stare down at the metal, fingers twisting in my lap, before looking over at Curly in the driver's side of the car. "You didn't have to handcuff me. It's not like I'll run."

Curly's face remains stoic, as if he can't hear me speak at all.

He's been like this ever since I spit in his face. But I don't regret it, and there's nothing I have left to say to him anyway—nothing I have left to say to *any* of them.

I close my eyes and lean my head against the window, allowing the rays of the sun to soak through the glass and into my skin. There's a constant heaviness that lives inside me now, but in this moment, I grasp on to the little bit of relief at *finally* being in the light. I have no idea how much time has actually passed, but when you're stuck in the dark with nothing but your thoughts, a second feels like a century.

My brain was scrambling like eggs, the isolation turning into a mental torture chamber—nothing but my thoughts and emotions to keep me company—so I started sitting in the middle of the room and trying my hand at meditation. I'm not sure if I've been doing it right, but it seems to calm the panic down. Allows time to pass in a way that doesn't make me feel as though I'm losing my grip on sanity.

It was during one of these introspective moments that I realized some of my pain isn't new; it's just fresh scratches on old scars. James—*no, not James*—Hook is another person in the line of people who think they can tell me what to do, who cut me down with words, tell me to sit and stay, expecting me to bite my tongue and smile. And it's true, it's what I've been doing my whole life. Never standing up for myself, swallowing down the insults from "friends" and the belittling moments from my father as if they were my cross to bear.

But I'm *tired* of being told to heel.

The car turns into the marina, and my stomach twists as I remember the last time I was here. It was only days ago, yet somehow, it feels like I was an entirely different person, one who still viewed the world and all the people in it as inherently good.

But the rose-colored glasses were stripped off my face in a millisecond, leaving nothing but shades of gray behind.

Curly parks the car and moves to my side in a flash, opening the door and lifting me by the arm before he unlocks my cuffs. "Don't do anything stupid."

As if I'd be dumb enough to put my brother in danger.

I follow behind him, down the docks and to the ostentatious *Tiger Lily* at the end of the marina, watching as Smee mops the sundeck and three white birds fly overhead.

The sun is shining, and the water is sparkling and crystal blue.

Everything is normal. Beautiful, even. Like my entire world hasn't been flipped, twisted, and dropped upside down. Like I wasn't seduced, drugged, kidnapped, and held in a stone basement. Despair creeps through me as I realize that I really am at the mercy of Hook's whims.

He called himself my *master*.

And at least until I formulate a plan that keeps my family safe, he's right.

"Move it, sunshine. Let's *go*." Curly's hand pushes the back of my shoulder, and even though my legs feel like lead, somehow, I force them to move, stepping onto the boat. He doesn't follow, just stands on the sidewalk, his arms crossed and his eyes narrowed, as if he's expecting me to do something wild, like jump off the side and try to get away.

Maybe I should.

But I can't swim well despite growing up in Florida, and I'm not stupid enough to think that I'd be successful.

Smee waves, and my eyes take him in, his boyish face and his bright red beanie making him look innocent as a lamb. My lips purse. I'm not sure how much he knows, but I'm done with putting my trust in people who haven't earned it. My stomach sloshes with nerves, hands shaking as I reach out and open the door, stepping into the living room and glancing around.

Empty.

Moving my way slowly through the cabin, I stop in front of the kitchen island, steps away from where the knives are sitting pretty, right next to the wood cutting board. My mind whirls a hundred miles a minute. The urge to grab one is strong, but I need to be smart, and the thought of what Hook will do if he finds me with a weapon makes my heart drop to the floor, a chill racing through my veins. I frown at the knives as gruesome images of how he'd kill me play through my mind.

"I wouldn't if I were you."

The voice makes my stomach jump, and I spin around, coming face-to-face with a blue-eyed devil. "Hook."

He inclines his head. "You can still call me James if you wish."

My jaw tightens and I cross my arms. "I *don't* wish."

He nods. "Very well. This way."

His hand comes to rest on my back and sends a shiver coasting through me, resentment coiling at the base of my spine for the way my body reacts to his touch. He moves us down the hallway and holds open the door to his room, allowing me to enter first before following behind. I lay eyes on his king-size bed with silk sheets and a fluffy burgundy comforter, the aches from sleeping on a cold stone floor flaring to life, making my bones weep.

"There are fresh towels in the washroom, and I've had a dress delivered."

My lips turn down, glancing at him from my peripheral. "How do you know my size?"

He smirks. "I have a very *hands-on* memory."

My cheeks heat, disgust curling inside me. He took my *virginity*. I let him basically strangle me half to death, and I trusted him to keep me safe.

Pathetic, Wendy.

"What do you want from me?" I ask. "What did I *do* to deserve this? I don't—" The words catch on the swelling in my throat, my hand coming up to cover my mouth.

His eyes flatten as he stalks toward me. I jerk on instinct, the backs of my legs hitting the edge of his bed, making me stumble and bounce off the mattress. I scramble up, leaning on my elbows as my gaze meets his.

He hovers over me, but it's not sensual like a lover. It's *intimidating*, his energy whipping around him like a lightning storm, making my hair stand on end.

He's so close, I can taste his breath as if it were my own.

"What I *want*," he whispers against my lips, "is for you to stop playing me for a fool." He presses in further, his eyes swirling with emotion. "What I *want* is to bring souls back from the dead and let them feast on your father's screams." His nose runs along the length of my neck, and I suck in a breath, my heart pumping so fast it makes my head spin. "Can you give me any of those things, Wendy darling?"

My middle squeezes tight. *How could I forget?* This isn't about me at all. It's about *my father*.

"You knew who he was?" I blurt out. "This whole time…"

His lips twitch, and he backs away, the fire in his eyes disappearing as fast as it came.

"Did you know who I was?" The question burns my throat, tears blurring my vision.

"Of course." He picks invisible lint from his sleeve. "I knew who you were the moment you walked into my bar."

My fractured heart cracks from the sudden pressure in my chest.

Of course he did.

Nodding, a grim type of acquiescence settles into my veins. It's thick and wet, like deep mud, and I know the more I struggle, the further I'll sink. "I think I'd like to take a shower now."

His brows lift as he points to the bathroom.

I stand up and move inside the room, closing the door behind me. My fingers grip the metal handle, my head resting against the cool wood of the frame. I hold my breath until my lungs cry for air, and even then, I don't let it out, afraid that once I do, I'll scream. I'm confused, my emotions tugging me in a thousand different directions. I don't know whether I'm stupid for not making a break for it or if I'm smart for trying to make a plan. I have no idea if after tonight I'll get thrown back into the dark and cold stone room, or if he's just going to kill me once and for all.

That would *definitely* send my father a message.

And then there's the guilt, and that, on top of everything else, is the strongest. It splits through my stomach and reaches up my chest, clawing its way through my insides until it attaches to my throat.

Because I feel so goddamn *relieved* to be here. To take a shower. To breathe in fresh air. To have human interaction, even if it's with the person responsible for everything. And what kind of person does that make me—to feel grateful for the good when the source is a man threatening everyone I love?

Everything will be fine.

A memory of leaving Jon at Rockford Prep flies into my head, Hook's words—although he was James to me then—playing on a loop.

"Just remember, that whenever things feel bleak, all situations are temporary. It's not your circumstance that determines your worth, it's how you rise from the ashes after everything burns."

CHAPTER 29

James

"WILL SHE BE STAYING TONIGHT, SIR? I CAN MAKE up the guest room if she is."

I look over to where Smee is standing in the kitchen, drinking from a mug of tea.

Cocking my head, I take a sip from my own cup, the liquid singeing my tongue as I swallow. "Why would you assume she'd be staying anywhere other than in my bed?"

His eyes widen the slightest bit, and curiosity sneaks through my thoughts at his sudden interest.

"No reason. I just thought I'd offer." He walks to the kitchen sink, placing his cup in the basin before spinning around to lean against the lip. "I won't be around tonight, and I didn't want to leave you with the setup is all. I know how you like your own space."

I lift my chin, my gaze soaking up his mannerisms. He seems on edge, almost like he's uncomfortable that she's here. "Big plans?" I ask.

I've never taken an interest in Smee's personal life, and quite honestly, I still don't care. But talking to him is a distraction from the girl locked in my room, and I find myself craving a break from the anger that surfaces whenever I see her face or think her name.

Smee grins, running a hand through his hair, the kitchen lights glinting off his dark brown strands. "You could say that."

"Well, I appreciate your hospitality, but it won't be necessary."

I'm undecided on what to do with her after the gala. Part of me wants to throw her back in the JR's basement and let her rot. It's no less than what she deserves. The other part wants to tie her to my bed and use *other* means of forcing the truth out of her. It *infuriates* me that she still acts as though she's innocent. Like she has no idea what she's done.

No matter, I'll be able to tell a lot from the way she interacts with her father this evening. I sent the twins ahead, ensuring that our places were at the guest of honor's table, and I can't *wait* to see what's on the menu.

Loud knocks pound from down the hallway and I smirk, draining the last of my tea and placing it back on the counter.

Smee's eyes widen as he looks toward the noise and then back at me. "Is she stuck in there?"

I stand, buttoning the jacket of my tuxedo and walking past him, pausing to squeeze his shoulder, the muscle tensing under my palm. "What I do with my toys is none of your concern, Smee."

His eyes go flat and he inclines his head. "Apologies, boss man."

I wave him off, smiling. "Forgotten."

My hand slips into my pocket, retrieving the skeleton key as I walk to my bedroom door. The banging is loud, the force of Wendy's knocking making the wood rattle against the hinges. I slide the metal into the lock, the door clicking as Wendy's flushed face greets me, her fist poised halfway in the air.

The corner of my lip lifts. "Is everything alright? You sound awfully frustrated."

The ruddiness of her cheeks makes a vision of her beneath me flash before my mind, and arousal spears through my middle. I shake off the thought and glance down her form, the dress I had Moira pick out hugging her every curve.

She looks stunning. The picture of grace and poise, a powder-blue fabric with a sweetheart neck and an open back. Sophisticated enough to be seen on my arm, yet ravishing enough that every man will wish he could have her.

My perfect little pet.

She grits her teeth. "You locked me in there."

"A precautionary measure."

I stare at her for a few more moments, drinking her in like fine wine, remembering what it felt like to be inside her. Blood rushes to my cock, making it jerk against my leg.

She puts her arms out to her sides. "Well, do I pass your approval?"

Frustration wells in my chest at my constant attraction to such a conniving wench. I force it from my mind, replacing it with the black mass that's been burning the fragments of my soul ever since Ru's death.

The death I'm wholly convinced she was part of.

My eyes narrow, vines of anger wrapping around my muscles like ivy. "You'll suffice," I say. She scoffs, and I turn my back. "Come along. It won't do to be late."

Her heels clack behind me on the polished wood floor, and I resist the urge to look back, keeping my focus on the fact that she's a traitor. She's out of her mind if she believes I buy her obedience ploy. It's a mistake to underestimate me, thinking I'll fall for such petty, silly tricks. Which is why I had to bring her brother, Jonathan, into the fray. I don't particularly like using children as bait, and in all truth, I don't plan on actually harming the boy. I didn't even make a true phone call. But the quickest way to acquiescence is to hit someone where they're most vulnerable, and Wendy has a soft spot for *family*.

The ride to the convention center is silent. Wendy's fingers twist together as she stares out the window, her face drawn and sullen. I sit across from her in the limo, hatred mixing with lust like a volatile cocktail, sparks flying through my body, making me vibrate with an energy that makes me feel as if I'm on the edge of combustion.

I find it extremely irritating that I'm not able to control my body's reaction to her. I was blinded by lust the first time around, both for her and the thought of my enemy's daughter choking on my cum.

Truthfully, that idea still appeals to me, only now my eyes are wide open, and they'll never shut again. I let her get too close, became too relaxed, even in that short amount of time.

Most likely because I never truly viewed her as a threat.

"I don't suppose I need to remind you what will happen if you misbehave tonight?" I ask as the limo pulls to the curb.

Her eyes narrow. "I've been going to functions like this since I could walk. I don't need a pep talk."

I can feel her ire all the way across the car, and it does nothing but fuel the flames.

"That may be so," I respond, leaning forward. "But now you're walking on a *leash*, pet. So don't do anything that forces my hand." I rise from my seat, moving next to her as I reach in my pocket and pull out a thin velvet case.

Her body cowers against the limo door, as if even being near me is too much for her to bear.

My fingertips trail along her neck, pushing her silky hair to the side. "You will not try to escape." I open the case, a whoosh of breath leaving her as she takes in the diamond-encrusted choker. "You will not say or do *anything* that could raise concern." I slip it from the box, the gems cool against my hand, and I lean forward, placing it around her neck, my fingers tracing her skin as I fasten it in the back. My eyes flick from her lips to her throat, a shot of desire pooling low in my abdomen. "There." My hand brushes over the jewels before resting on the swell of her cleavage, my palm rising and falling with her heavy breaths. "Every good *bitch* needs a pretty collar."

She rips her head away, gazing out the window.

I grip her chin in my hand, turning her face back. "You will not, under any circumstances, take that necklace off. Do you understand?"

Her jaw clenches. "I understand."

"Excellent."

I signal to the driver that we're ready to leave, and the door opens for me to stand. I exit the limo, turning around and reaching back into the car. Wendy's fingers tickle my palm as she places her hand in mine, and I lift her up and into my arms at the same moment as flashes of light go off from the cameras lining the red carpet.

Wrapping my arm around her waist, I tug her in close, watching as she transforms in front of my very eyes. Her face lights up, a megawatt smile gracing her features, her eyes warm as she gazes up into mine. My heart skips, revulsion following closely behind, because once again my body is out of control when it comes to her.

I lean in, my nose inhaling the scent of her hair. "Be a good girl, and I'll let you sleep in a bed instead of on a stone floor."

Her spine stiffens underneath my hand, and she grins up at me, but her eyes hold something cold and dark. "Lead the way, *master*."

As we walk inside, my stomach flips and twists in knots, anticipation flooding through my veins.

I'm so close I can feel it on my tongue. And it tastes like *vengeance*.

CHAPTER 30

Wendy

THE WAY HOOK SPEAKS TO ME CURDLES MY insides like sour milk.

Even though I *despise* what he's done, having his insults rain down like knives is a painful type of torture. It slices into my veins and bleeds me dry, leaving me brittle like fallen leaves.

My fingers tangle in the choker, wondering why he told me not to take it off. It's beautiful, but I can't imagine its importance goes far beyond its worth, and knowing I don't even have control over what I'm wearing is another slash against my newfound pride.

The heat of Hook's palm sears my hip as we walk into the main ballroom. It's beautiful, as these events usually are—chandeliers drenched in crystals and tables set for kings—but I'm not impressed. I wasn't lying when I told him I've been to a thousand. My father has deep pockets, and that makes him a renowned guest at many charity functions.

I wonder if he'll be here. The thought is fleeting as it whispers across my mind, but I grab on to it and hold tight, hope flaring in my chest for the first time in days.

We make our way through the tuxedos and ball gowns until we reach the open bar, Hook ordering a whiskey neat for himself and passing me a glass of champagne. I take a sip, relishing the way the bubbles fizz and pop on my tongue. Normally, I don't like the way alcohol makes me feel, but I'm going to need *something* to keep the fake smile on my face.

"Happy birthday, by the way." He clinks his glass to mine. "You'll forgive me for being a few days late. I was rather preoccupied."

A sharp jab of anger punches me in the chest. "How do you know that?"

He smiles, setting his whiskey on the bar. "You'd be surprised at how much I know."

"What's that mean?"

"That means whatever I *want* it to mean." He leans in, his eyes turning cold. "I know of your birth, Wendy Michaels." His lips press against my cheek. "And I'll know of your death."

My heart spasms, free-falling to the floor. "Is that a threat?"

He sighs, backing away. "I find threats to be terribly wasteful. I only speak of things I intend to see through."

Anger at this entire situation burns me from the inside out. "If you're going to kill me anyway, why should I bother being your obedient *bitch*?" I realize a second too late how loud my voice is—how well it carried across the room.

His hand moves fast, wrapping around my neck and jerking me into him. To anyone else, we must look like lovers in a passionate embrace. But all I feel is nausea and panic sloshing through my stomach and surging to my throat.

"Be very careful what you say next." His grip loosens. "You're a bleeding heart, darling. It's not your own life you should be worried about."

My face drops, teeth grinding so hard I'm afraid I'll break a molar.

He turns slightly, beaming at a couple who are walking toward us. "Perk up, dear. It's showtime," he whispers to me. Then louder, "Commissioner, so good to see you." His voice melts in the air like rich chocolate, tempting and sinful. "And your beautiful wife. Hello again, Linda. Always a pleasure." He leans in and kisses her cheek before reaching my way, wrapping an arm around my waist. "This is my date, Wendy Michaels."

I nod, smiling so wide my cheeks hurt.

The man grins, his bushy blond mustache twitching. "Wendy Michaels, as in Peter's daughter?" He chuckles, looking to Hook. "How'd you bag this one? She seems a little out of your price range."

My chest sears from the insult.

Linda giggles. "Oh, darling. Don't be rude."

I expect Hook to laugh, but he doesn't, his body tightening as he tilts his head. "I'm afraid I don't understand what you mean, Reginald. Are you insinuating something about *me*?" He points to himself. "Or about who I choose to have on my arm?"

The air thickens as the grin drops from the commissioner's face.

The tension lingers as Hook stares him down. "A gentleman knows when to apologize after insulting a lady." His brows rise.

My heart kicks against my ribs, my eyes volleying between them.

Reginald clears his throat, his gaze resting on me. "I apologize, Miss Michaels. I meant no disrespect."

My eyes widen, disbelief turning my stomach as I realize just how much power Hook really has. If he's able to speak to the police commissioner this way, how can I ever expect to be free?

The commissioner shifts on his feet, glancing around. "Ru's still avoiding these things like the plague, I take it?"

Hook's body stiffens, his grip tightening around my waist until I fidget, a small whimper escaping me. He looks down, his fingers stroking where he pinched.

"I'm afraid Ru took a very sudden and permanent vacation," he clips, his neck muscles straining like he had to force the words from his throat.

Linda sighs. "That sounds lovely. I've been trying to get Reginald to retire for some time."

The commissioner is staring at Hook, wrinkles forming between his brows. "That's a real shame," he says slowly. "I had a meeting with him next week about a possible donation."

Hook gives a thin smile, his Adam's apple bobbing. "I'm afraid you'll have to reschedule and meet with me."

The commissioner nods, sucking on his teeth. "Well, Ru was always someone who—"

My ears go fuzzy as Hook's fingers knead the curve of my hip, his arm wrapping me in closer to his side. I look up at him, wondering if he even realizes what he's doing. His jaw muscle twitches, but his eyes stay locked on Reginald and his wife.

I'm not sure what makes me do it, and I'm sure at the end of the night—when I'm forced back into the reality of my situation—I'll regret it, but I reach up, my hand rubbing his arm. "*Darling*, my feet are getting tired. Do you think you can show me to our seats?"

Hook's gaze lands on me, his brows jumping to his hairline and his eyes softening. He picks up my hand with his, bringing it to his mouth, skimming his lips across the back. "Of course, sweetheart."

Shivers dance up my arm, traitorous butterflies fluttering in my stomach.

What is wrong with me?

He nods to the couple. "Commissioner. Linda. If you'll excuse us."

My gut flips as we walk, nerves making my limbs tremble, wondering whether he's going to be angry that I interrupted his chat. *What was I thinking?*

"I'm sorry," I mutter as we reach the table. "I just—you looked uncomfortable, and he kept going on and on and I—"

Hook pulls out a chair for me to sit, leading me into it with his finger pressed against my lips. "Hush."

My mouth snaps closed, unease worming its way through me like a snake. I've never experienced as much anxiety in my life as I do around him. Most of the time, his personality is calm waters, still and sparkling and as clear as glass. But a single drop can disrupt the entire surface, and you never know when the rain will hit.

I glance around at the few other people sitting at the table. In the past, I've known most everyone at these events. But this is Massachusetts, not Florida, so all these people are strangers. None of them are paying any attention to me anyway. It's *him* they all have their eyes on, and I don't blame them. Even knowing what he's capable of—knowing what he's done to me—there's a certain type of feeling that comes along with being on the arm of the most powerful man in the room. I wish I could ignore it, but it's there whether I want it to be or not. The same way that I can't shake off the conversation between him and the commissioner. I've never seen Hook rattled before, and this. *This* rattled him. I try to push the thought from my mind, knowing I shouldn't give a damn.

But I do.

Before he showed his true colors, I was falling for him. Or for the version he presented anyway. And feelings don't just go away. They merely shift and change as your soul breaks, molding themselves into the cracks. *My* feelings for Hook may be mangled and unrecognizable, but that doesn't mean they've disappeared.

"I met Ru, didn't I?" I ask, unable to stop the words from leaping off my tongue.

His fingers pause from where they're drumming on the table. "You did."

"It's nice he got to retire."

Hook's face snaps to mine. His hand shoots out, gripping underneath my seat and pulling, my chair dragging loudly across the wood floor. I gasp, the air cold as it flows down my throat, clashing with the heatwave of embarrassment rising through my chest.

His nose brushes mine, the intensity of his glare freezing me into place. "I don't know what game you're playing," he whispers. "But it stops now. I suggest you don't test me."

My heart stutters. "I'm no—not playing any games."

He breathes in deep, his gaze flickering from my eyes to my mouth, then back, energy crackling in the space between us. And then he looks past me, and his entire demeanor changes.

I jump when his palm lands on my thigh underneath the table, squeezing in a bruising grip. "Remember what's at stake."

I scoff, anger brewing in my gut. "As if I'd forget. I—"

"Wendy?"

CHAPTER 31

James

WENDY TWISTS IN HER SEAT, COMING FACE-TO-face with Peter.

"Dad?" she gasps. She starts to rise from her chair, and my grip on her thigh tightens, holding her in place. She turns to me, her brows drawing in, and I cock my head, meeting her gaze and holding it.

It's obvious when realization hits; her eyes dim and her lips turn. She looks from me to her father and then over to Tina, who's standing there gawking in a sparkly green dress with gold trim.

Peter's face is a mask of confusion, his forehead wrinkling as he gazes between us. I move my hand from Wendy's thigh, draping my arm along the back of her chair. This is the moment he'll realize that their little plan didn't work.

That even though they took Ru from me, I still have her. She didn't get away.

"Peter," I greet. "What a *pleasure*."

His lip curls. "Hook."

"I'd make introductions, but I'm quite sure you're already well acquainted."

He stands still, his features frozen, until waiters bringing out salad force him to move. He clears his throat, pressing his hand against Tina's back and moving her toward their seats.

Wendy's body deflates. I look at her with a wide grin. *That's right, pet. Game over.* Nobody plays against me and comes out with the upper hand.

The servers drop off the salad dishes, and I pick up my fork, excitement thrumming through my veins as I spear a cherry tomato, reveling in the way Wendy fidgets and Peter glares.

Leaning in, my arm still on the back of her chair, I place the fork in front of Wendy's mouth. "Hungry?"

She presses her lips together, shaking her head.

I place it in my own mouth, the juices and seeds exploding on my tongue.

"Mmm," I hum. "I do love popping a good *cherry.*" I grin at Peter, my arm dropping from the chair onto Wendy's shoulders, my fingers tracing her bare skin. Wendy goes stiff as a board underneath me, her gaze trained on her plate. She's suspiciously quiet, the brazen girl who's been in my basement suddenly disappearing in her father's presence.

I find that it irritates me more than it should.

"Wendy," Peter sighs. "What are you doing here? Shouldn't you be at the mansion?" His eyes peer around the table. We have everyone's attention, and it's delicious, knowing he wants to make a scene but can't act out. But that's the difference between Peter and me. He has to operate within the constraints of civil society, while I make sure to pad their pockets and dance outside their edges.

Wendy's head snaps up at his question, her knuckles whitening as they grip her fork. "What do you mean *at the mansion?*"

Tina's hand reaches out to rest on Peter's forearm, Wendy's jaw setting at the movement.

Interesting.

"I think what your father is trying to say," Tina starts, "is that this is the last place we'd expect you to be." Her eyes glance over to mine. "And with the last...person."

I open my mouth to speak, but Wendy beats me to it, my hand falling from her shoulder as she leans forward, her eyes spitting lasers. "And why would it be so surprising to see me here? Because I wasn't given *express* permission?"

Peter clears his throat. "Little shadow—"

Wendy's glare cuts to him, and arousal rolls through me at her ire.

"Maybe you don't remember, *Dad*, but I used to come to these frequently with you."

Peter glances around, all eyes on the outburst of his daughter.

"And for the record," Wendy continues, her cheeks growing rosy, "I've never needed nor cared about Tina's opinion on *anything*, especially concerning where she expects me to be."

Tina's mouth gapes open.

I smirk at Wendy's outburst, heat swarming my body from how attractive she is when she's swirling in rage.

"Didn't you care to know where I was when your new security didn't find me?"

My hand moves to rest on the back of her choker, my fingers slipping underneath the clasp and tugging as a reminder to watch her mouth.

Peter's eyebrows raise. "Is that what this is? You running

away because you didn't like that I was trying to provide you protection?"

Wendy scoffs, stabbing the lettuce with her fork.

"Control your date," Tina hisses at me.

I grin, leaning back against my chair. "Now, why would I want to do that?"

This is a delightful turn of events. I hadn't expected her to be so upset with him.

"Wendy, this isn't the time or the place." Peter's voice is sharp, commanding, as if he's chastising a child. "Do we need to go somewhere and speak in private?"

Her eyes flick to me. I don't move, wanting to see what she'll do if given the opportunity.

She lifts her chin, inhaling deeply, and shaking her head. "No. We have nothing left to say."

Pleasure at her obedience trickles through me like a leaky faucet, and I have to remind myself that she isn't someone I should reward for being good. She's a *traitor*.

Although it's odd the way she's interacting with her father, as if they aren't on good terms.

His eyes stay on hers for long moments, something unspoken passing between them before Tina cuts in. "So how did you two meet?" She waves her champagne glass between us.

I take a sip of whiskey. *Because you sent her into my bar, you pathetic swine.*

"He already told you, didn't he?" Wendy cocks her head. "He *popped* my cherry." Gasps sound around the table, and I choke on the liquid of my drink, my hand shooting to my chest to stifle the cough.

"Wendy," Peter hisses.

She smiles wide. "What is it, Dad? Suddenly deciding to care again?"

Confusion slams into me.

I understand her anger at him not knowing she was gone—honestly, the thought of it does rankle a bit—but I can't imagine what she's getting out of this. They were already working together to destroy me. It shouldn't be a surprise that we've met.

Unless they had no idea.

My stomach cramps, my bruised heart twisting at the notion.

"I think the more important question," Wendy continues, "is how did *you* two meet?" She points her fork at her father and then at me.

Peter steeples his hands in front of his mouth, leaning back in his chair. "Nothing exciting there. We've met briefly for business."

I chuckle, the tips of my fingers caressing the side of Wendy's neck, my insides tightening with every pass against the choker. *My brand of ownership.* And a GPS tracker, but that's neither here nor there.

"Oh, don't be so modest, Peter," I quip. "We've more than *met*. In fact, I believe you were well acquainted with those I'm closest with. Seems only fair I return the favor."

The corners of Peter's eyes tighten as he nods, his lips breaking apart to show his gleaming white teeth. "Yes, that's true." He looks around. "And where are they tonight?"

My body stiffens, rage spiraling through me like a windstorm. Wendy's face snaps toward mine, her eyes trailing up and down before they go back to her father, narrowing the slightest bit. She drops her fork, and the noise of it clanking against the dish grates against my eardrums. Her hand reaches out, pressing against my chest and rising, until her palm cups my jaw. The shock of her touch is enough to clear the red haze filming over my eyes.

She leans in, pressing a kiss to my cheek. "Take a deep breath. People are starting to stare," she whispers.

My lungs expand as I collect myself.

Wendy sits back and pins her father with a look. "What is that supposed to mean?"

My chest pulls tight at her question. Because again, if she was part of Peter's plan, she would know *exactly* what that meant.

"Wendy, it was a simple question." Peter sighs.

"That's quite alright." I smile as I pull Wendy in close, my hand smoothing down her hair. "I've found much more *enticing* company."

Peter's jaw tightens and he leans in, his eyes pleading with his daughter. "You have no idea who you're sitting next to."

Her jaw stiffens. "I know *exactly* who he is. It's you I'm beginning to question."

My heart stutters, his phrase cementing what I've been theorizing for the past few minutes.

She doesn't know about her father.

And that means she never betrayed me at all.

CHAPTER 32

Wendy

THE REST OF DINNER IS FILLED WITH TENSE STARES, nothing but the scraping of silverware and the people who speak on the stage waxing poetic about solving injustices in the world by throwing million-dollar parties with thousand-dollar seats.

But my insides are raging.

"Shouldn't you be at the mansion?"

He didn't even know I was gone. I was *kidnapped*, and he didn't even know I was gone.

I've been telling myself for months that I need to admit he isn't the man I remember, but this is the moment when the piece of my soul that was clinging on finally breaks, falling to the floor and shattering into a hundred jagged pieces.

He didn't even know I was gone.

But of course, he could show up here.

God forbid his image ever take a hit. His public image, that is. It's clear as day to me now that he doesn't care how I see him.

And there's something going on with Hook's friend, Ru. The silent conversation with the commissioner, the way his name sends Hook into a tailspin, and now my father mocking his missing friends—it has my nerves wired and on high alert.

I know why Hook has me here, that's become very obvious, but I can't for the life of me figure out why my father is taunting *him*.

Why he even deals with someone like Hook in the first place.

Unless he's not who he pretends to be.

And that, more than anything else, has me feeling like the stupidest person on the planet. Because how can you live with someone, spend years breathing the same air, worshiping their every move, loving them with your whole heart, and not really know who they are?

The realization splits through me and breaks the lock on all the things I let go unsaid, all the times I've wanted to strike back but nodded and smiled instead. I know Hook is most likely going to hurt me for lashing out, but I can't find it in me to care. Finally—*finally*—being able to speak my mind is liberating. And when Hook not only allows it but encourages it, I feel like I have someone at my back.

As twisted as that may seem.

I glance over to watch him as he nods along to something a man next to him is saying, my stomach somersaulting from my completely upside-down emotions. How is it possible that this man—the one who threatened my life less than an hour ago, the one who chained me to a basement wall—is still the only one who seems to treat me as if I'm valid?

He made the police commissioner *apologize* for insulting me and rubbed my neck while I stood against my father and his bitch of an assistant. And that doesn't feel like Hook.

That feels like James.

I shake my head, reminding myself that he's putting on a show. Nothing about the way he's treating me is for *my* benefit, and forgetting that won't do me any favors.

My eyes slide past Hook's frame, noticing that one of the twins is walking in our direction. They reach us and bend down to whisper in his ear. Hook's fingers, which have been trailing along the top of my thigh, freeze in place, and he straightens. With a squeeze on my leg, he moves, placing his napkin on the table. "If you'll excuse me for a moment, there's a pressing matter that needs my attention." He stands, cutting a glare to my father before leaning down to press a kiss to my cheek, his fingers tangling in my hair. "Behave," he murmurs against my skin. "There's nowhere you can run that I won't follow."

Anxiety mixes in my bloodstream as he walks away, my stomach tightening with indecision. My father is sitting *right there*, and he's the one man on this earth who could save me, but at what cost?

I won't do anything unless I know that Jon will be protected, and my dad has proven time and time again that he doesn't make Jon a priority.

No. *What is wrong with me?* He wouldn't let him die. Jon is still his child after all.

My insides twist, disgust weaving its way through my middle at how easily my mind has gone from believing in the good of people to questioning what type of murder they'd accept. A few days around criminals and suddenly I've accepted it as fact.

It bothers me that it *doesn't* bother me the way it should.

"Wendy, I'd like to speak with you, please." My father wipes the corners of his mouth with his napkin before placing it down. "In private."

My heart stutters, knowing that's something Hook wouldn't like, but Hook isn't here. And I deserve some answers. I nod my head, pushing my chair back and glancing around, half expecting someone to jump out and grab me, but with every step I take, the easier I breathe, realizing that nobody is going to come.

We walk through the ballroom until we reach the back patio doors, my father allowing me to exit first before he follows behind. We're the only people out here, and a chill sets into my bones as I shiver from the cool breeze.

"He's using you to get to me."

I jerk from his sudden words, my hand coming to rest on my chest. I'm not sure what I expected. Maybe an apology for him not realizing I was gone or for being able to show up here but always missing everything else.

The fact that I clearly know nothing about my father pours down my throat until all I can taste is the bitter truth.

I shake my head, huffing out a laugh. "Did you really not know I was gone?"

"Wendy, be reasonable. If this is you acting out for attention, I—"

"Answer the question." My fists clench at my sides.

He sighs, rubbing his hand over his brow. "My security team told me you weren't home, and I assumed you were throwing a tantrum."

His words blast through my chest like a bomb, charring my insides black. A *tantrum*. Like I'm a child.

"If I would have known that you were busy frolicking around with a psychopathic criminal, I would have scoured the earth to track you down."

My mouth gapes as I stare at him. "How do you know that?"

"Know *what?*"

"That he's a psychopathic criminal." My stomach churns. "How do you know that?"

"How do you *not?*" He puts his arms out to the sides. "You're playing a very dangerous game here, Wendy. One you know nothing about."

The burn expands, scorching my throat. "Don't belittle me!" His eyes widen, and I step forward, my fingers running through my hair, my heart beating wildly in my chest. "I am so sick of everyone treating me like I'm some porcelain doll who's supposed to keep her mouth shut and look pretty. My opinions *matter.*"

His gaze softens. "Of course they do, little shadow." He moves toward me. "I'm trying here."

I scoff. "You haven't tried since Mom died."

His jaw sets. "You know nothing about your mother."

I throw my hands up. "So I'm just stupid then. I don't know Hook. I don't know my mother. And I sure as hell don't know *you.*"

"Is he forcing you to be here?" He steps even closer, his voice soft as if he's trying to lure an animal into a cage. "Has he... Has he *hurt* you?"

My breathing stutters as I grit my teeth, the urge to tell him screaming from the back of my throat. "How's Jon?" I ask instead.

His movements falter. "What?"

"I asked how Jon was. You know, your son?"

"What does that have to do with our conversation right now?" His brows draw in.

"A lot, actually." My heart swells with hope that he'll tell me he's been to see him. That he just spoke to him on the phone and he's settling in well.

He runs a palm over his face. "I'm sure he's fine."

Disappointment settles like a brick, crashing through my insides, making a sob lodge in my throat. He hasn't even talked to him. And if he can't be trusted to make a simple phone call, how can I trust that he'll make sure he's safe from Hook?

Guilt wraps around me, realizing that Jon's been all alone. Acclimating by himself.

Closing my eyes, I release a deep exhale, a sick feeling settling in my gut and expanding until acceptance of my situation fills me up and wraps around my edges.

"He isn't forcing me," I say slowly.

"He's *using* you to get to me," he repeats.

He's not wrong. Hook has all but told me that he only cares about getting to my father. But until this moment, I hadn't known how much that revelation hurt. The days leading up to this have numbed me to the pain, but with acceptance comes realization, and now the wounds are throbbing from where Hook dug his way into my heart only to carve himself out.

The faint sound of a door opening and closing comes from behind me, but I don't turn to see who it is. There's no need.

It's impossible not to feel him when he enters a room.

"Well." His accent floats on the breeze, wrapping around my neck like a noose. "Isn't this cozy?"

Heat envelops my back, Hook's arm slipping around my center and pulling me flush into his body. My heart jumps in my chest, dinner rising through my throat until I have to cover my mouth to keep it down.

"Trying to steal my date, Peter? Or just using her to plan your next foolish adventure?"

My father's eyes narrow. "Whatever you're trying, *kid*, it won't work."

Hook's body stiffens, the heel of his palm pressing against my abs. My hands reach up to cover his forearm, and then, quick as lightning, my head is wrenched to the side, the tendons in my neck stretching until they hurt. I whimper from the pain, my fingernails digging into Hook's skin.

"Are you *trying* to get her killed?"

My heart stutters at his words, my eyes widening as I stare at my father.

But all Dad does is smirk, his gaze landing on me. "I told you, little shadow. He doesn't care for you."

My insides burn.

A deep chuckle rumbles in Hook's chest, and it vibrates through my bones, setting my nerves on fire. He leans down, pressing his pillow-soft lips to the middle of my throat, his tongue swiping out to taste my skin.

Heat spreads between my legs, followed closely by the revulsion at the fact that my body can be turned on by this *sick* situation.

"Do not make the mistake of thinking I am like the other men you've dealt with." Hook releases my head, pushing me to the side gently as he stalks toward my father. "I do not care for my reputation. I do not care for the money or the businesses you *burn*."

My father's lips turn down, and my head spins, wondering what he's talking about.

"In fact, there is nothing you can steal from me that you haven't already taken." He steps closer until he towers over my father's frame. "These are *my* streets," he continues. "And I've been waiting so patiently for you to come and play."

His hand reaches in his pocket, the brown handle of his knife making my insides curdle with fear. My heart catapults into overdrive, my feet moving before I can stop them, and I run, shoving myself between them, my father stumbling back a step.

"Don't," I beg. *"Please*, just…don't hurt him."

Hook's eyes widen slightly, but he stands stoic, a slow grin creeping on his face. His fingers reach out, brushing down my jaw. "So loyal." He looks behind me to my father. "And where are your pleas, Peter?" His brows rise. "Or maybe you'd rather I spill her blood to cover your sins."

Silence.

Deafening, heartbreaking *silence.*

Hook's eyes lock on mine, and I hold his stare, my stomach rising and falling along with the uneven beats of my heart, my nostrils flaring from the agonizing pain of my chest cracking in half.

He exhales, bending his neck to the side until it cracks, and then nods, reaching his hand out. "Very well."

Relief pours through my veins, my body trembling as I place my palm in his. He tugs, and my body flies into him. My fingers press against his chest, his arm wrapping around my lower back and his mouth finding my ear.

"I want you to memorize this moment, darling. Remember how it feels to realize your father was willing to let you *die* in order to save himself."

And then he whisks me away while my soul shatters to dust.

CHAPTER 33

Wendy

HOOK IS SILENT IN THE LIMO RIDE, BUT I CAN FEEL the rage pouring out of him and infusing the air. It's thick. *Suffocating.* My eyes flick from him to the streets whizzing by, wondering if he's angry with me and asking myself why I care.

The car turns the street corner, and my breath stalls in my lungs as the familiar landmarks come into view. I *know* this street.

And it isn't the marina.

"You said you wouldn't bring me back here," I rush out, panic seizing my insides.

"And you said you wouldn't misbehave." He picks invisible lint from his suit.

My jaw drops. "I didn't! I did *everything* you asked for."

"You think gallivanting off with your father was something I would ask for?" he snaps.

My heart drops to my stomach. "That had—" I swallow. "That had nothing to do with you." I cringe, knowing how pathetic it sounds, even to my own ears.

He chuckles. "Darling, if you expect me to believe that, then you're truly a stupid girl."

My teeth grind, fists clenching. "I am *not* a girl."

His head tilts. "Just stupid then?"

I breathe deeply through my nose, trying to stem the roiling in my gut when I imagine being tossed back into that dark dungeon of a room. "Please, I don't want to be back in that basement."

He sighs, his fingers rubbing at his jaw. "You're not."

My head snaps up, relief flooding through me. "I'm not?"

The car rolls to a stop, blues and reds flashing over my skin through the windows.

What in the world?

The door opens, and Hook steps out, his hand appearing in front of me. My heart jolts when I place my palm in his, allowing him to pull me from the car. He's a dichotomy, threatening my life in one breath and being a gentleman in the next. It's terrifying how he can do both so flawlessly, as if they're integral parts of him, coexisting peacefully as one. It tosses everything I've ever been taught about good and evil out the window until it skews and blurs in my brain.

Shock spirals through my center as I exit the car, my breath whooshing from my lungs.

The smell of ash is strong in the air, making my nose tingle from the stench. There are fire trucks and ambulances, a few cop cars off to the side. And the JR is gone. Burned to the ground, nothing left but rubble.

My hand reaches up to cover my mouth. "Oh my god. What *happened?*"

Hook's face is stoic as he surveys the damage. "Your father, I would presume."

"No." My heart jerks, the defense spitting off my tongue

before I can even think through the words. "But he was with us tonight. He wouldn't…"

Hook looks at me then, and my words die out, the memory of this evening replaying in my head. I swallow around the sadness building in my gut and spreading through every limb.

A keening wail comes from down the sidewalk, and my head snaps over, the waitress from the JR running up to Hook and throwing her arms around his shoulders.

My chest pulls as I watch them embrace, but I step away, allowing them their moment. *What do I care if they provide each other comfort?*

Hook's arms come up slowly, peeling her off him. "Moira."

"Hook, it was terrible. I don't know—" She hiccups. "I have no clue what happened. I just—one second everything was fine, and the next…" She covers her mouth, breaking down again in sobs, and I glance around, my stomach sinking, hoping that no one was hurt inside.

But I can't help feeling relief too, at the fact that if there's no JR, then there's no basement with shackles and chains.

———

We don't stay at the site for long before Hook has us back in the limo and on his yacht.

Somehow, we ended up lying on his bed, still in full evening wear, not speaking, barely moving at all. My mind replays the past few days, going back and forth over everything, wondering if what Hook says is true.

If my father really *is* the one responsible for so much damage.

My stomach turns and my heart kicks against its cage. "Are you really going to kill me?" I ask, staring up at the ceiling.

His fingers are locked together, resting on his abdomen, rising and falling with his even breaths. "I haven't decided yet."

A heavy knot twists in the center of my chest. "Do you really think my father did it?"

He sighs, his hand rubbing across his forehead, his eyes pinching closed. "Darling, your questions are becoming very tiresome."

I bite the inside of my cheek until I taste blood, holding back the words that are dying to spew out. I risk a glance at his face. Sadness sneaks through his features, subtle, but there in the way his eyes turn down and how the silence sticks to his skin—an aura of melancholy, almost as if he's mourning.

"I'm sorry about your bar," I whisper.

"It wasn't mine."

My brows raise, surprise flickering in my chest. "Oh, I just assumed—"

"It was Ru's."

I chew on my lip, nodding. "And Ru is...where?"

His head turns, hair mussing slightly on his pillow, his gaze sizzling as it sits on my skin. I stay stock-still, hoping that he finds whatever he's looking for.

His tongue swipes over his bottom lip. "Dead."

The word—even though I expected it—hits me like a sledge-hammer, conversations from the evening slotting together like missing pieces of a puzzle. Ru's dead. And my father asked where he was with a smirk on his face.

Anger and disbelief war inside me, clashing together in a cataclysmic explosion of grief. Grief for the man who raised me. Grief for the father I've lost.

I don't apologize for Ru's death. Something tells me Hook wouldn't appreciate the words, that they'd tip the scale of his anger against me, and the last thing I want to do is upset him even more. Not when we've found some weird type of balance, a temporary truce.

"When I was a little girl," I start, "my dad used to bring me acorns."

Hook stiffens next to me, and I pause, but when he doesn't speak, I take the risk and continue.

"It was this…*stupid* thing, really. I was five and the biggest daddy's girl in the entire world, even though he was gone most of the time."

My chest pulls tight.

"But when he'd get back home, he'd come into my room and brush the hair from my face, leaning down and kissing my forehead good night." Tears blur my vision, and I squeeze my eyes shut, hot, wet trails streaking down my face. "I used to pretend to be asleep, afraid that if he knew I was awake, he'd stop sneaking in."

A knot lodges in my throat and I hesitate, not sure I'll be able to get the words out.

"What were the acorns for?" Hook's voice is low and raspy, his eyes staring straight ahead.

I smile. "I used to have breakdowns whenever he'd leave, worried he'd fly away and never come home. One night, when he was saying goodbye, something fell through my open window, and when I woke up in the morning, he had placed it on my end table with a note, promising he'd return." I laugh, shaking my head. "It was just a stupid acorn, but… I don't know." I shrug, reaching up to wipe away a stray tear. "I was a dumb kid. Put sentimentality on things that probably didn't deserve it. But from that night on, whenever he'd leave, he'd bring me another one and set it on my table, promising he'd come back." Agony sears through my broken heart and down into the deepest parts of my soul. "And I collected those acorns like kisses."

"Why are you telling me this?" he asks.

I turn to face him, resting my wet cheek on the back of my hand, my head molding to the pillow. "I don't know. To show you that he wasn't always so bad? That once upon a time, he really did care." A sob breaks free, and my hand flies to my mouth, trying to stuff it back down.

Hook turns to me then, his hand reaching out and cupping my face, his thumb swiping away the tears as they fall. "It's impossible not to *care* for you, Wendy. If it was, you'd already be dead."

A laugh bubbles in my chest at the absurdity of this entire thing—at the way the man holding me hostage is consoling me over my broken heart. At the way he can say something so vile and make it sound so sweet.

"Is that supposed to be romantic?" I wheeze out between giggles.

A small smile graces his face. "It's supposed to be the truth."

The laughter dies down, and we're stuck staring at each other, twisted feelings spiraling through me and branding every part of my fucked-up heart. And I know, I *know* I'm supposed to hate him.

But in this moment, I don't.

"Anyway." I sigh, breaking eye contact, wanting to ease the fire that's building in my veins. "The acorns disappeared when my mom died." I sniff. "And so did my dad, I guess."

He doesn't say anything else and neither do I. Eventually, he rises, going to the dresser on the far side of the room and passing me a pair of boxers and a plain black shirt. Clothes I couldn't imagine him in, even if I tried. And I take them without a fight, slipping them on and crawling back into his bed, knowing I don't have any other choice.

"Hook," I whisper through the dark.

"Wendy."

"I don't want to die."

He sighs. "Go to sleep, darling. Your soul is safe tonight."

"Okay."

I reach up, my fingers playing with the diamond choker that I was too afraid to remove. He told me to keep it on, and I don't know if that extends to when we're here in his home, but I don't want to ruin the calm that we've created. I've been on the end of his ire before, and I have absolutely no desire to be there again.

"Hook," I say again.

The room stays silent.

My stomach feels like lead, but I know if I don't get the words out now, I may not get another chance. "I watch you, you know? Wh-when you think no one can see?" My fingers move, tangling together underneath the covers. "And if my father has something to do with what makes you look so sad..." I reach out blindly, the side of my hand bumping into his. "I *see* you. I just wanted you to know that."

He doesn't respond, but he doesn't move my hand either. And that's how we stay until I fall asleep.

CHAPTER 34

James

I LIE IN BED WATCHING THE EVEN RISE AND FALL of Wendy's chest, admiring the way she looks so peaceful even as she whimpers in her dreams.

There will be no sleep for me tonight.

All my previous plans when it comes to Peter have been tossed out of the window, rage coursing through my veins, molding into my cells, and cementing into my heart.

The JR is gone.

Burned to a crisp, nothing but rubble and dust. And while everyone made it out safely, nothing else has been recovered.

Not that I keep anything of importance there. When you work outside the boundaries of the law, you learn quickly that keeping things where people expect them to be never works in your favor.

Still, the JR was our biggest front to clean the money, and in the end, it had more of a *personal* meaning. It was where I grew up, where I learned how to be *Hook* instead of just a monster bred inside a cage. Sure, there are other businesses we own, a few strip clubs on the edges of the city and a nightclub in the center of town,. but the JR was *home*.

Add to that I'm not sure what to do now with Wendy. I overestimated her and her father's relationship, stupidly assuming that the papers were telling the truth as they waxed poetic about their bond. But no man who has any sense of love in his heart would allow his daughter to stand in front of a killer and beg them for *his* life.

Pathetic.

I no longer believe she betrayed me. Yet for some reason, I don't want to let her go.

But if Peter Michaels thinks he can come into my town, steal my drugs, burn my businesses, and kill my people without facing my wrath, he's in for a nasty surprise.

I slip from the bed, leaving the room and locking the door behind me as I walk into the kitchen, stopping short when I see Smee sitting at the island, a cup of tea in his hand.

"I thought you said you were leaving for the night."

Smee turns, the red beanie on his head slipping back as he smiles. "I got done with things earlier than I thought. Do you need something?" He lifts his mug. "Cup of tea?"

I shake my head. "No, I have business to attend to. Listen, Wendy is here. And she is not to leave this boat. Understood?"

Smee's eyes glance down the hall before looking back at me. "Everything okay, boss man?"

I nod. "If she causes problems, call me immediately. You are *not* to touch her under any circumstances."

He takes another sip from his cup. "Understood."

"Good man." I grin.

I'm almost out of the room when I hear it.

Tick.

Tick.

Tick.

My head grows dizzy, heart pumping so fast my veins feel like they'll burst. I slowly spin on my heels, my eyes zoned in on where Smee is playing with something on the kitchen counter.

"Smee," I say slowly, my hands trembling against my sides. "*What* is that noise?"

Smee glances up, the side of his mouth lifting. "Hmm?"

I take a jerky step forward, the knot in my stomach twisting so violently it's ripping me in half, and when I reach the island, I inhale deeply, trying to maintain control.

"Oh, this?" He holds up an old-looking watch connected to a gold chain that dangles to the counter. "I found it at a pawnshop and just *had* to get it." He smooths his thumb over the face. "I know it's a little loud, but…"

My vision blurs from how difficult it is to keep from smashing every bone in his hand just to stop that *incessant* noise.

"Are you okay, boss?"

"Please," I grind out through my teeth. "Get that thing out of my home."

"I—"

My hand swipes out, smashing into his mug, the contents sloshing on the counter, the porcelain shattering against the wood floor. "I said *get. It. Out.*"

His eyes widen, his body jerking back. "Okay." He races to the deck, runs to the side, and throws it out to sea.

Closing my eyes, I focus on the beautiful silence, taking deep breaths as the red haze recedes, allowing me to regain control.

Smee walks back in, his eyes darting from me to the shattered contents on the floor.

I crack my neck, exhaling a heavy sigh. "Do not ever bring a clock on this yacht again. Do you understand?"

He swallows and nods.

I turn, walking out the door and shaking off the remnants of my rage, feeling the control slot back in place one step at a time.

The first thing I do is call an emergency meeting with the boys at the Lagoon—the strip club on the outskirts of town. I don't make much of an appearance there, but I need a temporary space, and this is the one with the best office.

The next thing I do is call Moira and tell her to meet me here. I should have talked to her immediately or had one of the boys keep her company until I could get away, but I was too wrapped up in Wendy and my conflicting emotions to think clearly. An oversight, to be sure.

But now that I know she's locked in my bedroom, I can breathe easier, allowing my focus to shift.

Thirty minutes after the boys have their marching orders, Moira saunters into the office, her eyes gleaming and her lips painted that garish red.

"Hook," she purrs. "It's been a while."

"I've been busy." She starts to walk around the desk, but I put a hand up to stop her. "You're not here for that."

Her lips turn down, brows furrowing. "Oh."

"Tell me what happened last night." I steeple my fingers in front of my lips.

She sighs, running a hand through her hair as she sits in the chair across the desk. "I already told Starkey everything I know, Hook."

I smile, my patience running thin. "Tell it again."

"I don't know, okay?" she bursts out, her arms shooting to the sides. "Everything was fine, and then it was like...*boom!*" She claps her hands together. "Explosion or something. To be honest, I was so worried about making sure everyone got out, I didn't think much of whatever else was going on."

My fingers scratch against my stubble. "Okay."

She smiles. "Okay."

I point to her. "Stay right there and don't speak."

Her forehead scrunches, but she does as I say. And at least at first, she's quiet, allowing me to click through business expenses of the Lagoon. I don't necessarily need to, but I *do* need to pass the time, and while in the past I may have been interested in using Moira's body to do so, I find that the idea repulses me now.

She sighs loudly, smacking her hands on her thighs. "Are we gonna do anything or not, Hook? This is *boring*."

My eyes snap to hers. "I said don't speak."

She stands up and saunters over. "I could think of something else I could do."

I watch her move toward me, irritation flaring in my chest. She drops to her knees, her red fingernails sliding up my thighs until she palms my cock, wrapping her fingers around the length through the fabric. I bat her hand away and grip her chin, pulling harshly until her face is level with mine. "Did I tell you to touch me?"

She attempts to shake her head.

The back of my free hand runs down the side of her cheek. "Don't you wish to *please* me?"

She nods. "Yes."

I lean in, my nose brushing hers. "Then sit down and stay quiet. Your mouth is of no use to me anymore."

Her eyes shutter as I drop her face, her body stumbling back as she rubs at her jaw and walks to the chair, crossing her arms and staring at the ground.

Over the course of the next hour, we sit in silence. I occasionally call for random employees to come to the back for no other reason than to make sure they see me here, with Moira, at this exact moment.

But this time, when someone knocks, it's who I've been waiting on.

"Come in," I say, relief bleeding through my chest as the twins appear. "It's done?"

They nod, glancing to Moira.

I lean back in the chair, satisfaction dancing through my insides.

See, what Peter doesn't understand is that while he has the money and the social standing, I have the *loyalty*. And loyalty is bred from respect. You take care of people, and they'll take care of you. And if there's one thing Ru and I have done in this town, it's take care of our people.

Bloomsburg, Massachusetts, isn't like anywhere else in the world, and its inhabitants don't take too kindly to new blood coming in and their town going up in flames.

As it happens, the security guard at the new NevAirLand airstrip is a personal friend. His child had a terrible bout with cancer a few years back, and Ru paid for her chemotherapy and every doctor's visit since.

He'll have to disappear, of course, after looping the security feed and allowing my boys inside to light every single plane on fire. But people are willing to do anything for those they love, and he knows his wife and children will be taken care of—protected by the Lost Boys until their last breath.

True love sometimes requires sacrifice.

Something Peter clearly knows nothing about.

I look to Moira, a grin spreading across my face. "You may leave now."

She stands, her chin red from where I gripped it, and turns to leave without a word.

"Moira," I say. She pauses at the door. "Feel free to tell people I gave you a nice ride today. Wouldn't want to sully your reputation after all."

She scoffs, slamming the door behind her, and I grin, jumping to my feet, the sudden urge to head back to my boat making me giddy.

Right as I reach my car, my phone vibrates in my pocket, a single text on the screen.

Smee: Your girl is gone.

CHAPTER 35

Wendy

WAKING UP, I STRETCH, MY BODY POPPING FROM the deepest sleep I've had in a long time—even before I was thrown in the basement of the JR. I yawn, rubbing my eyes and gaining my bearings, and I glance around, half expecting to see Hook sleeping peacefully by my side.

He isn't, of course.

I'm all alone. I sit up in the bed, wondering what I'm supposed to do. I make my way to use the restroom, splashing water on my face and using the toothbrush that was laid out for me yesterday before the gala.

It's odd, waking up in luxury and using the facilities here as if they're mine. It confuses me, tilts my insides off their axis, making it difficult for my brain to remember that I'm not *actually* free to do anything.

Even if my chains are now invisible, they're still there.

My gaze snags on the choker.

Well, almost invisible.

I walk back into Hook's room, my eyes going to the bedroom

door, expecting it to be locked the way it was last night. But when I walk over, grabbing the handle and tugging, it opens right up.

The yacht is completely silent, and trepidation fills me, making my nerves jump beneath my skin as I make my way down the hallway, padding into the kitchen.

When I get there, I stop short, seeing Smee standing next to the sink.

My hand goes to my chest. "Oh my gosh, hi."

He smiles. "Hi, Miss Wendy. I didn't mean to scare you."

"No, I should have known someone would be here." I wave him off, looking around. "Where's Hook?"

His brow lifts. "You mean James?"

I tilt my head. It's the first time I've heard anyone else call him that, and it makes me wonder just how close he and Smee are. He told me once that he doesn't pry into Smee's life, but I can't imagine he lets just *anyone* call him by his given name.

And if they're close, then that means Smee is just as bad as the rest of them.

I wait for the red-hot anger to spin through me, wanting to destroy everyone and everything responsible for my current situation, but it never comes. Instead, a resolute acceptance settles in my gut. A sick feeling follows quickly after, making me realize just how fast I've adjusted to this new reality.

"He's busy running errands. Told me to make you feel at home." He smiles. "Coffee?"

I watch him closely, unsure if I should take a drink from someone I don't know. After all, the owner of this boat drugged me, so I wouldn't put anything past anyone. This is *their* world, and I'm here, just trying to wade in their waters. I don't really know what rule book criminals go by.

Although technically, I guess Smee isn't a criminal. He only works for one.

Shaking my head, I force a smile. "Do you think it would be okay if I go sit outside?"

He watches me closely for a minute, his eyes shifting, almost as if he's debating how to answer. I hold my breath, hoping he'll say yes. I'm desperate to get some fresh air, to remind myself that I'm not still stuck in a dark, abandoned room with only my thoughts for company.

"Please, I promise I won't go anywhere. I just…" My fingers tangle together on the countertop. "I want to soak up some sun."

He nods. "Go ahead, Miss Wendy."

A smile breaks across my face, and I race out the side door onto the sundeck.

I lie on one of the loungers, but no matter how hard I try, I can't get comfortable, a jittery energy making my legs restless. I glance around, not seeing Smee anywhere. I see the edge of the dock a few steps away, and the idea of being able to walk around, maybe put my feet in the water, makes my muscles twitch with need.

I head back to the door, about to go inside and ask Smee if it's okay, but stop myself. *What the hell am I doing? It's not like I'm leaving.*

Anyone would be able to see me from the boat if they're standing on the sundeck and looking. I pull my hand back from the doorknob, and with my heart in my throat, I walk toward the exit, stepping off the yacht and onto solid ground.

Part of me expected that once I stepped off the boat, I'd feel the urge to run. But surprisingly, it doesn't come. And as I make my way to the edge of the dock, the rays sinking into my skin, it hits me that maybe I'm not desperate to leave because if I do, I'm not sure what I'll be going back to.

I can't imagine going to the mansion and living with my dad. Not after knowing the things I do. Not after hurting the way I am.

I'm sure I've lost my job at the Vanilla Bean. Not showing up to shifts is a sure way to get fired, and it's been days.

Angie is either worried sick or has written me off as a lost cause. We weren't be-all and end-all besties, and as much as we got along, she'd only known me for a couple of months.

Jon will still be gone.

And I'll just be alone. With no job, no prospects, and no family.

My heart clenches in my chest.

I'm not sure how long I sit here, my feet dangling above the water, but I'm snapped out of my self-reflection when footsteps sound from behind me. I turn, seeing Hook stalking down the wooden walkway, his mouth twisted and eyes narrowed.

He looks *extremely* unhappy.

My stomach curls in on itself.

I open my mouth to say hi, but before I get the chance, his hand is wrapping around my arm and ripping me up, his grip bruising. I stumble as I stand, grasping on to his suit to keep steady.

He doesn't say a word, just starts dragging me back toward the *Tiger Lily*, his jaw muscles clenching as I scramble to keep up. "Ouch, you're *hurting* me."

His fingers tighten when I say it, my feet taking three steps to every one of his. I glance around, wondering if there is anyone else at the marina who would maybe show some concern, but there's no one in sight. And if there is, I'm sure Hook has them all under his thumb anyway. He seems like he can go anywhere, do *anything*, and remain untouchable.

We make it back to the yacht, and he slides open the door, walking into the living room and flinging me onto the couch, my body bouncing as it hits the cushions. My hair flies into my face, and I reach up to wipe it away, irritation bubbling in my veins at his rough handling.

"Is that really necessary?" My fingers rub at where he gripped me, soothing the spot.

"Do you think this is a *joke*?" he asks, his voice cutting.

My brows furrow. "What? I—"

"You must," he continues. "Because I cannot, for the life of me, understand what would make you think you could leave this boat."

"I—"

He steps forward, his body towering over me. My heart pumps adrenaline into my veins.

His eyes lock on mine and my stomach flips.

"Do not mistake my generosity as weakness, Wendy." His thumb presses into my bottom lip. "Or I will tie you to my bed until I break you of the will to leave."

"Ugh!" I explode, anger scorching through my insides, exhausted from his hot and cold act. "You are so *fucking* insane!"

The second the words pass my lips, I know I've made a mistake. My hands shoot to my mouth, my eyes growing big and round.

He jerks back, his head cocking. "What did you just call me?" His question comes out as slow as thick syrup, controlled and dangerously sweet.

My palms drop from my lips, and even though I know I should take it back—apologize before it's too late, I don't—his

Jekyll and Hyde personality bending me past the point of breaking. I push up on my elbows until my nose grazes against his. "I called you *fucking* crazy."

His mouth parts, his breath leaving him on a slow exhale. It coasts across my face, and my tongue swipes along my bottom lip as if searching for his taste, my hands trembling at my sides.

He grabs my face and kisses me.

It catches me off guard, the feel of him so shocking I freeze in place. But when his tongue pries open my mouth, I lose myself to the feeling, releasing all my emotions and pouring them into him.

I surge forward, my arms flying to his jaw, our teeth clacking as I climb his body, trying to get closer, to taste *deeper*. He groans, one of his hands tangling in my hair, the other wrapping around my waist and squeezing.

The kiss is anything but sweet. It's twisted and toxic, a poison masked in sugar, making you love the taste of death.

But for the life of me, I can't stop.

His lips break away, trailing bites and nips along my jaw and down my neck, my head falling back on a moan as I cling to his shoulders. His fingers tighten their grasp on my waist, his hand leaving my hair as he lifts me up and spins me, the front of my body smacking into the back of the couch, my arms scrabbling for purchase. His palms run down my sides, his thick erection pressing into my ass, his face resting in the crook of my shoulder. He slides his arm across my chest until his hand wraps around my throat. My nipples harden, a spike of heat thundering through me.

Goose bumps sprout when he glides his touch down the flat of my stomach, slipping underneath the boxers I'm wearing until his palm cups between my legs, his fingers sliding through my folds.

My abs tense.

"You think I'm crazy?" he rumbles into my ear. "You *make* me fucking crazy." His teeth sink into the juncture of my neck right as his fingers plunge into my core, the sharp pain piercing through me and mixing with the pleasure of being filled.

My head flies back onto his chest, eyes rolling at the sensation.

"Tell me you like my hands on you, pet," he demands. "Tell me you missed the way it feels."

"I…missed—Oh god." His thumb presses firmly on my swollen clit, rubbing in sharp circles while his digits move in and out, his other hand manipulating the airways to my lungs.

My head is dizzy with lust, heat coiling tight in my womb and spreading outward, spinning me into oblivion until I'm on the verge of explosion.

"Do you apologize for breaking my rules?" He slows his movement.

My hips buck into him, desperate for the contact, *so* close to a release that I can't focus on anything else. "Yes," I breathe.

His fingers slip back in, curling inside and hitting something that makes my back arch, my mouth opening on a gasp.

"Good girl," he purrs.

Pleasure from his words bursts inside me like exploding stars, wetness dripping down his fingers and pooling in his hand.

His pressure on my windpipe increases, my breathing now constrained to tiny sips of air. Panic starts to seep into the moment, the darkest recesses of my mind screaming at me—begging me to remember that this man threatened my life less than twenty-four hours ago, that he could end it all right now if he wanted, and I'd die a pathetic, turned-on mess.

"And you're not going to disobey me again, are you?" His teeth nip my earlobe, tingles racing down my spine.

"N-no," I force out through the tightness of my throat. My insides squeeze, legs trembling, my hair matted to my face as pleasure makes my mind delirious with need. I whimper, my body screaming for release, teetering on the edge of bliss.

"That's my girl," he whispers against my skin.

He pinches my clit, his fingers tightening on my neck until he cuts off my oxygen, and that combined with his praise makes my body combust, millions of bright lights dotting my vision as I come apart under his hands.

Sucking in lungfuls of air, my inner walls flutter rhythmically around him, and as I come back down to earth, my logic slowly starts to seep back in.

My body trembles against his, chest heaving from my heavy breaths.

He removes his hand, bringing it to my mouth and sliding his cum-covered fingers between my lips. The taste of myself combined with the salt of his skin sends aftershocks of pleasure trickling through me, and I lick him clean while he holds me upright.

"Don't *ever* try to leave me again."

I want to argue. Want to tell him that I *wasn't* leaving. That it was his stupid "first mate" who said I could go outside. But I'm too tired to fight.

So I nod against his chest, choosing to live in my bliss for a little while longer before the shame and grief resurface and swallow me whole.

CHAPTER 36

James

I'M NOT QUITE SURE WHAT MY PURPOSE IS WITH Wendy anymore. When Smee told me she was gone, a hundred different scenarios played out in my mind. *Did Peter take her? One of my other enemies?*

It wasn't until I was all the way back to the marina that I realized my thoughts were centered around *worry* and not around the fact that, given the first opportunity, she would flee from me and never return.

And that makes me unbearably angry.

Both that she would leave and that I would care.

But avoidance is something that never gets you far in life; it only brings you trouble. True mastery of control is accepting your emotions and then learning to wield them despite how you feel.

My issue now is Wendy makes me *lose* that precious control.

And that's never happened before.

I release her and step back, logic filtering into my brain, even though my cock is throbbing against my slacks.

She slumps on the couch, her body rising and falling with her heavy breaths, and I stare at her, shock reverberating through my bones. She didn't fear me, even though I've all but promised her death.

She thinks I'm mad, but any person who allows their life to be so fragile in my hands is the one who's truly out of their mind.

I was angry that she made me worry.

I was raging that she makes me feel.

And I'm now left reeling with the thought that she's actually come to mean something, something beyond a tool or even simply a good time.

Somewhere along the way, I've started to care.

The realization that I no longer wish to use her against her father slams into me, sucking the breath from my lungs and making my tortured heart skip a beat. But if I give her freedom, she'll run far, far away.

She leans her head back, eyes closed and lips parted as she gasps in air. My heart kicks in my chest as I soak her in. "You're quite beautiful, you know?"

Her eyes pop open, and her tongue appears, slowly licking along the seam of her bottom lip. Blood flows to my groin, my already hardened length pulsing against my leg.

A lazy smile spreads across her face. "I bet you say that to all your hostages."

"Hmm," I hum. "Quite the mouth on you, though." I walk toward her. "You know, I believe your snark has gotten *worse* since you've been under my protection."

She snorts, her head lolling to the side as I take a seat beside her. "Is that what we're calling it now? *Protection?*"

I shrug. "Do you truly believe you'd be safer out there than you are with me?"

Her eyebrows draw in. "*Hook.*"

The nickname makes my stomach twist, the way it always does when she says it. I don't like her knowing me as Hook, especially when she's the only person in this world who makes me feel like James.

"You have literally threatened to kill me multiple times," she continues.

Leaning in, I brush her hair off the side of her neck. "That didn't stop you from coming all over my fingers, naughty girl." My hand trails along her collarbone, enjoying the flush that spreads across her skin. "Does it excite you when your life is in danger?"

She scoffs, jerking from under my touch, and I relax back against the couch, a smirk lining my face.

My phone rings, and even though I want nothing more than to ignore the world and stay in Wendy's bubble, I remove it from my pocket, seeing Starkey's name flash across the screen. "Speak."

"Hey, boss. Got some time today for a meeting? We've got an interview I think you'll be interested in being here for."

My insides squeeze, my focus leaving Wendy and centering once again on the problems in my life. Interviews only mean one thing. Something has happened, and they have people to interrogate.

"Very well. Where are they being held?"

"The Lagoon."

I blow out a breath, hanging up and tapping my phone against my chin as I stare at Wendy, unsure what to do with her. I could leave her here, but Smee has made it more than obvious he isn't capable of watching her.

And while I no longer wish to use her for nefarious deeds, I don't want to leave her alone and chance her running away. Not that it would matter much. Despite her snark and attitude, she hasn't taken off the necklace I've placed around her throat. And as long as she wears that, I'll find her anywhere.

But if she runs, then I'll lose her forever. And I've only just realized she's something I wish to keep.

"How did you get out of the bedroom?" I ask.

Her fingers run through her tangled hair. "What do you mean?"

"I mean exactly what I said. The door was locked. How did you leave?"

She shakes her head slowly. "The door *wasn't* locked."

My chest tightens. "*Yes*, it was."

"Not when I tried it." She lifts her shoulder.

Unease swims in my gut like a shark circling its prey. "Are you lying to me?"

"What reason would I have to lie to you?"

I lift a brow. "I can think of several, actually. I shouldn't, in theory, be your favorite person right now."

Her eyes narrow. "You're *not* my favorite person. You're actually my *least* favorite person."

Chuckling, I stand straight, my hand reaching out to help her rise as well. She puts her fingers in mine, allowing me to lift her from the couch, and I tug her body flush against me, my palm splaying across the width of her lower back, the cotton of her shirt bunching underneath my touch.

Her breathing stutters as I skim my mouth across her lips. "You have quite a funny way of showing it, darling." I pull back, seeing her eyes dilate, and pleasure courses through me. "I need to run an errand, and since you can't be trusted, you're coming with me."

She sighs. "Fine, but what do you want me to wear, *this?*" Her hands run down her frame, showcasing my clothing that sits on her supple body.

I grin. "I *do* find it quite arousing to have you in my clothing."

She huffs.

"I'll have Moira meet us and bring you something." My eyes take her in, my body delighting in the way her features pinch at Moira's name. "You both are about the same size."

Her eyes darken, a tight grin making its way on her face. "And you know this because you have a '*hands-on*' memory?"

My fingers brush against the apple of her cheek. "Jealousy is quite becoming on you. Unfortunately, we don't have time to entertain it."

She crosses her arms. "I'm not jealous. I just don't like her."

I grin, delight sprinkling through my chest, wondering if maybe she feels more for me than she wants to admit. If maybe I haven't irrevocably ruined everything.

The Lagoon, like most of our businesses, has a basement. We mainly use it for storage or temporary resting places for some of the less than legal things that pass through our hands.

Again, meeting here isn't ideal, but since the JR is gone, it's what we have.

Wendy is upstairs in the office, Curly watching over her, and I'm down here surrounded by boxes and crates, staring into the face of yet *another* low-level drug pusher who thought it was wise to betray me.

I'm not sure of his name, and quite frankly, I don't really care. What I *do* care about is the fact that my time is being wasted on trivial matters instead of focusing on the larger picture. But the boys aren't quite as skilled at retrieving secrets from traitors, and when it comes to someone trying to usurp me from the ground up, I need all the information I can get.

"Tell me." I walk toward the man, who is bound and gagged. I rip the white cloth from his mouth, making him sputter and cough as he inhales deep breaths. My knife slides across his cheek. "What is your name?"

"To-Tommy."

"*Tommy.*" I nod. "And, Tommy, what was it you hoped to gain from betraying me?"

He swallows, looking to the side.

My gloved fingers grip his chin, forcing him to meet my gaze, my knife pressing against his mouth, drops of blood forming from the pressure of the blade against his skin. "I do not have time for hesitation, *Tommy*. So let's stop wasting precious seconds and get to the point. You will not be leaving here alive." I pat his cheek, releasing his face. "But I'm a fair man." I back away, rolling my shirtsleeves up my forearms. "I'll let you choose whether your death is painful or swift."

He's silent.

I lift my arms to the side. "Well? What will it be?"

"It was a woman," he rushes out. "She came around a few months ago, started hanging out with us a bit, you know? Started, uh…" His eyes bounce around the room, to the twins and Starkey, who stand behind me, then back to me. "Started sleeping around. Telling us all about her boss and how he could take better care of us. Give us more than what we've been—"

He hesitates, and my chin lifts. "More than what?"

"Uh…more than what we've been given."

My jaw twitches, anger sizzling through my insides. I twist, looking to the boys. "Am I not a giving employer?" I turn back to Tommy. "Do I not allow you unfettered access to your product and to my streets?"

His eyes widen. "No—no, you are. It's just… Look, I wanted to say no. But I want to be part of something, man." He leans in. "I wanted to get the mark."

Interest settles deep in my gut. *Finally*, new information. "And what mark is this?"

"It's a tattoo. So fucking cool, bro."

Annoyance snaps at my senses, breaking away the vestiges of my control.

"I see," I say as I step closer. My hand slams down, the tip of my blade slicing through his tendons like butter, lodging deep in his thigh.

He screams, the sound grating against my ears and scratching down my insides.

My palm covers his mouth, muffling the noise, and I lean in, my face inches from his. "Do you know my favorite part about knives?" My other hand, still on the end of my blade, starts twisting slowly, pushing through the resistance of the muscle. "It's the ability to be so delicately *precise*. You see, three inches over, and I would have sliced into your femoral artery, allowing you to bleed out quickly. Your mind would have ceased consciousness, allowing an easy death."

Tommy whimpers, his body vibrating as he jerks against the zip ties.

"But since you've decided we're 'bros,' I think we'll spend some quality time." A grin cracks my face. "I can show you just how much I like to play with things that *slice*."

I remove my hand from his mouth, my stomach curdling in disgust at the way tears and snot streak down his face.

"It's of a crocodile," he spews. "Wrapped around a—a clock. It's…it's the mark you get when you join his ranks."

Shock punches me in the gut, my insides cramping from the vision his words create.

"What else?" I hiss, pressing the knife in deeper.

"That's it, man. I swear."

My fingers twitch. "Starkey, bring the salt please."

"They call him Croc!" Tommy yells. "Please, stop, I—"

My hand slips from the handle, but I regain the hold, fury racing through my blood, darkness blowing through me like a windstorm. I pull the blade from his skin and strike again, this time higher, dragging it through the flesh in sharp, jagged motions while he screams in agony.

"Liar," I hiss. "How do you know this name?"

"I'm te-telling you the truth. I swear." His face is white, blood pooling on the floor underneath us. "He goes by Croc. I-I've never met him, but the woman's name is—"

Boom.

CHAPTER 37

Wendy

MY HEART IS HEAVY AS I SIT IN THE COLD, DAMP office of a strip club and wait on Hook to do whatever business he has to do.

This sucks.

Curly sits behind the office desk, scrolling on his phone, and *Moira*, for some reason, has taken it upon herself to keep us company. Her glare is hot as it rakes down my insides, and I smile wide at her, hoping that it's tearing her apart to know that Hook has me here. She brought clothes, but I declined them, not able to help the spark of pleasure that simmered in my chest when she took in what I was wearing.

I've had the past couple of hours to come to terms with the fact that I'm emotionally screwed up. Allowing a man like Hook to touch me and *reveling* in the way it feels when he does seems unhealthy to say the least. He's made it abundantly clear that he's not an upstanding citizen. He does horrible things, most of which I hope I never see.

But despite what he's done both to me and, I'm sure, to others,

I can't change the fact that when I'm with him—when I'm truly with *him*—I discover more of who I am. Who I *can* be.

Ironic, how losing my free will helped me find my voice.

And maybe that makes me more like my father than I'd care to admit.

But we're all a little twisted, and there's no such thing as good and evil. There are only perspectives, and perceptions change depending on the angle.

People aren't static. Our morals aren't constant. They're variables, ever changing and molding into different versions of themselves, energy that can be shifted and realigned.

"Can I borrow your phone?" I ask Curly.

His eyes roll. "Sunshine, the answer now is the same as it's been the last twenty times you've asked me. *No.*"

"I just want to check in on my friends. On my brother."

Moira glances up from where she's been picking at her nails, her curious gaze settling on me. "Why don't you have your own phone again?"

Curly's spine straightens, casting me a warning glare.

"I lost it," I say, trying to cover up for my mistake.

"Oh." She nods. "That's a shame." A gleam passes through her eyes as she looks me up and down, her lips curling. "You know... I understand, though. I was actually worried I lost my phone last night too, but I realized I left in such a rush to meet Hook, I didn't even take it with me."

My stomach clenches. *She's lying.* "Last night?" Moira reminds me a lot of Maria, and I never got the chance to stand up for myself with her, too worried about being accepted. But I'm done with being the docile girl who took people's insults and wore them as a burden. "That's interesting, because Hook was with me last night."

Her grin widens, her head cocking to the side. "You sure about that?"

"I—" I pause as I realize I'm not actually sure where he went after I fell asleep. I assumed he just woke earlier than me, but there's a niggle of doubt curling through me, making my insides turn green.

"Moira, shut the fuck up," Curly snaps. "Nobody cares about your extracurricular activities with the boss. Leave."

"But I—"

He stands from the desk. "I said get the fuck out."

She shoots to her feet, stomping out the door. *Good riddance.*

"So he *was* here?" I ask after she leaves, my head snapping to Curly.

He looks at me, his jaw clenching, eyes drooping slightly in the corners, as if he pities me and doesn't want to answer.

I huff out a breath, crossing my arms. *I don't care.* It's not like it matters who he spends his time with. I am just absolutely disgusted with the fact that he may have been with her and then came home and put those same fingers inside *me*.

And I let him without a fight. I practically begged for it.

The door slams open, Hook storming through like a hurricane, immediately sucking up all the energy in the room. The guy from the first night at the bar—the one who let us in—follows close behind. "Hook, I—"

Hook spins around. "Starkey, do not *speak* unless you want to lose your life."

My stomach clenches tight. My eyes widen as they take in Hook's appearance. He has those black leather gloves on, and his button-up shirt is rolled to his elbows. There's red splattered along his skin, and his hair is mussed and disheveled, like he's been tugging at the roots.

Starkey swallows, his face pinching as he drops his head. Hook cracks his neck, and while, despite his appearance, he looks relatively composed, I can see the slight tremble in his hand and the way his features pull tight. And the air—it feels different. I don't know how to explain it, but whenever his mood shifts from one extreme to the other, I can sense it. Like it reaches out to touch me, wanting to drag me in and help save him from drowning.

I can feel in my bones that he's seconds away from snapping.

And when Hook snaps, I imagine it won't be good for anyone involved.

I'm not sure what makes me do what I do next. Maybe I have a death wish, or maybe I've resigned myself to the fact that if he wanted to kill me, he would have. But I rise from where I'm sitting on the couch and walk slowly toward him, not stopping until I'm right in front of his face.

He blows out a breath, dropping his hand from his hair, his nostrils flaring as they look down at me.

"Hi," I say.

His eyes darken. "Hi."

"I know this might not be a good time," I say, attempting to joke.

The corners of his mouth twitch.

I step in closer, hoping he keeps his gaze on me, worried that if he looks away, I'll lose him for good, and the little bit of *James* sneaking through will disappear completely.

Pressing my hands to his chest, the steady rhythm of his breathing makes my palms rise and fall, and I lean up on my tiptoes. "Can I speak to you alone?"

He grabs my sides, his eyes boring holes into me, his stare

wrapping around my chest and tugging. His fingers twitch against my waist.

"Please," I whisper, looking at him from under my lashes.

"Leave," he barks.

My senses are fuzzy, my focus lasered on him, but I hear the door as it clicks shut behind us.

His hands trace up my back, making tingles race through me. And suddenly, I'm not just trying to calm the situation down. Suddenly, I'm *desperate* to have him to myself, memories of earlier whipping through me and stirring up desire until heat boils in my veins.

This time, it's me who leans in and kisses him.

CHAPTER 38

James

I'VE NEVER DONE A DRUG IN MY LIFE, BUT I IMAGINE it feels similar to the way it does when Wendy courses through my veins.

All-consuming.

I grip on to her fiercely as her tongue tangles with mine, wanting to bathe in her taste to drown the memories that are overtaking my mind. I was *this close* to losing it. Fear and fury pumped through my blood until all I could see was red, but I held it together, waiting to hear the name *Tina Belle* drop from Tommy's lips.

And then Starkey, the blithering idiot that he is, put a bullet in Tommy's head, saying that his finger slipped on the trigger.

He must be foolish to think I believe such a pitiful excuse. But I'll deal with him after I deal with my demons.

Croc.

The name alone sends disgust racing through me, shame spiraling close behind. It's *impossible.* Peter doesn't know of him—*no one* knows of him.

Unless it was tortured out of Ru.

The thought of my closest friend spilling my darkest secrets to my mortal enemy creates an inferno of rage, one that I bleed into Wendy's mouth and she laps up like water, as if she likes the way it tastes.

My insides seethe and spit, my mind warring between breaking everything in its path or cutting myself open until the imprint of my uncle's memory is drained from my soul.

My mouth breaks away from Wendy's when a sharp pain sears across my chest, nightmares from my childhood flashing into the forefront of my brain.

Wendy grabs my hand and places it over her heart, teeth nipping at my bottom lip. "Give it to me," she whispers.

I shake my head, my body trembling. "I don't have anything to give."

Her mouth grazes along my jaw, pressing soft kisses to my skin. "So give me all your *nothing*," she replies.

Her words tap into the deepest part of me, mixing with my fury until I break. My hands grip her tightly and I flip us around, bending her backward over the top of the desk, raising her arms above her head, and locking her wrists in my hand. "Do not pretend you care for me," I spit. "Not now. I won't be able to stand it." My voice catches on the burn scorching up my throat.

Wendy's eyes widen as she stares at me, her lips swollen and kissed pink. "And what if I'm not pretending?" she whispers.

My stomach flips, chest squeezing at her words. "I've given you no reason to care." I press my torso into her, my hips settling between her thighs, the papers on the desktop crinkling underneath our weight. "I am not a good man."

"I know," she breathes.

"I have tortured." I dip my lips down, brushing them against her neck. "I have killed." Lifting her shirt with my free hand, my fingers skim up her side, my mouth tasting her collarbone, then trailing over the swells of her breasts. "And I'll do both again, without ever regretting a thing. I *enjoy* them."

Her legs tighten around my hips.

My hand releases her wrists, moving to cup her face, her skin soft beneath the pads of my fingers. My chest twists as my heart bangs against my ribs. "But I regret, with every fiber of my being, that for even one moment you suffered under my hands."

Her eyes widen, the beautiful shades of brown glossing over.

"You are, without a doubt, the only good I've ever known." I rest my forehead on hers, my shaky breaths ghosting across her lips, my thumb rubbing against her cheek. "So don't lie to me, Wendy darling. Because my heart won't survive it if you do."

She surges up, her mouth colliding with mine, passion exploding on my taste buds. I moan as she wraps her limbs around me, my cock hardening as it rubs against her.

All my turmoil is funneled into her instead of on the world, and I lose myself to the moment.

I reach for the neck of her shirt, jerking until it rips in two, exposing her nipples that are pink and hard and *gorgeous*. I suck one into my mouth, twirling the bud under my tongue as my hands strip the boxers down her legs.

She gasps, her back arching into me. My heart swells with the need to make her see. To show her how I feel because I've never been good with words. Not the ones that matter anyway.

I want her to *choose* me.

Not because I demand it but because she can.

My fingers dip between the folds of her cunt, slipping through the wetness.

I work my way down her torso with my mouth, kissing and nipping, apologizing with my tongue and my teeth for all the ways I've hurt her—for all the pain I know I've caused.

My face lands between her thighs, and I inhale deeply, the aroma of her arousal making desire coat my skin.

"Always so wet for me, pet." I slip two fingers inside, watching as her tight walls suction around them. "You're such a good girl. Do you know that?"

Her legs tremble as they spread wider, opening herself for me to feast. She gets off on the praise. Twisting her fingers in the strands of my hair, she tugs me forward. I go willingly, swirling her clit into my mouth, her taste exploding on my tongue. I groan, pressing my face into her deeper, wanting to drown in her essence until I feel her in my soul. I glide my fingers in, curling upward before easing them back out, then dipping them down lower, to coat a *different* opening with her arousal.

Her legs tighten around my head, and saliva collects in the front of my mouth. I rise up slightly, my hands pushing her thighs firmly apart until she's split wide open and on display. I dribble the saliva, watching as it drips from my mouth onto the top of her pretty pink cunt, then slides all the way down, past her pussy and farther down still until it finally drips onto the desk beneath us.

She shudders, and I smirk, my cock pulsing from the lewd vision. My finger presses into her slit, running down her labia until I reach the tight ring of muscle that's now slippery and wet.

"Such a filthy girl, aren't you?" I rasp, my stomach winding tight with desire. I suck her clit back into my mouth, swirling my tongue in a figure eight, my finger teasing around the rim of her asshole.

"Oh my *god*," she keens.

I open my mouth wider, my saliva mixing with her juices, drenching her until it's pooling on the desk.

"I don't thin—"

"Shh," I soothe. "Don't think, pet. Just take it."

I push the tip of my finger inside, making sure there's enough lubricant to make it feel pleasurable instead of painful.

"*Fuck*," she cries.

My mouth dives back in, tongue alternating from dipping inside her pussy to twirling around her clit. Unintelligible moans leave her mouth, her body jerking, and my free hand rises up, pressing down on the flat of her stomach.

When the staggered rise and fall of her breathing ceases, I know she's close.

She's holding her breath.

My finger dips in and out of her tight hole in tandem with my tongue in her cunt, my thumb pressing firm circles against her clit.

Her entire body starts to shake, and my eyes glance up, my cock jerking when I see the splotchy flush of her skin.

She opens her mouth on a silent scream, her body arching off the desk, and the inner muscles of her ass grip my finger like a vice.

I work her through her orgasm, drinking down her juices and groaning from her taste. The shaking turns to trembles, and I slowly lick my way up her body until my lips press against her ear. I slip out of her ass until just the tip of my finger is pressing against it.

"One day," I whisper. "I'm going to take you here. Feel your muscles milk the cum from my cock while you pleasure that sweet little cunt."

She sucks in a breath, her eyes wild and her cheeks ruddy.

"Would you like that?" I whisper, rubbing my nose along her cheek.

Her hands reach out and grip my face, pulling me toward her. And then she *licks* her juices from my mouth, her eyes heavy-lidded as she moans at the taste.

My insides clamp tight, my length jerking.

She moves her touch from my jaw as her tongue slips between my lips, her palms sliding down to grapple with my belt buckle. I help speed up the process, stripping off my pants until my cock springs free, thick and engorged, dripping with the *need* to be inside her.

Her fingers move to my shirt, and I freeze, my hands shooting to cover hers, not wanting her to see the imperfections of the past marring my skin.

"It's okay," she says. She sits up until her face is level with mine, the flat of her palm resting on my chest, directly over my heart. "I'm *not* pretending."

I breathe in deeply, my emotions running haywire, fear flooding my veins as she slowly undoes my shirt, one button at a time, until she slides her hands underneath the sleeves, the fabric slipping off my skin. I stand stoic, my jaw set, bracing myself for what I know she's about to see.

She scoots closer, her legs wrapping around my hips, nestling my cock against her center. "James," she whispers.

The name rolling off her tongue undoes me, something warm and needy exploding through my chest. I raise my arms, allowing her to lift my undershirt and toss it to the side.

And then I wait.

Her fingers trail over my torso, and I chance a glance down, terrified to see the look of pity on her face.

But I don't.

Her gaze is wide and open as she touches every scar, many of them from the nights my uncle decided to nick my skin, knowing the sight of my blood caused terror to paralyze me in place.

My heart pumps erratically in my chest. Her hand ghosts along my hip, the jagged line searing up my side, burning from her touch.

"What happened here?" she asks.

I grit my teeth. "Plane crash."

Her eyes glance to mine, and then she leans in and presses her lips to the mark. My lungs squeeze, my throat swelling from the gesture. I want to tell her that she's kissing the scar her father helped create and that somehow, with just her touch, she's eased the pain.

But I don't know how, so I pull her face up to my mouth instead, and I show her with my body.

I suck her breath into my mouth, slamming her back on the desk, my shaft slipping between the folds of her pussy and creating a friction that has my stomach tensing, pleasure pricking along my spine.

"Say it again," I murmur against her lips.

"Say what?"

"My name." I grind into her, heat spreading through every cell.

Her eyes roll back as the tip of my length presses against her clit. "James," she breathes.

My cock slides inside in one thrust, all the way to the hilt.

We gasp simultaneously, the feel of being surrounded by her overwhelming every sense. I'm afraid if I move, I'll explode, and I want this to last forever.

Slowly, I ease out before pushing back in, the power of my

hips matching the surge of my emotion, making me delirious with the need to get as deep as I can.

I lean down, my tongue licking along the shell of her ear. "You're so perfect. Feel so *fucking* good."

She groans, her fingernails digging into my shoulder as her hips rise to meet mine.

There is no exchanging of power here, no demand for obedience or a need to keep everything under my control.

There's just Wendy.

Only ever Wendy.

Doing what she does best: consuming every part of me.

My torn-up heart rattles against its blackened cage, beating just for her, hoping she'll learn to love it through the dirt.

"Again," I demand.

"James," she moans.

I bite my lip, my insides raging with heat as my hips piston into her, balls slapping against her ass with every inward stroke. "I want you to tell me that you're mine."

She cries out as I change the rhythm, my cock seated fully inside her, my hips grinding against her clit.

"I'm—"

I cut her off with a kiss, needing her to understand what I'm asking. "I want you to tell me but not because I say to, not because I ask." I drop my head in the juncture of her neck, my breathing shallow and hot, my orgasm building deep in my gut as I pull out, then slide back in, rotating my hips against her. "I want you to say it because you *are* mine. Because you're going to stay, even though we both know you should leave."

Her breathing stutters, her hands framing my face as she stares deep into my eyes. "I'm *yours*, James."

Heat bursts inside my chest, and I pick up my pace, her words pouring into my soul and filling up the cracks in my heart.

The sound of our skin slapping mixes with her moans until she tenses and then explodes. Her pussy walls clench around me, urging my balls to tighten, my muscles seizing until they ache. Cum pulses through my shaft, my cock jerking wildly inside her as I coat her womb with my seed.

I collapse on top of her, breathing heavily, my mind finally at peace.

It's in this moment that I know, as wild as it seems, that I love her.

And that terrifies me more than anything else ever has.

CHAPTER 39

Wendy

I'M IN FRONT OF THE MIRROR, ADJUSTING THE ill-fitting clothes Moira bought since what I was wearing is now shredded on the floor—something I've noticed James loves to do. My eyes flicker to him through the mirror as he stands behind his desk. He's finally washed the blood off his arms and is now buttoning up his shirt, covering the scars that mar every inch of his torso. My heart twists, wondering how they got there and feeling a heavy sense of purpose, knowing that he let me see.

He opens a drawer and pulls out a gun, slipping it behind his back in the waistband of his pants before grabbing his suit jacket and sliding it up his arms, buttoning it in the front.

My abs tense at the sight.

"You're really too attractive for your own good," I say.

His head snaps up, a grin sneaking on his face as he saunters over, stepping behind me and pressing kisses to my neck.

"James?" My heartbeat pounds in my ears.

I'm not sure where we stand, part of me feeling as if I'm

balancing in the middle of a teeter-totter, unsure which way it's going to shift.

"Hmm?" he hums against me.

"Can I…" I spin around, my hands resting on his chest. "I want to see my brother."

He nods. "Alright."

Relief pours through me. "And…" I bite my lip. "I'd like my phone back."

"Done." His brow lifts. "Anything else?"

"And I want you to tell me you weren't with Moira," I rush out, heat singeing my cheeks.

He pauses. "Ever?"

I cringe. "Well, obviously not now. I know you'd be lying."

His fingers tilt my chin up until I'm staring into his eyes. "I haven't been with Moira, or any other woman, since the moment I touched you."

I blow out a deep breath, my stomach slowly unraveling from where it's tied itself into knots. "Okay."

His lips twitch. "Alright."

"Okay," I say again.

"And just so we're clear." He presses his thumb into my chin. "If someone *else* touches you, I'll cut off their hands so they can never *touch* anything again."

My chest spasms. "You're so violent."

He grins. "It's just who I am, darling."

"Am I? Are we… I'm not still being held…"

"Wendy, you're free to do as you wish. Your father, he—"

"No, I know," I cut him off, not wanting to talk about my dad, the wounds still too fresh.

"You *don't*." He touches his side, where the jagged scar mars his skin. "This plane crash?" His nostrils flare. "It was on one of your father's flights."

I gasp. "What?"

He shakes his head. "This isn't the place to talk about this, darling."

Irritation flares in my gut, not wanting to be brushed off, the way I always have been when I've wanted to know what was going on.

I open my mouth, but his finger covers my lips. "I'll tell you whatever you wish, just not here."

A heavy feeling sinks through my insides. "Are you going to kill him?" I whisper.

He sighs. "You need to understand, your father, he's taken almost everything from me." His thumb brushes across my lip. "And while I would do *anything* you asked, please, don't ask me for this."

My heart pinches, desolation running through my veins. "But I…" Tears well behind my eyes. "He's my *father*."

"Yes, well." His head cocks to the side. "He's the one who killed mine."

I'm back on James's boat, sitting on the sundeck in the exact same spot he brought me for our first date. It's been two days since he fucked me on the desk at his strip club and then shredded my mind to pieces when he opened up about his past. About my father.

Bile burns on the back of my tongue when I think of James, a child, going through what he did at the hands of his uncle. Living through the pain of losing his parents and watching the person responsible for that loss smile on magazine covers for years without any repercussions.

My soul is sick from the thought of the torment that has *scarred* up his heart.

Still, I can't reconcile him killing my father and me just accepting it. But how can I ask him not to after what I know my father has done?

And I don't understand *why*. Why would my father kill his own business partner? Why would he kill Ru?

It just doesn't make sense.

That being said, knowing the root of the issue does lessen the sting of James having done what he did to me. It doesn't make me forget, but I do understand his anger, at least a little bit.

And maybe that makes me stupid. Maybe I'm still naive, but James is the only one who has ever trusted me enough to tell me the truth. To let me in on what the hell is going on so I can gain some understanding. He's taken a risk by telling me. So I can take the risk by trusting when he says he cares.

I've had my phone back for over forty-eight hours. I've gone through the messages and calls from Angie and from the Vanilla Bean firing me for being a no-show. But there wasn't a single missed call from my father.

Not a *single* one.

Nothing from Jon either, although I texted him and asked how everything was.

The sliding door opens, Smee walking onto the deck with a tray of sliced veggies and a smile on his face. He sets them down and sits. "Boss man said to make sure you eat while he's gone."

"I could have gotten something for myself." I grin at him.

Smee waves me off. "It's no big deal. This is my job, remember?"

He pushes the tray toward me on the table, and I reach out, grabbing a green pepper and popping it in my mouth as he cracks open a beer, taking a long pull.

"Where are you from, Smee? How'd you end up working for James?"

He picks up a carrot and takes a bite, relaxing against his chair. "Oh, it's really not all that interesting. I came up on some tough times years ago, and he helped me out."

My heart swells. "He did?"

He nods. "Got me off the streets. Put me up in this place and told me I could stay, as long as I learned everything there was to know about yacht maintenance."

"And did you grow up here in Bloomsburg?"

I'm not sure why I'm asking him so many questions. Maybe it's because if I'm planning to stay on the boat, I'll feel more comfortable if I get to know its inhabitants, or maybe it's because I'm desperate for a distraction from the upheaval James's recent revelations have caused.

He takes another sip of his beer. "I sure did. Been here my whole life."

"That's nice," I hum. "Any family?"

Something dark coasts across his eyes.

"I'm sorry," I cringe, my stomach souring at the look on his face. "I'm being nosy."

He chuckles, adjusting the red beanie on his head. "No, it's fine. My mom's probably still around somewhere, looking for her next fix."

Guilt for prying trickles through me. "Oh, I'm so sorry."

He waves me off. "I came to terms with who she was a long

time ago. My father was a good dude, though. Although I didn't know who he was until a few years before he passed."

"My mom passed too," I say, my heart aching. "The pain of lost time never really gets easier, does it?"

His lips turn down, his fingers tightening on the neck of his beer. "It sure doesn't, Miss Wendy."

Footsteps draw my attention away, James stepping onto the deck, looking impeccable as always in his three-piece suit.

Smee stands up, dusting off the front of his shorts. "I should get back to it. Thank you for the company."

I grin. "Thanks for the snacks."

They pass by each other, James barely giving him a second glance.

"Don't you get hot in that?" I ask.

He ignores my question, swooping down and meeting my lips for a kiss. His tongue slides into my mouth and my eyes flutter closed, losing myself in his taste.

"Mmm." He breaks away, resting his forehead on mine, his thumb caressing my cheek. "Unfortunately, I have business that needs my attention. Will you be alright here?"

"Yeah. I'll be fine. I was thinking about stopping by the Vanilla Bean anyway."

His mouth twists.

"James, you *told me* I was free to go, and now you're—"

"Darling, please." He sighs, pressing another peck on my lips. "You are. Forgive me for wanting to keep you to myself. I'll leave the keys to the Aston if you want to use it."

The knot in my chest loosens. "Thank you."

"Do me a favor? Don't take off that necklace."

My brows furrow. "*Still?*"

"Humor me." He grins. "I like knowing jewels are decorating your skin." His fingers brush along the diamonds. "Make it back home by dinner? I have a surprise."

"Okay." I smile, butterflies fluttering in my stomach.

Home.

He says it effortlessly, as if this place is mine and it's where I belong. But I'm still teetering on the edge, unsure if this is all too good to be true—if maybe he's still using me for some master plan.

I push the thoughts aside and head inside, choosing to ignore the whispers of doubt.

CHAPTER 40

James

I SIGH, FLIPPING THE STATION FROM THE NEWS. They've been speaking of nothing besides the NevAirLand fires, and while it does bleed a bit of satisfaction through me each time I see the rubble and destruction, I can't help but be frustrated that nothing has come of it.

In fact, for a man who's as popular as Peter, he seems to have disappeared off the face of the planet. It leaves me feeling *uneasy*. Everything, as of late, seems to be leaving me unsettled—a foreboding feeling, a storm brewing, and without radar, no idea of when it will hit or the destruction that will be left behind.

The twins sit across from me, their faces grim as they tell me of yet another shipment that never arrived, a million dollars in pixie just disappearing into thin air.

Rage curls through me as I sit behind the desk, feeling as though I'm staring at a giant puzzle and missing the center piece.

And where the fuck is Peter?

I look at the twins, blowing out a deep breath as I try to contain my growing ire. "I need you to make the rounds. *Today.*

You will go to every single street corner and collect *every single* person who's ever touched our product, and you will strip them down and search them. If you see a tattoo of a crocodile, a watch, or any variation of the two, you will bring them here, and you will chain them up in the basement. Is that understood?"

"You got it, Hook."

"Good." I crack my neck. "Will you please send Starkey in on your way out?"

They leave, and my stomach twists at the reminder of the tattoo, as if it were plucked directly from my nightmares and drawn into my skin with ink. But that's *impossible.*

Starkey opens the door, his eyes wide and cautious. "Sir."

My jaw clenches as I stand up, buttoning the front of my suit and walking around the desk toward him. It's silent for long moments until I finally speak. "Remind me again, Starkey, why it is you interfered the other night?"

"It was an accident, Hook. I didn't *mean* to." He looks down. "I'm willing to take whatever punishment you think is fit."

The corner of my mouth curls up, although inside, my stomach is rolling. "And what if I see fit to end your life? After all, the punishment should match the crime, don't you agree?"

He swallows, his fingers twitching at his side. My eyes track the movement. "It was an accident," he repeats.

I nod, stepping toward him. "I don't pay you to have *accidents.*"

My nostrils flare, fingers itching to grip my blade and sink it into his skin. But it wouldn't look good for morale if I killed him now. Up until this point, Starkey has never been a bother, and between Ru's death and the whispers on the streets, the last thing I need is for my inner circle to feel as if they aren't safe in my presence.

"You've always been extremely loyal, Starkey. One of the best. One that up until the other day, I would have trusted with my life." His jaw clenches, and I take out my knife, flipping the blade and using the tip to tilt up his chin. "Do not do something so foolish again, or next time I won't be as lenient."

He bobs his head, his eyes glancing down at where my fingers press metal to skin. "Thank you," he says. "And I'm sorry. I didn't mean—"

I hold up my hand, stepping back. "I want you to find Peter Michaels's assistant, Tina Belle. And I want you to bring her to me. Do you understand?"

He swallows and nods.

"Go."

With every minute that ticks by after Starkey leaves, my body winds itself tighter, my brain feeling as though I'm watching a TV with static. *I have to be missing something.* But for the life of me, I can't figure out what it is.

When I finally make it back to the marina, having had a pit stop on the way home, grabbing a bottle of champagne and a bouquet of roses, I'm exhausted. I want nothing more than to lose myself in Wendy's presence.

Walking into the kitchen, I set the champagne on ice, the silence in the air making my heart stutter, wondering if maybe she changed her mind and decided to leave me after all. I rub my palm against my chest, not liking the way my pulse is suddenly out of my control.

"Romantic."

I spin at the voice, Smee waltzing into the room.

"Yes, well, I guess you could say I'm turning over a new leaf." I give him a tight smile.

His eyes spark as he steps toward me, his head tilting as he takes me in. "You really care for her, don't you?"

My chest twinges, but I nod. I'm not one to speak of emotions plainly, but I imagine it's rather obvious the way I feel, especially when we're here, in my home. There's no sense in trying to deny it. "She has come to be *paramount* to my happiness."

"Hmm." Smee stops in front of the bouquet, leaning in to smell the roses. "Well," he sighs, straightening. "I've been waiting a long time for you to bring someone here."

My brows lift. "Oh?"

He grins. "To see you happy, I mean."

Unbuttoning my suit jacket, I slip it off, setting it on the back of one of the kitchen barstools. "To be honest, I don't quite know what to do with myself." I run a hand through my hair. "We didn't necessarily get off on the best foot."

Smee chuckles. "Sometimes, boss man, you just have to be patient and let everything play out."

I rub the scruff of my jaw, nodding at his words.

"Is she here?" I ask.

He angles his head toward the bedroom. "I don't think she's left all day."

The urge to see her is too strong to resist, so I rise, pausing before I hit the hallway. "Smee," I say.

"Yes, sir?"

"You're a good man. And I appreciate everything you do. I'm sure I don't tell you enough."

He inclines his head, and I make my way to the woman who's become the center of my universe.

CHAPTER 41

Wendy

I CHICKENED OUT AND DIDN'T GO THE VANILLA
Bean, not wanting to come face-to-face with an angry, outspoken
Angie. If her text messages are any indication, she's not exactly
happy with me, assuming that I bailed and disappeared, deciding
I didn't need the money. So I took the coward's way out and sent
her a text instead. She hasn't replied.

Not that I blame her. From her perspective, it seems like I'm
a flake, a temporary fixture, leaving them all high and dry. And
maybe it's for the best that I allow them to remember me that
way. I'm not sure I can come up with an excuse as to why I disappeared, other than the truth. Somehow, I don't think showing up
and telling them that I was held hostage, but it's okay because I
think I'm in love with the kidnapper, would go over well.

I scoff, rolling my eyes and leaning back on James's bed, laughing as I remember one of the first conversations we had here. Joking
about *Stockholm syndrome*, of all things. Talk about the irony.

A giggle bursts out of me just as the door opens and James
walks in, his eyes hollow and haunted.

"What's so funny, pretty girl?" he asks, coming to sit next to me on the bed. His hand reaches out, brushing underneath my eyes, and my insides melt like butter from his words and his touch.

I grin. "I'm just thinking about the first time I woke up in here. Do you remember?"

He leans in, brushing his lips against mine. "I remember every single moment between us, darling."

"Well, isn't it kind of funny that we talked about nice kidnappers, and then you went all *Hook* on me and did it?"

His brow lifts.

I laugh again. "I'm just saying." My hand flies up. "It's funny when you think about it."

He tilts his head. "Are you alright?"

Sighing, I lean against the pillows. "I'm fine. Just trying to find some humor from our less-than-ideal start. What a story for the grandkids, huh?" His eyes flare and I realize what I just said, my chest pulling. "Not that I think we're going to have kids, or that *they'll* have kids. It's just a phrase, really. I know we're still super new, even though we *are* technically living together, aren't we?"

A smile grows on his face and he stands, stripping out of his suit and climbing in the bed, hovering over me. "I'm not sure I've ever heard you ramble before, darling."

I lean back, his body weight settling on top of mine.

"For the record." He dips his head down, the tips of his hair tickling my neck as he presses kisses to my skin. "I would give you the world. You simply have to ask. You want kids? Done." He presses his lips to my jaw. My stomach tightens. "You want to stay here and never work again?" Another kiss, this time just beneath my ear. "Done."

My core flutters, heat spreading through me.

"You want to watch the world burn?"

"Let me guess, you'll set it on fire?" I ask.

He chuckles, the sound vibrating through me and settling into my bones. "No, darling. I'll hand you the match and stand at your back, watching you become queen of the ashes."

My breath stalls at his words. At what he's really saying. And *that*, as morbid as it seems, hits me in the center of my chest, making warmth spread with every beat of my heart.

Because James sees me as his equal. As someone worthy to stand at his side.

His lips meet mine, and I sink into the kiss, fully giving in, accepting that this is what I want.

All his deep, dark, and slightly unhinged pieces. I choose every single one.

I choose *him*.

He pushes up my oversized shirt—another one of his that I put on—his fingers dipping between my legs and groaning when he meets naked skin. I pull his face back to mine, staring into his eyes, taking in the white lines that run through the cerulean blue. Leaning in, I kiss him.

He groans, pushing down his boxers, his fingers sweeping through my folds. "I have dinner planned, but I feel as if I deserve a treat."

My stomach jumps, my body lighting up with heat and love and *acceptance*.

I'm done fighting it.

James may not be a hero, but even villains can feel. And you can't help who you love.

He grips his length, running the tip of himself up and down my entrance, pleasure snaking its way through my middle.

"You're such a good girl, ready and waiting to take my cock," he rasps into my ear.

Butterflies fly through my stomach and up into my chest, my hips rising to force him inside, *desperate* to feel him fill me in the way only he can.

"James, *please*," I beg.

He circles his tip on my sensitive nerves until my legs start to tremble, and only then does he move himself down to my opening and slide all the way inside me. He leans back, his hips flush with mine, and he rips off his undershirt, his scarred body hovering on top of me.

"You're beautiful," I gasp as he pulls out and thrusts back in.

He smirks. "Am I?"

"Yes." My heart swells in my chest, and my hand reaches up to trail along his jaw. "You're dark and moody and mysterious. But beautiful."

Leaning down, he sucks my tongue into his mouth and sets a steady pace, my walls squeezing around his length as if my body wants him closer. *Needs* him deeper. His lips break away, his hand wrapping around my throat the way he knows I love.

"Darling, if I'm the dark, then you're the stars."

And then he squeezes, cutting off my air supply, my vision going blurry moments later. My hands dig into his shoulder blades, fingernails cutting into his skin as I give in to the burn of my lungs, my middle winding tighter with each second that I rim the edge of consciousness. I explode, my vision going black, my head growing fuzzy, and my walls contracting around his cock. Euphoria sizzles beneath my skin.

He groans in my ear, continuing his rough pace as I come back to myself, my lungs expanding with every breath.

"Do you want my cum, pet?" he asks.

I moan. "Yes, *please*."

"I do love it when you beg." He pulls out, moving up my body until his knees rest on either side of my chest. "Be my good girl and suck it out."

His length bobs in front of me, glistening from my juices and throbbing from his need for release. I grasp it in my hands, feeling it pulse beneath my fingers, and pull it into my mouth, moaning at the taste of my cum on his skin.

I swirl my tongue around the head and relax my jaw as he pumps his hips, his length hitting the back of my throat. My eyes water, but I breathe deep through my nose, his hands fisting my hair and his head thrown back, mouth slightly parted.

Seeing him in the throes of pleasure sends a rush of power spiraling through me. I suck hard as he thrusts, gagging as he pushes past the back of my mouth and slips down my throat, spit dribbling from the corners of my lips and sliding down my face. My eyes burn, tears blurring my vision as his hips push until they're flush against my face.

"That's my girl," he coos. "Taking my cock down your throat like a perfect little slut."

The insult slices against my middle, but the way he says it makes me *want* to be his whore. To be filthy and depraved just for him.

Only ever just for him.

Suddenly, he pulls out of my mouth, and I gasp in a breath, my jaw aching. He grips himself and strokes, his hips thrusting into his fist. I watch, desire pooling low in my belly as his body tenses, the vein on the underside of his shaft physically pulsing as thick ropes of cum shoot from his tip. They land, hot and sticky, along my face, dribbling down my cheek and dropping onto my chest.

He lets out a long moan as he paints my skin with his pleasure, and the sight of him coming undone above me makes my insides clench with need.

His chest rises and falls as he catches his breath, his palm coming up to stroke my hair and brush across my face, rubbing his seed into my skin.

"So good to me," he praises. "So absolutely perfect."

My chest warms, satisfaction wrapping around me like a heated blanket on a winter's night. I lean into his touch. "James?"

"Yes, darling?"

"I think I love you."

CHAPTER 42

James

SHE LOVES ME. AND SHE'S THE FIRST PERSON, apart from my mother, who's ever said those words.

I hadn't realized until now just how much I needed to hear them. But instead of saying it back, I kissed her silly and gave her food and roses, like that would make up for the fact that I couldn't get the words to pass my lips. Not that I don't feel them; I do. I just don't know how to *say* them. And therein lies the problem.

But even though fear beats against my soul, worried she'll take the words back or still think I'm using her for some other purpose, I push it deep down, because what I'm about to partake in has nothing to do with love.

My eyes take in the three men who are bound and gagged, chained to the walls in the basement of the Lagoon. They're naked, their pathetic bodies shivering from the dank concrete floors and the cold AC that blasts through the vents.

I walk toward them, the clack of my shoes the only sound other than their whimpers, and my fingers flex inside my gloves.

My eyes glance down, scouring along their skin, searching for the mythical *mark*.

And when I find it, I wish I never had.

It's exactly as Tommy described: a gold pocket watch with a crocodile wrapped around the face. The sight of it makes me *ill*. This seems personal. But how is it possible that someone knows? Then again, how is it possible for this to be a coincidence?

The twins walk up to the three men, ripping the black cases off their heads and tearing the tape from their lips. Their eyes widen as they see me, standing in the middle of the room, watching them.

"Hello, boys." I grin. "Lovely tattoos. Tell me…" I tilt my head. "Where did you get them?"

None of them speak.

"Ah." I click my tongue. "The silent treatment. I see." My hands rest on my hips as I blow out a breath. "Well, I was hoping to do this the easy way, but I can see now that isn't going to work."

One of them spits at my feet. "Get fucked, Hook."

I raise my head to the ceiling, chuckling. "Now, there's no need to be rude." I slide my knife from my pocket, twirling it in my hand.

Turning, I nod to the twins, who walk to the far wall, retrieving three buckets.

"Normally, I enjoy this type of back-and-forth. But you see, I'm a little perturbed, because there's somebody trying to ruin my good mood. And *I* heard that you gentlemen might know who that is?"

The buckets clank against the floor as the twins set them down by the men's sides.

I walk forward, crouching in front of the one who spit, rage twisting my features into a wide grin. "Twins," I say without breaking my stare from the man before me. "Would you mind bringing me our guests?"

"You got it, boss." A fourth bucket appears, scratching sounds and squeaks coming from the inside.

"Do you hear that?" I cup my ear with my hand. "They sound *excited*." Reaching inside the bin, I pick up a small, furry animal, its tail flicking against the sleeve of my suit. I bring it up to my face, staring at its small, beady eyes. "Probably on account of how hungry they are." My gaze slides back to the pathetic traitor who's chained to my wall. "After all, rats always know when they're on the brink of death."

I place the first rodent inside the bucket next to the man before grabbing another one from the bin and repeating the process until there's half a dozen there, scratching at the sides, attempting to escape.

The twins appear, handing me a long lighter before moving forward, picking up the bucket, and flipping it upside down until it rests on the man's stomach. They crouch down, their forearms resting along the rim, ensuring it stays in place.

The man squirms, no doubt feeling the rats skittering along his skin.

"Now," I say. "I'm going to ask one more time nicely. Who gave you that tattoo?"

The man's body shakes, pathetic whimpers leaving his mouth, but still he doesn't speak.

"Very well. I do wish you had shown that type of loyalty to *me*, but I respect it all the same." I flick on the lighter. "Do you know what happens when you starve a rat?" I ask, smiling at the pathetic waste of space. "They don't generally need much food.

But if you withhold for long enough, you'll find that they become rather *ravenous*."

The first scream pierces the air shortly after I put the flame to the bottom of the bucket, heating it from the outside in.

I raise my voice to talk over the noise. "Add a little bit of heat, and they become frenzied in their need to escape." I chuckle. "I think you'll find they're quite the survivalists. They'll even take to chewing on flesh…and intestines…and bone."

"Stop!" he screams, "Please! God! It was a wo-woman!"

I keep the flame lit, the bloodlust overtaking my brain until red seeps in the corner of my eyes and my heart pumps out nothing but *vengeance* against all who dare to go against me.

"I already know it was a woman, you blithering fool. Tell me something useful before I let them eat you whole."

But it's too late, his eyes rolling back in his head, losing consciousness as the rats feast on his middle.

Sighing, I take away the flame and look to the other two chained-up fools. "Who's next?" I smile, twirling the lighter between my fingers.

"The woman," one of them rushes out. "She worked at the bar."

My movements freeze, insides squeezing tight. "What bar?"

"Yours!" he cries. "The JR."

I crack my neck, letting out a long, loud laugh, disbelief running through my veins. Because there's no way this man is saying what I think he is. That the woman is not Tina Belle, nor is she a stranger. I rush over to him, my fingers gripping his jaw, my knife out in a flash, slicing against his cheek.

"Please," he begs.

"Do not lie to me," I demand. "Are you insinuating that

someone has been taking advantage of my hospitality?" I ask, fire brimming behind my eyes. "What is her name?"

His body trembles beneath my grasp, his hiccups and heavy sobs making his words sputter.

"Tell me!" I spit, my knife pressing deeper, drips of his blood running down his face.

"Moira!" he cries. "Her name is Moira."

CHAPTER 43

Wendy

"WENDY?"

Relief flows through me when I hear Jon's voice. I was in the shower, and when I got out and saw that I had missed his call, I started blowing him up until he answered, not wanting to do anything until I heard him speak.

"Jon, hi," I breathe down the line. "How are you?"

"I'm okay."

"I miss you so much, my dude." My voice cracks, the emotions from the past few weeks bubbling over. "I'm so sorry I haven't been able to call until now."

"Oh, it's okay. James told me you were sick."

My breath stalls. "Ja—what?"

"Yeah, he said that was why he was calling to check on me instead. Listen, I really don't need babysitters."

My heart explodes in my chest, my mind racing at what he's saying, at what that means.

"When did—" I clear my throat. "When did you talk to James?"

"Almost every freaking day since I've been here, Wendy. That's what I'm trying to say. It's a little overbearing."

"He calls you?" My throat swells.

"Yeah. Did you not know?"

My chest cracks wide open, tears rimming my lower lids. Even when he was threatening me, he was checking on Jon. *Does that mean he was always bluffing?*

"No, I knew," I sniff. "I'll let him know to back off."

"Okay, thanks. Hey, you gonna be home tonight?"

My brows pull in, and I glance around. "Yeah, why?"

"Dad said he's picking me up and to call and let you know."

My stomach twists when I realize he's talking about the mansion. "Dad's coming to get you?" I repeat, unsure I heard him right.

"Yeah. Said there's something he wants to tell us. I don't know, but I don't really want to be with him by myself."

My loyalty splits in two, wanting to stay true to James and knowing he wouldn't want me anywhere near my dad but also wanting to be there for Jon. And as much as I want to say no, wait for James to come home and pretend my dad doesn't exist, I know I can't. Not if it gives me a chance to see my brother. "Okay. I'll head there now."

"Cool."

"Cool," I repeat back, smiling as I hang up.

There's a lightness floating through me from the anticipation of seeing him, even though guilt wraps around my middle, knowing James will hate that I'm there. But hopefully, he'll be able to see things from my point of view.

I was feeling off all morning. I told James I *loved* him, and he couldn't say it back. Not that I was expecting it, but still, when you lay out your emotions, it hurts when they aren't returned. But him checking in on Jon, even while he was spinning a different tale to me? That means more than any words ever could. I pull up James's number on my phone and dial, my heart swelling with gratitude for what he's done. I want him to know that *I* know, and I also want to tell him where I'll be. He won't be happy, but he promised not to control my life.

I'm not a hostage anymore, and I won't let him tell me who I can and can't see.

His phone rings and rings, but he doesn't answer. I frown, trying to dispel the unease that trickles into my gut. I leave him a message and then send a text, just in case, and blow out a breath, brushing off the anxiety.

An hour later, I'm pulling James's Audi into the mansion's drive and being stopped at the gates.

My brows draw in at the new, extensive security features that line the perimeter. Four men are stationed on the outside, and one walks up to my window, knocking on the glass.

I roll it down, confusion spiraling through me. "Uh, hi. I'm Wendy."

His brow raises.

"Peter's daughter? He's probably expecting me."

The man doesn't speak, just nods and walks away, whispering into another guy's ear before they open the gates and let me through.

What the hell?

Nerves snap and crackle beneath my skin, like ants scurrying through my veins. I'm so disgusted with my father I can hardly see straight. Not that I'm the gatekeeper on morals. After all, I'm in love with a man whose morals are severely lacking at best. But at least he owns who he is. My father puts on a show, fooling the masses.

Fooling *me*.

I park my car and walk up the brick walkway, opening the front door and making my way inside. It's eerily quiet, and my stomach tenses with nerves.

"Jonathan? Dad?" My voice echoes off the high ceilings in the foyer, but nobody responds.

Odd.

I walk into the formal living room, pulling out my phone to bring up Jon's number.

"You came."

The voice shocks me, and I spin, my phone flying across the room, cracking as it hits the floor. My hand shoots to my chest, my heart banging underneath my palm. "Jesus, Tina. You scared me."

Tina smiles, walking into the room until she's only a few steps away. "Sorry."

"Where's Dad?" I ask, glancing around. "Is he picking up Jon?"

Her eyes are slightly unfocused, her pupils round and dilated as she grins.

"Tina." I wave my hand in front of her face.

She jerks, snapping out of her daze. "What?"

"Is my father here?" A warning tingle races up my spine as I take her in, something feeling off about this whole encounter. Suddenly, I wish I would have waited for James to get home so he could have at least attempted to talk me out of coming at all.

This just doesn't feel *right*.

"Mmm, nope." She laughs. "He told me to wait for you, though."

I tilt my head, my heartbeat whooshing through my ears, my eyes taking in my surroundings. "Okay."

She steps toward me, stumbling before she regains her footing. "Are you okay?" *Is she drunk?*

"I'm fine. Your father has a new business partner. Brand new, actually, and I was the tester to make sure the product was on point." She taps her nose.

My eyes widen, stomach dropping. "You're *high?*"

"Just a little bit of pixie." She grins. "Pete doesn't like to touch the stuff, but someone has to make sure he's not being robbed." Her eyes narrow. "And there's no one your father trusts more than me."

She throws her barb, and it hits the mark, but it doesn't rip me open the way it once would have. It merely stings, a phantom ache for what could have been.

Not that I would *ever* agree to do drugs to benefit his business.

My eyes narrow. "You're disgusting. How can you be okay with what he does?"

She huffs out a laugh. "That's rich. Tell me, do you ask yourself the same thing as you let Hook split you with his cock?"

Heat rushes to my cheeks, and I grit my teeth. "That's none of your business."

She stares at me, the grin dropping off her face. "Ugh, this really sucks. I was told not to hurt you."

My hair stands on end, alarm racing through me at her words, and I back away slowly, not wanting to make any sudden moves. "Who told you that?"

"*Everybody.*" She glares, stepping toward me. "Wendy *this,* and Wendy *that.* 'Don't hurt her, Tina.' 'We *need* her, Tina.' 'She's my *daughter,* Tina.'"

My back hits the wall, the table next to me shaking from the thump, anxiety swarming my insides as she continues to move closer, her eyes small slits.

"Do you know how exhausting it is always coming in second place?" she says.

I shake my head, putting my hands in front of me, my eyes glancing to my phone across the room. "I never asked to be put first."

"Liar!" she screams. Her hand shoots out and slaps me across the face, my head swinging to the side, cheek stinging from the burn. I grit my teeth, desperately trying to keep my composure. Blinking slowly, I inhale a breath, and when I reopen my eyes, I realize how big of a mistake it was to close them at all.

Because Tina is right in front of me, and a blue glass vase is in her hand, high in the air. My arms reach up to try and stop her, but she's fast, and it crashes into my head. I fall to the ground, pain searing through my skull as she brings it down again, and everything goes black.

CHAPTER 44

James

MY OFFICE IS DESTROYED.

I stare at Curly, Starkey, and the twins as they watch me pace back and forth. They're smart enough to know there's nothing they can say that will calm the rage wreaking havoc on my insides. I called Curly in specifically because I know he and Moira are close.

Moira.

Unbelievable.

Turning, I point at Curly, my finger shaking. "Did you know?"

His nostrils flare, his fingers popping as he puts his fist in his other hand. "Hell no, Hook. I would never let that bitch get away with this."

Nodding, I rest my palms on the edge of the desk, my grip so tight my knuckles leach of color. "Bring her to me."

"I don't know if—"

My arm sweeps across the desk, everything crashing to the floor, wires ripping from their sockets and pens rolling across the wood. "Bring her to me. *Now.*"

Curly nods, pulling out his phone and walking away. But he needn't go anywhere, because as he opens the door, Moira stands on the other side. "Hi, boys."

My head snaps up, untapped fury ripping through my muscles and bleeding from my bones. "Moira," I purr. "How lovely of you to make an appearance." I walk around the desk, my fingers gripping the handle of my knife so tight it bruises.

She makes her way inside, meeting me halfway, and smirks.

I brush her hair off the side of her neck, the back of my hand resting against her cheek. "Tell me, sweetheart, did you think you would get away with it? Or do you simply wish for death?"

She looks me straight in the eye and smiles. "I still think I'm getting away with it. *James.*"

The back of my hand connects with her cheek in a sharp crack, her body flinging onto the floor. My nostrils flare as I step over to her, the heel of my shoe digging into her back. I lean into my body weight, reveling in the way she whimpers beneath me. My eyes snag on that disgusting crocodile tattoo gracing the back of her neck as a memory flashes in my mind.

"Sorry, new tattoo. Still kind of sore."

I shake my head, chuckling at my own stupidity. Reaching down, I flip her over, pinning her with my forearm on her chest. "Ah, such memories of you beneath me like the filthy whore you've always been."

Her hands smack the floor, and she lets out a scratchy scream. "Fuck *you*, Hook. This is exactly why I flipped. You treat people like shit."

"Spare me the theatrics. I treat *you* like shit because you've never been worth anything more." I press my blade against her jugular. "Tell me what I want to know."

"I'd rather die," she sneers.

I grin. "Oh, rest assured you will." I lean down, my lips at her ear. "You made a mistake choosing Peter."

Her brows furrow and then she *laughs*, her head smacking against the floor until tears seep out the corners of her eyes. "Oh my *god*, you don't even know, do you?"

My jaw clenches, my free hand reaching up and grasping her hair, lifting her head up and slamming it against the ground. She cries out as I push her face into the floor, my knife back at her throat. "Speak in riddles again and I'll cut off your lips."

She winces. "I don't know Peter, okay? *My* man is Croc." She pushes her neck into the edge of my blade. "And he's coming for your head."

I remove the blade, replacing it with my fingers, squeezing until I feel her trachea in the palm of my hand.

She coughs, her eyes bulging at the pressure. "You don't— don't want to do that," she wheezes.

"I promise you, I do."

"He has your *precious* Wendy. And I know where she is."

Before this moment, I always thought I had known fear. Had assumed that staring down the face of my uncle—hearing the ticks of his watch as he locked my bedroom door—was the epitome of the word.

I was wrong.

Because I have never known the icy grip of true terror as I do when Wendy's name passes Moira's lips.

The blunt end of my knife comes down on her head before she can speak again, knocking her out cold. I drop her body to the floor, rushing to find my phone and pull up the GPS tracker installed in her necklace, hoping beyond hope that she still has it on.

She does.

And she's at Cannibal's Cave.

But if it isn't Peter, then why are they there?

Once I have her location, I'm out the door, Starkey and the twins coming with me and Curly staying behind. He's waiting on my call. Once I make sure Wendy is really there, he's to put a bullet in Moira's head.

I'd like to prolong her torture, but Wendy's safety is paramount, and I don't want to leave loose ends.

The drive to Cannibal's Cave takes half the time it normally would, my foot like lead on the pedal, my mind spinning in a thousand different directions.

I am so stupid for believing that my enemies wouldn't take her from me.

That *Peter* wouldn't use his own daughter. I underestimated him once again.

The boys are relatively quiet in the car. Starkey sits in the passenger seat with a pistol in his lap, and the twins speak quietly to each other in the back. And my insides are raging, my mind praying to a god who's already sentenced me to hell, bartering my soul as long as it keeps Wendy safe.

She has to be safe.

As soon as we hit the cave's entrance, I throw the car in park. "Okay." I blow out a breath, slipping on my gloves and checking the chamber of my gun. "Are you ready, boys?" I grin. "The time has come to pay the piper." I don't wait for them to follow, knowing they'll have my back. I'm solely focused on finding

Wendy, getting her to safety, and then killing every person who thought they could use her against me. Surprise flickers at the realization that revenge doesn't even matter to me now, not if it's at the cost of her life.

Walking past the charred trees, I ignore the way my chest pulls from the memory of Ru's body lighting up in flames and head into the entrance of the cave. I go through the narrow rocky hall and into the large opening, my steps faltering when I see Wendy, unconscious, tied to a chair with dried blood on the side of her face.

My heart falls to the floor, fire decimating my insides at the sight.

I will *burn* them all.

"Hook, nice of you to make it!"

My chest cramps at Peter's voice. I had been holding out hope that it wasn't actually Wendy's own father who would go to such extremes just to get to me.

"Peter." I place my hands in my pockets. "Funny seeing you here, being a disastrous father figure once again."

He chuckles as he looks at his daughter. "Yeah, well, sometimes sacrifices must be made."

I tilt my head. "You would harm your own daughter?"

His eyes darken. "She wasn't supposed to be hurt. Tina got a little carried away."

"Hmm." I glance over at her again, focusing on the even rise and fall of her chest, the relief from seeing her breathing making me able to focus on Peter instead. "Maybe you need to keep a tighter rein on your bitch."

He runs a hand over his mouth, his shoulders lifting. "You're probably right. But what can you do? Women."

I sigh. "I tire of playing these games, Peter. Tell me why you lured me here." I put my arms out to the sides. "I assume that's what all this is for?"

"He didn't."

A new voice comes from behind me, and the blood in my veins freezes over at the familiarity.

It's not possible.

I resist the urge to spin around, not wanting to turn my back on Wendy, even for a moment. But before long, he moves to stand in front of me.

He looks different. His hair is slicked back, a solid black suit fitted to his frame. He looks *like me.*

A smile cracks along his boyish face. "Hello, boss man."

My mouth opens, and I blow out a breath, betrayal sinking deep into my chest, splitting apart the cavity. "Smee."

"Surprise!" He lets out a cackle, spinning around in a circle. "Wow, this is *so* much more than I hoped it would be." He presses a hand to his chest. "You'll forgive me, of course, for my excitement. I've been waiting for this moment a long time."

My stomach churns, anger and hurt mixing together until my vision blurs. My eyes flicker past him to Wendy, her head shaking back and forth, her body fighting against her restraints as she comes to. Relief floods through me.

Good. That's a good sign.

Smee snaps his fingers in my face. "Pay. Attention. To. *Me.*"

I grin, my teeth clenching together as I reach in my pocket and pull out my blade, twirling it slowly through my fingers. "You know," I start, "it's incredible that after all these years, I'd find you here." I step closer to him. "Betraying me."

His eyes narrow. "You're right. We *have* been together for

years. And every day was torture, knowing who you were and not killing you in your sleep," he spits, a sneer marring his features.

I press a hand to my chest, sticking out my bottom lip. "That hurts, Smee. I thought we were friends."

He laughs. "Oh, we're more than friends, James Andrew Barrie."

My lungs compress at the use of my full name.

"We're cousins."

CHAPTER 45

James

THE BREATH FREEZES IN MY LUNGS, MY HEART
faltering from where it beats against my chest.

Cousins means that he's my uncle's child.

But my uncle didn't have any children.

"Impossible," I say.

"*Improbable*. But it's the truth." Smee shakes his head. "I was
there the night you killed my father."

My brows rise, surprise flickering through me as I think back on
the night I took my uncle's life. I was in a bit of a rage, so I suppose
it's not beyond the realm of possibility that someone was looking in.

I glance behind Smee to where Wendy is looking around, her
arms moving as if she's trying to free herself from her constraints.
Peter stands in the corner, but his eyes are locked on me, his face
pinched and his eyes hard.

"You'll meet him again soon enough," I reply. Lunging
forward, my blade is at Smee's throat in a matter of seconds. "It's
very stupid of you to bring me here, thinking you would make it
out alive."

He laughs, his Adam's apple pressing against the hooked edge. "You've always overestimated your own importance. It's what made it so easy to come into your life, pretending to be homeless as I sat next to the bar where you work." He grins. "It's also why it was so easy to sway people to work for me instead."

My knife presses deeper into his skin. "My people are loyal to me."

"Your people are *afraid* of you." His eyes flash. "But I didn't go after them. I found the ones who were wronged. And when I told them that I would bring you to justice, taking over and treating them right…well." He smirks. "It was easy after that."

"It's a shame," I say. "I tried so hard to keep you from this life." A dull throb smarts against my insides. "I won't enjoy killing you."

"I wouldn't kill him at all if I were you." Heat surges through my blood as my eyes meet Starkey, red stains covering his shirt and a bruise swelling on the side of his face—I'm assuming from the twins. I would say I feel betrayed, but the truth is, with Starkey, I should have known.

However, none of that matters, because all I can focus on now is the fact that he has his gun pressed to Wendy's temple, his finger poised and ready on the trigger. My eyes soak her in, trailing along her person to see if she's been hurt again. But she seems okay. Her jaw is stiff, and she's glaring at her father.

"Sammy." Peter straightens from where he's leaned against the cave wall, pulling his own gun from his waist. "This was *not* part of the plan."

Smee's head twists from where it's still pressed against my knife. "Plans change, Peter. I told you the only way to get James to heel was to put her in danger. You knew the risks, and you agreed."

Wendy's eyes widen, her mouth parting on a gasp. "You *what?*"

"Hello, darling," I cut in, my gaze flicking to Starkey. "It's extremely wonderful to hear you speak. Are you alright?"

Her eyes soften. "You mean besides the gun to my head?"

I smirk, and Starkey's body stiffens, his hand moving the barrel before pressing it under her jaw. "This *isn't* a fucking joke," he seethes. "Let Croc go."

Wendy winces as Starkey pushes his pistol into her chin, and a shot of fear surges through my insides.

Her eyes widen as she locks her gaze on mine. "James. *No.*"

Starkey snaps, his hand ripping open her jaw and shoving the gun in her mouth.

Rage consumes me, and a terror like I've never known follows close behind. Because as much as I would love to pry the skin off Starkey's body and break every bone for thinking he could *touch* her, I'm halfway across the room.

And I'm not willing to risk her life on the off chance he's bluffing when I know, deep down, he's not.

Licking my lips, my fingers tighten around the handle before I step back, raising my palms in the air, the knife clattering to the ground.

Smee grins, immediately swooping down to pick it up. He flips it over a few times in his hands, his eyes soaking in every detail. Looking back up at me, he points the tip of the blade in my direction. "Any other weapons I should know about?" He glances behind him to where Wendy sits, her cheeks wet, Starkey's gun still held inside her mouth. I reach behind my back, pulling out my pistol and dropping it to the floor.

Laughing, Smee turns to Peter and claps his hands. "What did I tell you, Pete? The boy is *in love.*" He sighs, looking back at me, reaching in his pocket and pulling out something bulky, covered in a cloth. Slowly, he starts to unwind the fabric. "To muffle the noise." He winks. "For dramatic effect."

The cloth drops to the ground, and with it, my mind does as well.

Tick.

Tick.

Tick.

My fists clench at my sides.

Smee holds up a glass pocket watch, his grin so wide it touches his cheeks. "Do you like my new toy? It's *almost* as loud as the one you made me throw overboard the other day." He chuckles, shaking his head.

My lungs squeeze tight at the noise, flashes of crocodile boots and the clicking of locked doors flashing inside my mind, making my chest rip open, my memories being flayed and sliced into fresh wounds.

He walks toward me until the tips of his shoes meet mine, bringing the watch up and pressing it to my ear. "Do you know how difficult it is to find a watch that actually *ticks*? The one I used to have was special. It was just like my father's." He frowns. "But I needed to make sure that what Starkey told me was true."

My hands fly to my head, trying to drown out the noise, my nerve endings clawing at my skin like a thousand bugs, desperate to escape. Red starts to soak into my vision, the haze bringing rage and shame—a volatile mix that constantly lives inside me. My palms shoot out, gripping Smee's shirt in my hands, balling the fabric and lifting until his feet barely touch the ground.

"Ah, ah, ah," he sings. "You hurt me, and he'll kill her."

Immediately, I release him, my heart slamming against my

ribs as I fight the manic thoughts. I briefly consider grabbing my knife from his hand and trying to cut off my ears, anything to stop the torment.

He moves away, the ticking becoming slightly less intense before his arm comes swinging back, the glass face smashing into my cheek, my body slamming into the ground as an aching sting spreads up my jaw. He crouches down, dangling *my* knife between his knees. "I was there the night you killed my father," he whispers. "I watched you through the windows as you took *this* knife." He lifts it up to my face, tracing it down my body before jamming it into my side, *deep*. "And bled him out on the floor."

Searing pain flares through my torso as he twists the handle, my teeth gritting against the burn.

"Do you regret it?" he asks.

My face is on the dirt floor, but I turn my head just enough so he can see me grin. "I'd kill him a thousand times over and force you to watch every time."

He pulls the knife from my side, blood spurting from the wound and soaking my shirt, my skin growing clammy.

"He was supposed to be mine," he says. "He *promised* he would take me in as soon as you were gone. He was going to send you away, but then suddenly he changed his mind." The blunt edge of the handle cracks against my cheek. "So I waited *three years* for you to turn eighteen, and then you fucked everything up."

Copper pools in my mouth and I spit on the ground, pushing up until I'm sitting, my head growing fuzzy from the sudden movement. I lean back on the wall, my hand immediately pressing against my side to try and stanch the bleeding. "I did you a favor."

"You took *everything* from me!" he screeches. "So I'll take everything from you."

Although I'm sure he meant for his words to inspire fear, they only bring realization. Because I have thought that exact same phrase. Imagined it a thousand different ways as I visualized my final words to Peter. A laugh bubbles up my throat, the pain in my side twinging, although it's nothing compared to the devastating truth, that Smee is just like me.

And to him, I'm just like Peter.

"You want my life?" I cough, blood bubbling in the back of my throat. "All you had to do was ask. It's yours."

Smee's brows turn down. "That's not good enough." He stalks toward me, bending down until his face is directly in front of mine. "I want to see the look on your face as I kill the only person who would show you love."

He's talking of Wendy. *Of course*, it's her. Because life is full circle, and it's only fitting that he would take from me what I longed to take from Peter.

Pop. Pop.

My heart thumps in my chest as the gunshots ring out, my stomach cramping as my eyes swing to Wendy in fear.

No. Not her. *Anyone* but her.

Relief pours through my veins when I see she's fine, the gun gone from her mouth, her eyes wide as she stares at the crumpled form of Starkey, dead at her feet.

Another pop rings through the air, Peter stepping forward as he shoots Smee in the back of the head, and he too drops to the ground.

I don't feel satisfaction from his death. I understand all too well the all-consuming rage of seeking vengeance. How it bleeds into your pores and poisons your blood until you can't think of anything but seeking revenge. I only hope that in death, he finds peace.

"Morons," Peter mutters, walking over and untying Wendy. "Tina, you can come out now."

Tina stands from where she was crouching behind a large rock, *hiding* this whole time. I cringe as I stand, my hand pressing against my side, the burn radiating through my torso. My feet stumble from the way dizziness overtakes me, but I breathe deep, trying to keep my eyes focused.

"Your name is James Barrie?" Peter asks, tilting his head.

"It is," I reply.

I have imagined this moment for years—the look that would cross Peter's face as he realizes just who I am. But now, I only feel hollow. I force my feet to move as I walk toward my knife, grunting from the pain of bending to pick it up, a gush of fresh blood spurting from my wound and seeping through my shirt. I'm not sure how deep the puncture is, but my body is becoming chilled, and I'm sure I'm losing more blood than what anyone would deem a reasonable amount.

"You look just like your father," Peter continues. "And your brother looks like you."

CHAPTER 46

Wendy

HOW MANY SECRET FAMILY MEMBERS DOES JAMES have?

My wrists burn from where the rope was tied around them. I shake out my fingers, ignoring the throbbing in my head and the dried blood that pulls the skin on my face.

I woke up in a fog, a gun pressed to my temple and Smee threatening James's life. There are cuts on my wrists from where I fought against the rope, and honestly, I've never felt as helpless as when I saw James fall to his knees—a slave to his trauma.

If my father hadn't killed Smee, I would have.

Anger floods through me like hot lava at how my father tricked me. Used my brother to get me here and allowed Tina to abuse me and tie me up.

That's not love.

James laughs, his eyes wincing as he hunches over. Worry grips my chest tight, wondering just how badly he's injured.

"You're fucking with me," he says. "A cousin *and* a brother? Must be my lucky day."

My eyes snag on Tina as she inches closer to where I am.

My father taps his gun on his leg, his stance rigid, his eyes as hard as steel. If you had asked me a month ago, I would have told you there was no way my father owned weapons. Yet here he is, looking every bit the gangster.

"I *wish* I were joking," he says.

James shakes his head and stumbles, his hand dropping his knife to the ground. My stomach falls to the floor, and I start to move, but I'm yanked back by the hair, Tina gripping me tight. "I don't think so."

I briefly consider fighting against her hold, but I don't want to take my eyes off James, afraid that if I do, something terrible will happen. Panic spreads through my veins.

My father steps forward, kicking the knife out of the way and moving in front of James, pushing the gun into his forehead until he drops to his knees.

"Dad," I plead, my heart slamming against my chest. "Stop it."

He looks back at me. "Can you not see the resemblance, Wendy?"

"Resemblance to *who?*"

Tina pulls on my hair, making me wince.

"To Jon!" he snaps. "The bastard child of your mother and my old business partner, *Arthur.*"

My breath whooshes out of me, shock ramming my gut. "What? No, Mom would nev—"

"Please, Wendy," my father laughs. "You're always so naive."

James's lips part, his face growing pale. "Jonathan is...my brother?"

"Technically, half." My father crouches down, taking two fingers and jamming them into James's side. "I thought you had died with them."

James curls over, groaning in pain, his face screwed up tight.

My stomach jerks as I choke out fumbled words. "Dad, *please*," I beg. "If you've ever loved me at all, you'll st-stop." My chest burns, and Tina giggles from behind me. "Haven't you done enough?" I gasp, my tears hot as they stream down my face.

My father pauses, removing his bloodied fingers and standing straight. He looks at me, his gaze growing soft. "I do love you, little shadow. But I cannot let this man survive. He *burned* all my planes. He disrespected my offer of business. He spit in my face and paraded my daughter around like a cheap whore on his arm."

Fury and grief war together for first place in my soul.

And as all his declarations slot into place in my brain, any confusion I've ever had drains away, clarity overcoming every sense. I understand now why my father never paid any mind to Jon.

Why Jon has black hair and dark features, so similar to our mother's but also a lot like *James's*.

Disbelief coasts through me, a whispered question dancing inside my brain.

My father turns back to James, pressing the barrel of his revolver against his head and clicking back the hammer. "Any last words, Hook?"

"Bad form, Peter," James grits out. "Not quite a fair fight."

He looks past my father, locking his cloudy eyes on me. He licks his lips, blood dribbling from the corner of his mouth.

"Don't say it," I hiss, my stomach twisting until it tears. "Don't you *dare* say it."

He smiles, and I swear to God the sight makes me want to die.

"The greatest thing I've ever done in my life was to love you, Wendy darling."

My heart cracks in my chest, agony ripping through me so deep it brands my soul. A guttural sob escapes my throat, making my father spin around. I thrash my body violently against Tina's hold, my head snapping back into her skull, her grip growing slack.

Ripping myself away, I stumble on the ground, rising on my hands and knees to crawl toward Starkey's body, reaching out at the same moment as Tina grips my ankle.

She was fast.

But not fast enough.

I twist in her hold, raising the revolver to her face, and without another thought, I shoot.

Blood explodes from the side of her head, my stomach heaving as it splashes on my legs, her lifeless body falling back and crumpling on the floor.

I wipe my mouth with the back of my hand, slowly standing, focusing my eyes on where my father has James on his knees.

They both stare at me, frozen with eyes wide.

Tears stream down my face, the fragments of my heart slicing through my flesh as I lift my shaky arms, aiming the gun at my father. "It didn't have to be this way," I whisper.

"Wendy," James says, his voice the strongest it's been all night. "Stop this."

"Did Mom die in a car accident?" I ask, my finger curling around the trigger.

"Little shad—"

"Did she?" I scream, my throat scratching from the force of my yell.

My father's face drops, all pretenses gone, a blank and hollow look entering his eyes. "No."

"And Jon?" I continue, though the anguish is splitting me in half.

His chin lifts. "Jon is not my son. He's a *bastard* and the living embodiment of your mother's disrespect."

My face screws up, the truth excruciating as it gores its way through the center of my chest. I breathe deep, welcoming the pain, allowing it to fuel me.

I look to James, then back to my father. My hands tremble so violently, I'm surprised I can even hold them up. But I grit my teeth and push through the tremors. "Don't make me do this." My voice catches on the torn-up edges of my throat.

My dad chuckles, but his eyes dart nervously between the weapon and my face. "Wendy, don't be ridiculous. I'm your *father*."

I take slow steps forward.

"Wendy." James's voice is sharp. His gaze is wide and open, resolute acceptance in his eyes. "It's alright, darling," he purrs. "Put the gun down."

Tears blur my vision, pain ravaging my soul, but I do as he says, lowering the weapon.

My father's shoulders relax, his brows drawing in. "I'm sorry it has to be this way, little shadow. But in time, you'll understand this was for the best."

He spins around, pushing his revolver against James's head. James closes his eyes, as if he's ready and willing to accept his fate.

But I'm not.

"Dad?" I lift the gun and cock it. "I'm sorry too."

And then I pull the trigger.

My body hits the ground before his, heaving sobs racking through me as I collapse in on myself, the anguish of what I just did more than I can bear. My arms wrap around my stomach, nausea making my skin sweat and my body heat, and I heave, vomit rising through my esophagus and pouring from my mouth onto the floor.

My throat burns and my soul is shattered, my eyes so swollen I can barely see.

Soft touches caress my back, and then I'm pulled into a lap, James's lips coming down to press against my face. "Shh, darling. It's okay. It will all be okay."

His hold is shaky and weak, but it's there.

And right now, it's exactly what I need.

CHAPTER 47

Wendy

IT'S BEEN A WEEK SINCE I'VE KILLED, AND GRIEF sits heavy on my soul.

I'm not sure there will ever be a time that it doesn't, but I don't regret what I've done. I was mourning my father long before now, and if I had to do it all over, we'd still be where we are today.

At his memorial service, sitting in the front row, with hundreds of people behind us.

The tears that stream down my face are real, remembering the father who brought me acorns and always said good night. But that man didn't exist in the end, and I pray I helped his soul find peace. Because he wasn't finding it here.

I'm not sure how everything was covered up, and I don't care to know. But to the rest of the world, Peter Michaels was killed by a low-level criminal named Sammy Antonis, the secret child of the late Senator Barrie, known to the underworld as *Croc*.

James somehow got us out of Cannibal's Cave, finding the twins tied to trees, broken and bruised but alive.

And by the time we made it back to the *Tiger Lily*, James

was no longer conscious. Curly met us there with their in-house doctor, and although I screamed until my voice went hoarse to take him to a hospital, they refused.

Too many questions and too many witnesses.

Forty-seven stitches, a few blood bags, and a week of rest later, and you'd never know he was so close to losing his life.

I, on the other hand, have had to come to terms with the fact that my soul is now stained in red. A heavy mark, but one I'll wear with pride.

James says that sometimes true love requires sacrifice. Well, I'll sacrifice my soul a thousand times over in order to stay with his.

After the service wraps up, we settle into the car, James's arms wrapping around my shoulders and dragging me into his side. He tangles the fingers on his free hand with mine, bringing them up to his mouth and kissing every knuckle. "Are you alright, darling?"

"As good as I can be, I suppose."

"Have you checked on Jonathan?"

I sigh, shaking my head. Jon didn't come to the service. When he found out about my father's death, he seemed *happy*. And when we told him the truth about his own father, he seemed relieved.

It's odd, knowing that James and I share a brother, but now that he's out of Rockford Prep and living with us on the yacht, I'm excited for them to get to know each other. To love each other as much as I love both of them.

If there's anything I've learned over the past few months, it's that family is what you make it.

"Hey, do you think we can stop by the Vanilla Bean?" I ask, suddenly wanting to see the smiling face of a friend.

Angie reached out after hearing of my father's passing, and

we picked up right where we left off. She hasn't asked what happened while I was gone, and I haven't offered an explanation. Although we haven't seen each other in person yet, so who knows if that will change.

James leans in, pressing his lips to my ear. "We can do anything you like, darling. All you have to do is say the word."

"Okay." I grin, turning toward him. My hand reaches up to cup his face. "And you? How are you doing?"

He smirks. "I'm ready to go back home and tie you to my bed."

"Behave, *darling*." I press a kiss to his lips. "Hey, not to change the subject, but do you want to have a service for Ru?"

His eyes darken, his jaw tensing underneath my palm. He opened up about his relationship with Ru over the past week. He said he was just bored from being bedbound and needed to talk, but I have a sneaking suspicion it was his way of helping me grieve.

When my thoughts would overwhelm me and my heart would ache with pain, James would wrap me in his arms and tell me tales of the Lost Boys, led by Ru and his bright red hair.

And it did. Help, that is.

He shakes his head. "No. He wouldn't have wanted that."

My heart clenches in my chest. "Okay, but we always can. If you want."

He presses his lips back to mine, his fingers trailing down my dress and dipping underneath the hem. "You're a very caring woman, pet. Allow me to show my appreciation."

"James," I gasp. "You're still *healing*."

He smirks as he slides off the limo's seat, his hands forcing my legs apart so he can settle between my thighs. "You're absolutely right about that," he says, his fingers moving my panties to the side and dipping into my folds. "You would deny an injured man some pleasure?"

"I just think you need to be—" My voice cuts off as he leans in, the flat of his tongue swiping up my core and swirling around my clit. My fingers reach down, gripping his hair, my hips pressing into him.

My heart rate speeds as I glance to the driver, but the partition is up and the windows are tinted, so I'm sure that he can't see. Still, the thought of him hearing is enough to make my body coil tight.

James's finger dips inside my core, curling against my inner walls, drawing a long moan from my mouth. A few more passes of his tongue and that's all it takes, my orgasm cascading through me like an avalanche, my thighs pressing harshly against his face.

He places my panties back in place, pressing a soft kiss on top of the fabric before gliding his body back up my frame and meeting my lips for a kiss.

"That's my girl," he says.

I grin against him, warmth spreading through my chest, my arms wrapping around his neck. "Only yours, James Barrie."

"And always yours, Wendy darling." He kisses my jaw. "Every night."

"And straight on 'til morning."

EPILOGUE

James

Two years later

I USED TO HATE THE SEA.

Not that you would know it from the way I stand on the sundeck of the *Tiger Lily*, the saltwater breeze blowing on my face.

It's Wendy's second year by my side and the first full year as my wife. And she promised she'd *finally* let me take her out on the water.

She didn't used to like it either, but I think it's growing on her now.

I glance to the table where we had our first date, back before I knew she would soon eclipse my world and become the sole reason for my existence. She sits there now, her belly swollen with our second child, the first one just old enough to waddle around on his own.

We didn't know it then, but she was pregnant when we buried her father.

A little boy. Named Ru.

She and Jon laugh at our baby while he wiggles his hips to music as it croons through the speakers, and a warmth spreads through my chest, happiness infusing every pore.

I never thought I would have this.

A family.

A life.

But then Wendy swept through with her unfailing loyalty and her selfless way of forgiving even the worst of mistakes, and she showed me that even the most damaged of hearts can still learn to love.

Eventually, we'll have to go back home, of course. I still have an empire to run, and Jon is starting his first week of college to get his engineering degree.

He wants to build planes, of all things.

Shortly after the dust settled on everything, Wendy attempted to get her job back at the Vanilla Bean, but they said no, citing the multiple times she failed to show. Which was my fault, really.

So I bought it for her.

And before little Ru came along, she spent her days brewing coffee and bonding with her best friends, Angie and Maria.

Maria took a while to come around, but once she started dating Curly, she softened up, and these days, they're as thick as thieves.

I look back out on the water, closing my eyes and looking toward the future where adventure awaits, feeling grateful for how far we've come.

And to think, it all started with a little bit of faith.

Misplaced trust.

Missing pixie dust.

And a villain who just needed to steal a little love.

EXTENDED EPILOGUE

Wendy

"DARLING."

I turn around at the term of endearment, my eyes crinkling with a smile when I see James walk into our bedroom on the yacht. My heart skips a beat as he makes his way toward me, and as I take in his crisp black suit and perfectly styled hair, my fingers tingle, remembering how I was tugging on the strands two hours ago when he snuck into my shower and shoved his head between my thighs.

My stomach flutters.

You'd think after a decade together, our passion would have waned, but it's only grown. When you're with someone for as long as we've been together, when you *love* someone for as long as we've been lucky enough to love, they become etched in your skin, their wants and needs a muscle memory instead of a road map.

They say it takes doing something ten thousand times before you become a master at the task, and I can say that when it comes to James, he's an expert in everything that has to do with both my pain and my pleasure.

"I didn't think you'd be ready so soon," I say, quirking a brow as I spin back toward the mirror and push the last pin into my hair, watching his reflection.

He smirks, his blue eyes sparkling as he moves behind me, wrapping his arm around my waist and tugging my back to his front. Another shot of desire whips through my middle and I bite the inside of my lip, trying to stifle my reaction to my husband's presence, not wanting him to ruin my makeup when he promised me a night on the town.

But James doesn't miss a thing.

His hand trails down the front of my skintight baby-blue dress—the one I'm wearing just for him—bunching the silky fabric in his grip and dragging it up my thigh until he slips beneath the hem. Goose bumps sprout along my skin when his fingertips graze against my clit.

"No panties?" He presses down and my arousal leaks down the inside of my thighs. "Naughty girl," he whispers against the shell of my ear. "It's almost as though you *want* me to lose control."

I blow out a shaky breath, leaning my weight against his solid frame, my heart beating so loudly I can hear it in my ears.

He isn't wrong. I *do* want him to lose control.

His free hand glides up my torso and over the swell of my chest until his palm wraps around my throat like a necklace. "Are you trying to get somebody killed? I assure you that's what will happen if I see a man so much as look at you while I know you're bare beneath this devastating dress."

"It's just for you," I say, my breaths puffing out in a stuttered rhythm. "Only for you."

"Is that right?" he rumbles.

His fingers glide through my folds until they slip inside of me, and my eyes roll back, my head falling on to his shoulder.

"You're needy and exposed just for me?"

"Ye-yes," I gasp out.

He hums, his grip tightening around my throat and tension coils in my abdomen. His thumb presses against my clit, causing my back to arch against him.

"That's it, perfect girl. You're doing so well."

Fire licks up my thighs and settles in my groin, and I move my hips against his hand, desperate for relief. My insides pull taut and I don't think I can take a second more, but then the pressure snaps, and I explode into a thousand fragments, light blinding my vision and my soul soaring out of my body.

I ride his fingers through every single moment, my nails digging into his wrist to hold him in place. Slowly, the pleasure recedes and my eyes clear.

"Stunning," James purrs into my ear, his thick erection pressing into the middle of my back. "Angie is here to watch the children, darling. Keep the panties off. I want to sit across from you at dinner and know your pussy is on display *just* for me."

He grins, a wicked gleam coasting across his eyes, and I turn toward him, pressing up on my toes and pecking his lips. Before I can pull away, his powerful grip is at the nape of my neck, dragging me back in, his tongue slipping between my lips and kissing me until I lose my breath. My sensitive core clenches and spasms, begging for more. I'm always needy with him.

When he releases me, he rests his forehead against mine, and as he rolls it slowly back and forth, my arousal deepens into something else. Something more vulnerable. An intense, all-consuming feeling that presses beneath the surface of my skin and seeps out of every single pore.

"I love you," I breathe against his mouth.

His hand moves, jostling at his side before sliding up my spine. A cold sensation drapes around my neck, and then there's a soft click. I glance down, my eyes widening at the blue sapphire necklace.

"Happy anniversary, Wendy darling." He pulls back and grabs my hand, pressing it against his chest, over his beating heart. "My life wasn't worth living before you were in it."

Tears prick the corner of my eyes and I swallow around the sudden knot of emotion. I spent most of my life hoping to have a man who loved and cherished me. And James? He's everything I could have asked for and more.

James

THERE ISN'T MUCH THAT I REGRET.

But I will spend every second for the rest of my life making up for all the ways I failed Wendy so many years ago. She is my perfect half, my *better* half, and I know no matter what I do, a man like me will never deserve her.

She softens my edges, although I'd never admit it out loud. In fact, if you ask any of the lost boys, they'll tell you I'm *more* ruthless now than I was before her. But now I have a family to protect, and I don't take any risks when it comes to them.

It took being on my knees with a gun pressed to my temple to realize that my poor decisions and blindness to my surroundings were a byproduct of things that happened to me as a child. That my trauma made me incapable of thinking logically, and as a result, almost had me losing everything that mattered. And while I know I don't deserve it, I thank God every day that my wife was just broken enough from her own issues to forgive me so easily. Maybe that makes me a poor excuse of a man, but I am *only* a man. As it is, I like to think I've spent the last ten years making up for the mistakes I've made, even if they do still haunt my dreams.

After so many years of looking back on all the things you've done wrong, you start to see the world through a sharper lens.

She's given me everything. I have beautiful children and a younger brother I love dearly, but it doesn't change the fact that *having* them at all is dangerous. So I work in the shadows, the same as I always have, and I keep my family there with me.

And when I'm with Wendy, I leave everything else behind. She consumes me just as much now as she did that first night I saw her walk into my bar.

She sighs, undoing the straps of her heels as she walks through the master bedroom in our penthouse apartment. We've just arrived after going out for a candlelit dinner, and I intend to keep her up and screaming my name all night long.

I bought this place for us eight years ago, after I decided we needed somewhere *other* than the yacht to build our lives. I could live every day on the boat, but I know Wendy still has problems on the water, even though she'll never say it out loud, and more than anything else, I want to make sure she's taken care of. Besides, it's advantageous to have a place I can take her with no one there to interrupt. I quite like being able to sink inside of her for as long as I wish.

My cock jerks as I watch her fingers run over her new sapphire necklace.

"It's so beautiful, James," she says.

I walk up behind her, wrapping my arm around her waist and pulling her into me just as I did earlier tonight, making sure she can feel every single inch of my hardness against her. I want her to know what she does to me. What *only* she does.

She pushes her ass into me, moaning as her hand sneaks back and grips me through my slacks. I let out a slight growl, thrusting my hips into her hand, pleasure curling through me like a slow fog as she strokes my length.

"Strip," I demand. "And then move to the bed. I want you wearing nothing but that necklace, with your legs spread wide, so I can see your pretty cunt."

She sucks in a sharp breath, her cheeks flushing, and my stomach flips in response, loving the way she still turns so pink for me after all these years.

Slowly, she peels off her dress and then unclips her bra, my chest tightening as her skin is exposed inch by torturous inch. I stay still and watch her, lust clouding my vision as she sways her hips and walks to the bed, crawling on the mattress and then flipping over until she's sitting on her knees.

I bite back the groan as heat pierces through me, and I undo my belt, dropping my slacks until my cock bobs free, throbbing and ready. Reaching down, I stroke myself from root to tip, my balls tensing when Wendy licks her lips like she's desperate to have me on her tongue.

She looks up at me from beneath her lashes as I walk toward her, and when I reach the foot of the bed, I let go of myself and reach out, grasping her chin between my thumb and forefinger and tilting her face up to meet my gaze.

"You've been a very good girl tonight. Do you know that?"

She preens beneath my hand and it makes my cock twitch, eager to slip between her pouty lips so she can suck me down, the way she knows I love.

My touch moves from her chin, grazing down the front of her throat, until it hits her collarbone. I use a bit of force to push her back until she's laid out in front of me, her chest heaving, bare breasts lush and nipples hard, begging for me to pull them into my mouth.

"Do you know how much control it took for me to not slaughter every man who had his eyes on you tonight?" I rasp, leaning forward to press kisses against her sugary skin. "It was torturous. None of them were worthy enough to so much as look at you."

I circle my tongue over a nipple, drawing the bud into my mouth and biting until she arches into me.

Delicious.

I move my hand down until I'm palming the wetness of her cunt, collecting her arousal like a treasure and bringing it up to my lips as if it's the sweetest ambrosia. I groan when her flavor hits my tongue and then I'm on her, diving and sucking her clit into my mouth, my fingers plunging into her until she lets out a harsh moan.

"James," she mewls, her fingers threading through the strands of my hair.

"That's right, pet," I murmur in between licks of her pussy. "It's *me* who makes you feel this way."

I release her from my mouth, continuing the rhythm of my fingers, my lips wet with her taste as I move up and hover my body over hers.

Her eyes are dark and wild, her pupils blown, and the sight of her this way, so unrestrained and lost in how she feels, makes cum bead at the tip of my cock. I'm aching to sink into her until she makes me lost. The same way she always has.

"Tell me," I say, removing my fingers and lining my cock up to her entrance. My other hand grasps her throat.

"I'm yours," she whispers as she lifts her head, pressing her lips to mine.

My hips press against hers as I surge forward in one deep thrust. I fuck her hard, long and steady strokes as I tighten my grip on her neck, careful to avoid her windpipe.

The sound of our skin slapping is loud, and the smell of our sex permeates the air. Her cunt massages me on every forward motion, and I bite the inside of my lip to keep from coming.

"I want to feel us," she pants, reaching down and spreading her fingers around the base of my shaft. The added sensation of her hand slipping along my length with every thrust makes me spiral quickly.

"Such a perfect girl," I coo. My knuckles look beautiful against the creamy expanse of her neck. "You're taking my cock so well. You were made for me, darling."

Her head falls to the side, and she opens her mouth on a gasp, and then she's coming hard, her walls pulsing around me.

Heat spreads through my body and collects at the base of my spine, then explodes, and I shoot deep inside of her, my balls spasming as I pump her full of my cum.

My ears ring as I catch my breath, and after a few moments I slip out of her, rolling onto my back. She exhales and cuddles up against my side, our sweat slicked skin evidence of the way she still drives me mad.

"I love you," I murmur.

"Every night?" she replies.

I smirk, something warm expanding into my chest. A decade later and she still says it almost every day. I'm not sure if it's to keep Ru's memory alive or if she's adopted it as her own, but either way, who am I to deny her?

"And straight on 'til morning, Wendy darling."

Character Profiles

James "Hook" Barrie

Name: James "Hook" Barrie

Age: 26

Place of Birth: London

Current Location: Bloomsburg, Massachusetts

Nationality: British

Occupation: Businessman/Crime Boss

Income: Millionaire

Eye Color: Cerulean blue

Hair Style: Jet black, slightly messy

Body Build: Trim, tall. Fit but not bulky.

Preferred style of outfit: Suit

Glasses? No

Any accessories they always have? Hook blade (Karambit knife)

Level of Grooming: Impeccable

Health: Healthy

Handwriting style: Perfect cursive

How do they walk: Swagger, radiates power

How do they speak: To the point and charming when needed. He likes to tell stories with his words, especially right before he tortures or kills someone.

Style of speech: Proper

Accent: British that's been slightly Americanized

Posture: Perfect

Do they gesture? Yes

Eye contact: Always

Preferred curse word: He doesn't curse much

Catchphrase? Darling. Pet.

Speech impediments? No

Laugh: Like silk, low and deep

What do they find funny: He doesn't find humor in much

Smile: Dazzling, slightly higher on the right side, perfectly straight teeth

Emotions: Emotive when he wants to be because it's useful in manipulating people

Childhood: Wealthy and sheltered when he was young, then terribly abusive and neglectful after his parents death

Schooling: Heavily involved in school, always felt it was important and continued self-educating after he graduated; named in the yearbook as most likely to become a politician

Jobs: Always worked for Ru

Dream job as a child: Didn't have a dream job; he just wanted to kill Peter

Role models growing up: Ru

Greatest regret: Letting his unhinged emotions blind him from reason, resulting in him losing Ru; not seeing things that were right in front of his face; and jumping to illogical conclusions about Wendy that made him cause her harm

Hobbies growing up: Soaking in everything Ru taught him

Favorite place as a child: Anywhere away from his uncle

Earliest memory: His mother tucking him in at night when he was a small boy, telling him fairy tales

Saddest memory: Losing his parents, then losing Ru

Happiest memory: The moment he realized Wendy was his and he had gained back the family he had spent his life tormented over losing

Any skeletons in the closet? Some things are better left in the dark

If they could change one thing from their past, what would it be? Keeping his parents alive

Major turning points during childhood: Meeting Peter; his parents' deaths; being sexually and physically abused by his uncle

Personality: Charming, unhinged, handsome

What advice would they give to their younger self? Deal with your trauma before it causes your downfall

Criminal record? Would be extensive if he were ever caught

Father

> **Age**: Deceased
>
> **Occupation**: Businessman
>
> **What's their relationship with the character like?** It was a strong relationship, but not very emotional. James looked up to him, knew that he would one day take the reins of the family business and wanted to be just like him.

Mother

> **Age**: Deceased
>
> **Occupation**: Stay-at-home mother

What's their relationship with the character like? Close relationship, the only woman he loved until Wendy

Siblings: None that he knows of; Jon is a half-sibling
Closest friends: Ru
Enemies: Peter
How are they perceived by strangers? Dangerous and alluring
Any social media? No
Role in group dynamic: Leader

Who do they depend on:
    Practical Advice: Nobody (although he should)
    Mentoring: Ru
    Wingman: Ru
    Emotional Support: Nobody
    Moral Support: Nobody

What do they do on Rainy Days? Business as usual
Book smart or street smart? Both, although his street smarts can be overshadowed by his trauma, which leads to making glaring mistakes and bad decisions
Optimist, pessimist, realist: Realist
Introvert or extrovert: Extrovert when needed, introvert at heart
Favorite sounds: Silence; Wendy's submission
What do they want most? To kill Peter, because he thinks that it will cure the emptiness he feels
Biggest flaw: His unresolved trauma and his inability to allow others in—he lets his past shape his decisions, makes his mind jump to sometimes wild conclusions, or makes him lose control and do rash things without forethought

Biggest strength: His unpredictability, because it makes people afraid of him

Biggest accomplishment: Loving Wendy

What's their idea of perfect happiness? In the beginning, he isn't after happiness, so he doesn't have an idea of what it could be. In the end, it's when his character arc is full circle and he regains the type of family he never thought he would have again.

Do they want to be remembered? Yes

How do they approach:
    Power: Demands it
    Ambition: Ruthlessly
    Love: Thinks he's above it
    Change: Is not a fan of it

Possession they would rescue from burning home: Hook blade

What makes them angry? The ticking of a clock

How is their moral compass, and what would it take to break it? Nonexistent

Pet peeves: Ticking clocks, people not giving him respect

What would they have written on their tombstone? Every night and straight on 'til morning.

Their story goal: James spends the majority of his life lamenting what was stolen from him and wanting power so he would never feel as powerless as the way he did when he was being abused by his uncle. He feels nothing but vengeance, doesn't think he will ever have a family again, and although he doesn't realize it at the time, he is seeking revenge because of the loss of his "normalcy" that comes along with the type of childhood and family he once had. The type of life he longs for.

In the end, after allowing his trauma and his anger to almost completely ruin everything (he will make rash and sometimes stupid decisions because he can't look past his own issues to think logically), he will overcome and will realize that revenge doesn't cure the damage; it only creates more. He will be willing to give up everything, including his life's goal, in order to keep Wendy safe and happy. To him, she is the family he never thought he would find again.

In the epilogue, even though he is a villain, he will have the picture-perfect family with Wendy, Jon, and children because that is the full circle of his story. What was lost is once again found. It won't change who he is at the core—his past has shaped him, and he enjoys being who he is, but he will have allowed himself to heal from the wounds of his past and will get what he was longing for all along.

Wendy Michaels

Name: Wendy Michaels

Age: 20

Place of birth: Florida

Current location: Bloomsburg, Massachusetts

Nationality: American

Education: High school

Occupation: Barista as a hobby more than a need

Income: Heiress

Eye color: Brown

Hairstyle: Long, straight, and brown

Build: Petite

Distinguishing features: Nothing that stands out, but James loves her in blue

Preferred style of outfit: Summer dresses

Glasses? No

Any accessories they always have? No

Level of Grooming: High

Health: Healthy

Handwriting style: Loopy

How do they walk? She walks to blend in, not stand out

How do they speak? Doesn't speak her mind often—she has learned to bite her tongue and stay silent; has random outbursts, especially when upset with her father and whenever she's around James

Style of speech: Normal

Accent: American

Posture: Good

Do they gesture? Yes

Eye contact: Sometimes

Preferred curse word: She doesn't have one

Catchphrase? Doesn't have one—at the beginning of her character arc, she isn't quite sure who she is

Speech impediments? No

Laugh: Loud and light.

What do they find funny? Rom-coms and her little brother's jokes

Smile: Shy and beautiful

Emotions: Tries to keep them hidden but isn't always successful, especially once she starts to break out of her shell

Childhood: Wealthy and sheltered; raised by nannies and constantly craving her father's attention

Schooling: Only involved as much as she was expected to be; named in the yearbook as most likely to never work

Jobs: Barista, only to pass the time

Dream job as a child: She never really thought of what she wanted to do beyond what was expected of her

Role models growing up: Her father

Greatest regret: Not speaking up for her little brother sooner

Hobbies growing up: She's always been a people-pleaser who didn't have her own backbone or identity, so whatever anyone else wanted her to do

Favorite place as a child: At home when her dad was there from a business trip and was tucking her in

Earliest memory: Her father leaving her an acorn when she was a little girl

Saddest memory: Having to kill her father

Happiest memory: Finally standing up for herself

Any skeletons in the closet? No

If they could change one thing from their past, what would it be? She would have protected Jon better, and she would have found her voice sooner

Describe major turning points in their childhood: Her mother dying and her father's change in behavior

Personality: Innocent, sweet, naive

What advice would they give to their younger self? You deserve to be in every room you walk into.

Criminal record? Nonexistent.

Father:

   Age: Middle aged

   Occupation: Businessman

   What's their relationship with character like: Strong relationship when she was young and then strained as she grew older. He became distant and a workaholic and she longed for the attention and parenting she used to have. Created a lot of issues for her in her adult years.

Mother:

    Age: Deceased

    Occupation: Worked with her father

    What's their relationship with character like: Always strained.

Siblings? Yes, one half-sibling, Jon

Closest friends: Angie

Enemies: None

How are they perceived by strangers? Naive and young

Any social media? Yes, but only because she's expected to have it

Role in group dynamic: People-pleaser

Who do they depend on:

    Practical advice: Her father

    Mentoring: Her father

    Wingman: Angie

    Emotional support: Jon

    Moral support: Angie/Jon

What do they do on rainy days? Read a book or hang out with her brother

Book smart or street smart? Book smart

Optimist, pessimist, realist: Slight optimist

Introvert or extrovert: Introvert.

Favorite sound: Laughter in her home

What do they want most? To have a loving family that spends time together

Biggest flaw: Her naivete and her daddy issues, which make her desperate for attention and love

Biggest strength: Her loyalty

Biggest accomplishment: Standing up for herself

What's their idea of perfect happiness: Her family being under one roof and spending time together

Do they want to be remembered? Only to the people she loved

How do they approach:

    Power: Shies away from it

    Ambition: Average ambition

    Love: Aches for it

    Change: Isn't bothered by it

Possession they would rescue from burning home? A picture of her and Jon

What makes them angry? Her dad not being a parent to Jon

How is their moral compass, and what would it take to break it? Fairly strong, but if someone manipulated her need for affection, they would bend it easily

Pet peeves: Disrespect

What would they have written on their tombstone? Whatever someone else decided to write—she'd be too afraid of speaking up to pick something for herself

Their story goal: Wendy is a naive girl raised in a sheltered, wealthy home. Her father is the only love she's ever known other than her younger brother, and when that starts to disappear, she lacks purpose in her own life.

She loves hard and wants nothing more than for her family to be whole, happy, and safe. When she meets Hook, she finds in him what she's lacking in her personal life—attention, affection. Because she's desperate for it, she falls fast, and because she's lived most of her life sheltered, she isn't used to people like Hook who are known to manipulate things to get their way. She mistakes his manipulation for genuine emotion.

She forgives James's transgressions quickly because she's never known another way to be, and she loves him despite everything he's done because she's spent her entire life seeing situations from other people's perspectives and putting them above her own. It's allowed her to empathize with someone she should consider a monster, and she *does* empathize with people, even if it's to her own detriment.

As the story goes on and James falls in love with her for real, he will help her blossom. She will grow into someone who learns that sometimes you have to stand up for yourself, even if it means letting go of what you've always wanted. She'll learn that she is *worthy* to be anywhere she chooses and that her voice deserves to be heard, that she's the one who truly holds all the power.

She'll lose her innocence and be tarnished with stains of black, but she'll end with exactly what she's always wanted—a strong voice, a man who treats her as his equal, and a family that's happy, healthy, and whole.

THANK YOU FOR READING!

Enjoy *Hooked*? Please consider taking a second to leave a review!
Come chat about what you read!
Join the McIncult (Facebook Group) at
facebook.com/groups/mcincult.

GRAB BOOK TWO IN THE NEVER AFTER SERIES

Scarred: A Dark Royal Romance

She lives in the light.
He plots in the land of shadows.
And she doesn't belong to him.
She belongs to the crown.

Available at Amazon:
https://www.amazon.com/Scarred-Never-After-Emily
-McIntire/dp/B09PHBXP18

JOIN THE MCINCULT!

EmilyMcIntire.com

The McIncult (Facebook Group): facebook.com/groups/mcincult.
Where you can chat all things Emily. First looks, exclusive
giveaways, and the best place to connect with me!

TikTok: tiktok.com/@authoremilymcintire

Instagram: instagram.com/itsemilymcintire/

Facebook: facebook.com/authoremilymcintire

Pinterest: pinterest.com/itsemilymcintire/

Goodreads: goodreads.com/author/show/20245445.Emily_McIntire

BookBub: bookbub.com/profile/emily-mcintire

Acknowledgments

To my husband, Mike, thank you for being my rock and for supporting me even at the beginning when I wasn't sure what the hell I was doing. None of this would be possible without you.

To my best friend, Sav R. Miller. Thank you for always being there every step of the way, for overgifting me on every occasion, for talking me off the ledge and down from spirals, and for being a genuinely loyal ride or die friend and one of the best people I've ever known. I'm honored to know you.

To my alpha and beta readers: Sav R. Miller, Anne-Lucy Shanley, Michelle Chamberland, Ariel Mareroa. Y'all are the most amazing humans, always working on my ridiculous deadlines and making sure I'm not writing complete trash.

To my editors and proofreaders: Thank you for making my words so pretty.

To my cover designer, Cat from TRC Designs: You are incredibly talented. Thank you for taking my vision and bringing it to life.

To my Street Team: I genuinely cannot express how grateful

I am to have you by my side. Thank you for everything you do, all the ways you show up, and all the light you bring to my life.

To my ARC readers: Thank you for always reading my words and helping spread the word about my books with your reviews. So much of my success is thanks to you.

To the McIncult: Thank you for joining my groups and picking up everything I write. Having people who love my words is a dream come true, and I'm so happy to have your support. I am living my dream because of you.

And saving the best for last, to my daughter, Melody: You are now and always will be the reason for everything.

About the Author

Emily McIntire is an international and Amazon top-fifteen bestselling author known for her Never After series, where she gives our favorite villains their happily ever afters. With books that range from small town to dark romance, she doesn't like to box herself into one type of story, but at the core of all her novels is soul-deep love. When she's not writing, you can find her waiting on her long-lost Hogwarts letter, enjoying her family, or lost between the pages of a good book.

ALSO BY EMILY MCINTIRE

Be Still My Heart: A Romantic Suspense

THE SUGARLAKE SERIES
Beneath the Stars
Beneath the Stands
Beneath the Hood
Beneath the Surface

THE NEVER AFTER SERIES
Scarred: A Dark Royal Romance
Wretched: A Dark Contemporary Romance